The Dragon Wakes

the dragon wakes

jim wingate

dinas

Illustrations: Insight Illustration Ltd

ISBN: 0 86243 690 7

Dinas is an imprint of Y Lolfa

Printed and published in Wales
by Y Lolfa Cyf., Talybont, Ceredigion SY24 5AP
e-mail ylolfa@ylolfa.com
website www.ylolfa.com
tel. (01970) 832 304
fax 832 782

Y Ddraig Sy'n Cysgu

The Sleeping Dragon

DEDICATION

To you

You might be from any village or town or city neighbourhood which seeks
to take control over its own destiny.

You might be a person alone or with a group of friends or colleagues who wish
to repossess the power over your own lives.

You might be a person who is ready, or has a feeling that you are ready,
to revalue yourself and free yourself from your limitations.

If so, this book is for you.

It is the story of four friends who help one another to new freedoms and strengths.

The four friends are helped and confronted and challenged and entertained by the forty two stories contained within this book.

Maybe many or some or one of these stories will speak, also, to you ...

Y Ddraig Yn Deffro
The Dragon Wakes

What the reviewers say:

'Highly original... an intriguing story... a novel approach that works... the people become friends of the reader... it has pace and keeps one interested to the end."
The Welsh Books Council

'I found myself laughing out loud at this story of ordinary people in Wales attempting to do the extraordinary: transforming their lives and their community's life in the face of many difficulties. In this cynical age people would say that it cannot be done but the art of the storyteller made me believe that it would be possible. Stories are powerful things and I felt that power while reading this book.'
Lyn Davies, National Library of Wales

'This is a fine contribution to the themes of cultural imperialism and cultural resistance. Marshalling the forces of the bardic storytelling tradition, hwyl, multi-sensory wordplay, and humanistic passion, Jim Wingate spins a tale that is deep as a mountain lake, and as incisive as the darting runs of a great scrum half.'
Nick Owen, author of The Magic of Metaphor

'I couldn't put it down – a wonderful read, a brilliant piece of writing. I wondered if I'd be interested in seemingly stereotyed characters but I *was*, and in the Project, I *had* to find out what happened to them all. I loved the stories.'
Marianne Rankin, Chair of the Alister Hardy Trusts, University of Wales

The Dragon Wakes

International Introduction

Here is some background to the culture and economics and characters in this book. **(If you know Wales well, skip to the end of this introduction, to 'The Author', and skip that, too, if you like!)**

The Threats

1) Language and Culture

In common with many cultures, Welsh culture is under threat. In mainly the western parts of Wales there are many towns and villages where Welsh is the main language spoken. When incomers move into such towns and villages and don't learn and use Welsh, the use of Welsh as the normal, daily language is threatened. When the Welsh speakers are diluted by incomers to 60% or less of the population, then the daily language tends to become English, and the Welsh language begins to die out.

2) Jobs

In common with many rural communities, Welsh villages have few jobs for young people. The young people therefore move away to cities – and often out of Wales altogether – and the age profile of the villages increases.

3) Services

With ageing populations and few jobs, there is little tax-income locally to support services such as public transport and hospitals, yet these services are what older and jobless people increasingly need.

4) Housing

The local people have low incomes. The lack of jobs in an area make house prices low, and incomers from rich cities are tempted in to buy larger houses than they can afford in the cities. The city-fleeing incomers' higher incomes then force up the rural house prices, and the low-paid locals cannot afford to live in their own villages.

The local, rural young people, particularly, can only afford to live in the poorest housing in city centres, moving **into** the very conditions the incomers to their villages are fleeing **from.**

5) Housing Policy

When a Welsh-speaking village of fifty houses is faced with a housing policy to add a hundred and fifty new houses to their village, the village knows it is looking at its destruction as a Welsh-speaking community (or as any community at all).

The Characters

The Incomers

To the Welsh-speaking village in this book have come two incomers.

Sally is English, but has gone on many courses to learn Welsh, and has read lots of books by which she has sensitised herself to Welsh culture. Sally trained as a vicar (Protestant church pastor or minister). She does counselling on the internet.

Brum (his nickname) is also English, but he sees no reason to learn Welsh. "Every Welsh-speaking person, after all, also speaks English!" Brum finds, though, that there are many aspects of Welsh culture which he (therefore) finds impossible to understand. Brum has been a successful businessman and engineer.

('Brum' is the colloquial name for Birmingham, the second city of England. It is a large industrial city and many 'Brummies' (people from Birmingham) come to Wales for cheap holidays (for example in caravan parks). Later, when they get rich, or retire, the Brummies often move to Wales as incomers.)

The mother-tongue Welsh speakers

Myfanwy is a Welsh name. (The first 'y' is pronounced 'u' as in 'cup', the second as in 'i' in 'ski'. The 'f' is pronounced 'v' as in 'very'. The 'w' is pronounced 'oo'.) Myfanwy is landlady and gloomy owner of the village pub **The Sleeping Dragon.** (There is a lovely Welsh love song about 'Myfanwy'.)

Dafydd is a very Welsh name too. The patron saint of Wales is Dewi Sant, Saint David or Dafydd (the dd is pronounced as the 'th' in 'there'). The daffodil is Dafydd's lily, the national flower of Wales worn on Saint David's Day, the first of March. 'Dai' is the nickname for Dafydd.

Dafydd and **Myfanwy** spoke Welsh at home, but all their lessons in school were in English, except 'Welsh', which they learned as a school subject. They use their English almost as fluently and expressively as their Welsh. They were friends at primary and secondary school. Dafydd was an international rugby player and also traveled the world working as a storyteller, among other things.

The three friends (Brum, Sally and Dafydd) are the only regular customers of Myfanwy, who is also their friend.

Cultural Icons

The Dragon

The red dragon is on the flag of Wales. It is a powerful symbol to all Welsh people of Welsh national identity. Notice that the 'British' flag, the 'Union Jack', contains the English cross of Saint

George, the Scottish cross of Saint Andrew and the Irish cross of Saint Patrick – but no symbol for Wales!

'Welsh', 'Wales'

The word 'Welsh' is Saxon for 'foreigner'. The Saxon invaders drove the British (Welsh-speaking) people to the west and called them 'foreigners' in the Welsh people's own land! Imagine being called 'foreigner', or 'barbarian' in your own native country! Imagine your native land being called 'Foreign Place'!

Church and Chapel

(Scene 22) The (Protestant) Church of England in Wales used to be 'established', i.e. part of the government, the State Church. It used to have all services in English and the vicars were often English people appointed by the rich English-speaking landowners in Wales. All people were compulsorily required to pay 10% tax (tithe) to the church.

It is therefore no surprise that in the 18th, 19th and 20th centuries there were great waves of Welsh-speaking non-conformist* (non-established, independent) 'revivals' with hundreds of thousands of Welsh speakers being converted, deserting the churches, and building chapels where the services were in Welsh.

The Church of England in Wales was run by bishops. The chapels were run by the people themselves, the elders. They appointed their pastors and it was the people's money, voluntarily given, that paid for the building of the very many chapels and for their pastors.

In many ways chapels were (and are) democratic, socialist, egalitarian republican, and express Welsh-speaking national identity.

In many ways the churches (now the Church in Wales, disestablished), were (and are) hierarchical (with bishops), conservative, class-based, royalist and express an Anglo-Welsh or English identity.

(* Baptist, Calvinist Methodist, Primitive Methodist, Wesleyan Methodist, Presbyterian.)

Rugby
Next to religion, rugby expresses the spiritual life of the Welsh nation. Rugby is nothing like football (soccer). The crowds at Welsh rugby matches sing in four-part harmony the Welsh National Anthem in Welsh, and Welsh songs and hymns. There is no hooliganism, but when the Wales national rugby team plays the English national rugby team it is as if the soul of Wales is put to the test. And when Wales (a nation of three million) beats England (a nation of fifty million) there is great rejoicing in Wales!

The number '8' (Scene 14) is the tallest, largest player, the 'scrum half' usually the smallest.

Storytelling
In Celtic culture there have always been professional storytellers and there still are many in Wales, Scotland and Ireland. The 'bards' of Welsh medieval culture travelled from chief to chief, living as honoured and paid guests at the courts of chiefs and princes, and creating poems and songs of praise and love and grieving, and preserving and telling the culture's history in stories.

The Eisteddfodau, the local Welsh cultural festivals, culminate in the National Eisteddfod, where the best poet is given a magnificent chair and is 'chaired as the bard'.

Places
The Plas (Scene 16) is the name for a large house, a 'country house'.

Birmingham's 'heart' (Scene 8) in the Second World War the centre (heart) of the city of Birmingham was destroyed by aerial bombing. In the 1960s the centre was rebuilt as 'The Bull Ring'. 'The Bull Ring' was built for cars, with small areas of green and pedestrian walkways under the maze of roads. It became a centre for drugs and muggings and became a place to avoid. Decades later it was replaced.

St Fagan's (Scene 10) is the Museum of Welsh Life, near Cardiff, a wonderful collection of vernacular period buildings and enterprises.

The Pits (Scene 6). The coal mines were a major industry in Wales until all were closed down by the actions of Margaret Thatcher. Suddenly many villages lost nearly all the jobs.

Tŷ Bach (Scene 24) is the 'little house', the non-flush toilet up a path up the back garden.

The Author
Jim Wingate is half-Welsh and half-Scottish, living in a small village in the hills of mid-Wales. He is a professional, international storyteller, telling sixty traditional stories in English each year to twenty-thousand young people aged three to nineteen in six countries. In Welsh bardic convention he works completely in the oral tradition, never telling a story he has read or written, only stories he has heard. The oldest story he tells is eight thousand years old, and all the stories he tells have been passed from storyteller to storyteller to storyteller, down the generations.

In the Welsh tradition, bards complete their seven years' training as storytellers and then train for the next seven years to be healers. Jim also works as a healer and distance-healer and also releases ghosts who are trapped by their pasts.

Jim has worked in 42 countries, often in peace and reconciliation. He is a registered non-violence trainer and registered British Council International teacher trainer and has been plenary speaker at 37 international conferences in 19 countries. He has written over 40 books for teachers and 4 sets of course books for learners.

"My work," says Jim, "is all in helping people to treat other people as human beings." He has lived in several communities where the participants have exemplified their beliefs through co-operation, collaboration, self-awareness and self-development.

In *The Dragon Wakes,* Jim has created all these stories, except three, from his experiences and dreams.
Jim's books and services can be seen on his website
www.jimwingate.co.uk

CHARACTERS IN ORDER OF APPEARANCE

Myfanwy – small, dark, Welsh-speaking,
owner and landlady of the pub

Brum – fat, bald, rich, early-retired incomer from Birmingham

Sally – tall, blond, self-employed internet counsellor, incomer,
has learned Welsh and has integrated

Dafydd – very tall, grey-bearded, Welsh-speaking,
has travelled widely and tells stories

SCENE ONE

Y Ddraig Sy'n Cysgu

The Sleeping Dragon

The Pub – *The Sleeping Dragon*

"This pub's going to close," said small, dark landlady Myfanwy in her usual glum tone, as she washed the one glass used in the last two hours.

"Close! It's early!" Fat, bald, Brum looked startled. Here was yet another culture shock from moving to Wales! He looked at the clock for reassurance. At least that had English numbers….

"No, close, shut down, cease, stop." Myfanwy's light reading was her Thesaurus. She often spoke in oppressive lists rather than sentences. The longer her face, the longer the dire lists.

"Oh, no, Myfanwy. We must **do** something! **Why** will you close?" asked tall, blond Sally in her acquired Welsh accent. She dreamed of a community here, but it seemed it was crumbling to dust.

Myfanwy's next list was mercifully short but mercilessly consistent. "No customers, no trade, no money, no income, no future." She pointed to the three half-empty half-pint glasses of her three regulars, her only three regulars. There was a pause. Not one of the three offered to double her trade by ordering an extra round. For them three rounds a night were enough. Sally and Brum turned, desperate for hope, to their friend Dafydd, the third drinker, who sat between them looking deeply into his half-hour drawn beer. In spite of her anxieties, Myfanwy smiled inside herself, knowing well, before he spoke, what he would say: "I knew a…, once…." Each of his stories started the same way…

"I knew a pub once…" said very tall, grey-bearded Dafydd in his deep, resonant voice with its unstoppable tone. The other three gladly leant a little more heavily on the bar and settled themselves to listen. Their eyes, though open, closed a kind of inner lid on which their minds got ready to project the pictures Dafydd's words would conjure.

The Sleeping Dragon

It was a tired pub. The paint was peeling on the sign. There were old, dead cars in the courtyard at the back of the pub, and the small, tired village seemed to have turned its own back on the tired pub. Instead, the small, tired village had turned to face television, with cheap, supermarket beer cans.

It was the time of the Tiredness. As some say, 'Tiredness marched the land', but Tiredness was actually too tired to march, certainly too tired to put up candidates for anything, or even to vote.

There were four people in the village, the select four, the only four who were not too tired to meet in the tired pub and not too tired to buy three half pints of beer …

"Too **mean** to buy more!" landlady Myfanwy interrupted in her glummest voice, but as she looked at Dafydd there was a wistfulness in her eyes.

"This isn't a 'story'," Brum added, mystified, "This is **us**. Nothing happens!"

"It could," said Sally, brightly, "but go on, Dafydd. What's next?"

"Nothing," said Dafydd with a sigh.

"I told you!" said Brum, smiling, but irritated. "It's **not** a story! Please, Dafydd, tell us a **real** story. You know, one of the **old** stories you normally tell ..."

"Is that all I am?" asked Dafydd in mock despair, "an old teller of old stories?"

"Well ..." Brum didn't know how to respond to Welsh irony. As a result, his one, hesitant word hung in the air like a damning with the faintest of faint praise.

The four friends all heard the unintended meaning of "Well ..." and laughed.

"A real, Welsh story," Sally begged, trying to soothe the situation.

The 7 Sovereigns

It was the time of the Plague. As some say, 'death marched the land'. There were seven families in the village and there were seven members in each family. And from each family, all but one died. Well, when the last funeral was over, the seven exhausted survivors met in the pub...

"I could stay open with seven!" muttered Myfanwy, but Dafydd acknowledged her interruption only as a music maestro acknowledges a cough in the back row of the audience.

The seven looked from one to another, much as we are looking now.

Nobody's heads moved but they could all see the gaunt survivors' faces in their mind's eye.

'We are here,' said the oldest, taking the lead by stating something all the others could agree upon. 'We must decide what to do.' Well, they agreed, but their agreements were hope mixed with despair. Yes, they must all help one another to look after all the animals.

But so many people in the whole area had died, so nobody would want to buy those animals. Yes, they agreed to help one another to harvest all the crops. But likewise, there would be no market for their produce and the prices would, subsequently, be very low. They agreed to maintain the seven houses. But with only one person living in each house, living would be very lonely. They looked at one another in desperation. What would be their future? They could see only hard, lonely, work for no reward.

"Now there was one among them…" Myfanwy had known Dafydd all her life, so she was first to mouth that phrase, but Brum and Sally were only a fraction of a second behind. Always Dafydd would fill his lungs at this point and repeat the phrase as if inspiration had entered the dark and dingy bar.

Now there was one among them, Iolo, who delved deep in his pockets and laid on the bar seven gold sovereigns. 'These are all my family's savings. Every week,' he said 'I will pay each of you one sovereign.' At that moment, true to his word, he gave one to each. 'You will each sell me something I need for that week, a lamb to eat, vegetables, wheat for bread, beer, something that I will use up and need again the next week.'

The oldest one, the one who always stated the obvious, pointed out, with pleasure, the flaw in Iolo's proposal. 'But you have now spent all your seven sovereigns already! You have no money for next week!'

'Ah!' replied Iolo, grinning, 'you will each do the same and each buy from me something **you** need each week.'

'Aha!' exclaimed the oldest one, now triumphant, 'That is a gross injustice! You will then have **seven** sovereigns for one week's work! We will have made you rich!'

'Indeed so,' replied Iolo, grinning more widely, 'And each of you will be as rich as me, each earning seven gold sovereigns each week!'

'No, no, no,' the most pessimistic one among them murmured (I seem to remember he was a distant ancestor of Myfanwy, our esteemed landlady).

Dafydd's voice betrayed no smile, but Sally and Brum conjured to their inner eye Myfanwy's face at its longest, and they grinned.

'I will save my money!' said the pessimist. 'I will eat my own lambs, eat my own vegetables and bake my own bread.'

'Then,' said the oldest one – who, to give him his due, could always see the most obvious facts most clearly even when these facts were new – 'you will be poor and we will all be rich!'

There was a long pause. There was always a long pause in Dafydd's stories, and automatically the three regulars' elbows bent in unison as they each drank one more mouthful of beer.

It was normally Brum who asked the question first. He always tried to fill the Welsh silences with some healthy, English noise. Sally was normally too busy running back what she had just heard in order to collect Welsh cultural insights she could memorise and use again. Myfanwy never asked the question. She could wait. She knew Dafydd himself would ask it soon enough if nobody else did.

"But what about the **pub**?" said Brum.

"The pub?" said Dafydd as if it was a new thought all together.

Of course the pub became the richest pub in the whole country. Each person paid the pub a sovereign each week, and in the pub was where all the buying and selling were done...

"Like a shop," Interrupted Sally. "That's it, Myfanwy! We'd spend more here if your pub was the shop…. And the post office… and the bank…." Their village had lost all three over recent years, bank first, then post office, then shop.

… and the brothel!

Dafydd's voice always got louder when a story was interrupted before the end.

"Why a brothel?" Brum's eyes were wide. Was this another tradition the secretive Welsh kept from incomers, that each village had a brothel?

"Well," said Dafydd, his voice quieter now he had the story back in his grip.

Nobody **paid** for the services, but of course the seven survivors of the Plague had to make as many new Welsh babies as they could, and it was in the pub that they did it.

"Like a honeymoon hotel," chimed in Sally, and because Dafydd said nothing, she knew the story was over. "I would bring my babies up Welsh-speaking," she said as an after-thought. This was unlikely. She was in her fifties. So were her three friends.

SCENE TWO

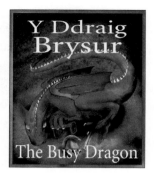

Y Ddraig Brysur

The Busy Dragon

The Pub – Shop – Honeymoon Hotel
– *The Busy Dragon*
a month later

The next time all three regulars met together at Myfanwy's bar was a month later. Brum had been visiting his new grandchild in Wolverhampton. Dafydd had been at the National Eisteddfod. Only Sally had been in the pub every day, putting all sorts of pressures on Myfanwy.

"Good God!" said Brum, panting with the exertion of walking from his car. "It's a shop!"

"**The** Shop," said Sally. The village shop had closed the year before. "And Myfanwy has already applied to have the Post Office."

"I don't know where I will get the money from to open," said Myfanwy gloomily in her new green and white striped overall.

"Money?" asked Brum, eyebrows raised, "No, Myfanwy. **Customers** pay **you** money in a Post Office."

Sally put on her kindly voice. Brum often feared she would pat him on his bald patch when he heard that voice. Sometimes he quite wished she would. Sally had nice hands…. "No, Brum, Myfanwy has to buy a computer, modem, a safe, alarms **and** put up a bond."

"I'll be your bond!" said Brum, grinning "James Bond!" He drew and fired a fast finger.

"Now there's an idea!" exclaimed Sally. "Brilliant, Brum! Yes we'll each put up a third of the bond and I'll teach Myfanwy the IT skills."

"You know if I'm robbed in the Post Office, I have to pay the missing money myself!" said Myfanwy, but there was an unprecedented note of optimism in her voice.

Dafydd, silent till now, took a deep breath. They all knew the phrase that would come "I knew a … once…" Brum silently signalled Myfanwy to set up the first round and to have one herself. His fast finger returned to his pocket to pay.

"I knew a Post Office once," said Dafydd, fixing his eyes on the new shelves of goods which had turned the bar into a shop, **the** shop. The sign '*Honeymoon Hotel*' pointed upstairs. He knew that spare room. He knew it well.

The Young Post Office

I knew a Post Office once. It was young. It wanted to be a coaching inn, but it was too young and too small. 'It's not fair', said the Post Office to anyone who would listen, 'just because I'm small and young the stage-coaches pass me by! One day I will be big and old, then they'll be sorry!'

There was a pause. All four friends took their first sip of beer, and Myfanwy's hand slid over the money Brum had laid on the bar. Brum, as usual, asked the question. "Why would they be sorry?"

Dafydd's voice obligingly continued.

'When I'm big and old,' said the Post Office, 'I won't let any stage-coaches stop here. Then they'll be sorry!'

"That doesn't make sense!" said Brum. Was this another Welsh secret?

"When you're small and young you don't know sense," said Dafydd, smiling "And when you're big and old you don't have to make sense."

Sally was memorising that. Was it a Welsh proverb? Had she heard it in Welsh in her Welsh classes? Dafydd's voice went on.

Then Iolo, who was of middle years, when sense is what you live by, said to the Post Office, 'Now then, Post

Office, by how much are you too small, and by how long are you too young?' And step by step the person of middle years persuaded the small Post Office to grow a stable block, an inn yard, a kitchen and a long table for sixteen people to sit at and eat. The young Post Office was also persuaded to grow older by six replacement horses, an ostler and a cook.....

"What's an ostler?" asked Sally. It didn't sound like a Welsh word, but then some Welsh words didn't.

"It's a heavy overcoat," offered Brum, trying to remember his grandfather.

"No, that's a hustler – no, no, a holster, no, a bolster, no, an ocelot," Myfanwy added.

Dafydd's voice was considerably louder after three interruptions.

An ostler looks after the horses. In those days Ulster overcoats were unknown. (The ostler made and remade a rain-proof cape of straw and tied old grain sacks around his body in the winter.) And the small, young Post Office became a big, old coaching inn, and it is so to this day, and all the customers were satisfied....

Dafydd took a deep breath.

"Now there was one among them," said Brum aloud, and clapped his hand to his mouth. In Wolverhampton you all spoke at once. Here in Wales, he remembered… Dafydd's deep breath was ready. Dafydd spoke on, unperturbed:

Now there was one among them who said, 'You sell two stamps a week, but two stage coaches stop here every day. Forget the post. You have grown to be a coaching inn.' And for many years the big, old coaching inn forgot the post, until the people said those words, generations later.

The elbows bent. The mouths sipped. Brum looked round, mystified.

"What words?" asked Brum.

"Why, **your** words, Birmingham." Dafydd was a great one for never using nicknames.

"You agree, then, Dafydd!" Sally was excited.

"To the Post Office, restored!" said Dafydd, raising his glass.

"Oh, thank you!" said Myfanwy, and there were tears in her eyes.

"What words?" asked Brum. What had he missed? Had a whispered word of Welsh appeared when he hadn't been listening? Sally turned a beaming smile to him. Behind her smile he saw '*Honeymoon Hotel*' and he grinned back in hope.

"We three," Sally said, grasping her two friends' shoulders in those nice hands, "are going to put up the money to make the pub-shop-honeymoon hotel into the pub-shop-honeymoon hotel-Post Office."

"And bank" added Dafydd, "or so I understood at the Eisteddfod. Local Post Offices can act as branches of a bank."

SCENE THREE

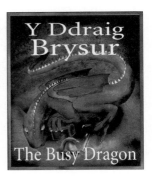

The Pub – Shop – Honeymoon Hotel
– *The Busy Dragon*
the next evening

The next evening Brum was startled to see 'Villages, Invasions' as the newspaper hoarding outside the pub-shop. As he stepped into the bar he turned his head sideways to try to read the headlines on the piles of newspapers for sale.

"Isn't it terrible!" exclaimed Sally signalling to Myfanwy to set up Brum's beer.

Brum nodded his agreement, hoping he would learn why, and looking nervously over his shoulder. Why couldn't the pub have loud music like a nice, English city pub? Then you wouldn't have to know about the invasion until it was all over? Dwelling **in** Wales was great if you didn't dwell **on** social disintegration.

"A hundred and fifty new houses, households, homes!" murmured Myfanwy shaking her head in disbelief at the thought, as her hands automatically counted Sally's money.

"Er, where?" asked Brum, looking at Dafydd whose concentration seemed to be fixed on the six new, different kinds of condoms on offer at the shop counter at his elbow.

"Here, Birmingham, my friend," said Dafydd, solemnly, "in our village."

"Ah!" said Brum cheerfully, "drinks are on Myfanwy then! More customers eh? First the builders. They're thirsty buggers! Then the families in the new houses. You'll have to expand your shop!" He looked around beaming. A bit more noise, he told himself, would help him sleep better.

"Oh, Brum!" said Sally, kindly. Brum moved his head towards her, hoping for the feel of her fingers. "You don't understand. A hundred and fifty incomers – maybe three hundred – who don't speak Welsh! Nor want to! And they'll be wanting jobs, the local jobs."

"Jobs!" Now jobs were what Brum knew. He'd had twelve different jobs in his life, each more highly paid than the last, each enabling him to move to bigger and bigger houses with more and more land. "Having more people **makes** more jobs! There'll be, what? – several new kids, that's jobs for more teachers! There'll be more people sick and old, needing nurses and doctors. People always argue, so there's more jobs for lawyers and house agents."

"But **local** jobs" said Sally, ignoring her drink in her kindly passion, "for the community, for **local** people."

"Cleaners," said Brum, feeling touchy and feely under Sally's glowing gaze, "gardeners, cleaners, repairers…"

"And Welsh?" Sally's eyes were looking deeply, appealingly, into Brum's eyes now, and her eager, blond eyebrows were raised high.

If Brum had learned one thing that Sally hadn't, it was to keep quiet in Wales when the issue of the Welsh language was raised. Desperately he turned to Dafydd.

Dafydd's eyes moved from the **A change is as good as a rest!** slogan above the varied condoms. He began to speak, and the tension in the shop bar relaxed.

The Walled Village

I knew a village once. There were fifty houses in the village, as in ours, and the powers-that-be or rather the powers-that-were. (All powers-that-be become powers-that-were. That's the only good thing about powers-that-be.) Anyway, the-powers-that-were insisted on a hundred and fifty new houses being built.

"The same number as here," sighed Myfanwy, more as a liturgical response than in interruption.

"The same number as here" repeated Dafydd, echoing Myfanwy's fatalistic tone.

And the original fifty households hurried together and first built a great wall, then took in a year's stock of food, then rowed out to the Russian, refrigerated, fishing ships...

At this point even Myfanwy's lips formed a question, but Dafydd was speaking rapidly, communicating the panicked pace of the original households,

And bought on the black market, unused land-mines which they buried around the great wall. Next they trained their sheep dogs to attack anyone who didn't speak Welsh, and they sat....

"The dogs?" asked Brum. Dafydd ignored him.

... and waited. Yes, the building work was noisy and dusty. Yes, the hundred and fifty new houses were built, but the new people didn't seem to notice the fences and the dogs and the ring of mines and the great wall.

After a few months the original inhabitants ventured out through the great wall, through the mines, through the dogs and the fence, and there on the outside they saw it all...

There was a long pause.

"Saw what?" Brum asked. Even as he asked it he wondered suspiciously at Dafydd. Was this some kind of Welsh magic by which Dafydd could always get him to ask the right question. Next time... he thought, but after a quenching of thirst, Dafydd was continuing:

What they saw was as if they had entered a different country. They saw new shops, new notices, a new bus timetable, new, cheerful people, a new playgroup, a new primary school, and not a word of Welsh anywhere, written or spoken! The fifty original households retreated, shocked, back inside their wall and conferred together...

Sally whispered Dafydd's next seven words as he spoke them,

Now, there was one among them who said, 'Let them pay at the door in the wall. We will sell them **The Welsh Experience**, food, songs, poetry, prayers.'

There was another among them who said, 'They will pay **more** to be **made** Welsh with courses in Welsh language and Welsh culture.'

Yet another said 'They want **nothing** of us! See! None of them has even knocked on our great door in the wall to ask why we are so different. They don't care! We have made ourselves into exiles in our own land! Let us keep ourselves to ourselves inside our wall and ignore them.'

Now the oldest, who was the intellectual as well as the plumber, said, 'Ah, to make it **worthwhile** to be separate, we must be **pure**. I will teach all of you pure medieval Welsh, and we will get rid of all modern possessions and additions until we are purely Welsh, back to the times of Glyndŵr , and we will obey only the ancient Welsh laws.

'Aha!' said the first. 'Then we will open our doors and sell *The Pure Welsh Medieval Experience'.*

'Yes,' said the second, 'It will be our new crusade to make them become **pure** Welsh through courses in our medieval Welsh language and culture. It will be the great new revival of the twenty-first century!'

The third one sighed. 'They don't care for us as modern Welsh people. They'll care even less if we become a living-dying museum. Let's just be ourselves. I **like** my modern possessions and additions.'

'But don't you see?' said the plumber, thumping his fist on the overstuffed arm of the chair, 'Even within this wall we will be gradually diluted, drip by drip, by television and radio until there are no more Welsh words left in our Welsh language and we'll look like and be like them, just like them, out there, outside! To remain ourselves, we **must** advance, marching swiftly backwards through time!'

There was a long pause. Brum had told himself 'next time….' And here was that next time, but the Welsh magic had, for the first time, failed. He didn't know what question to ask! He looked at Sally and Myfanwy. Their eyes were down. Was the story over?

"What did they do?" Brum asked, but he already sensed it was the wrong question, even as he said it. Dafydd was silent.

"It was too late!" said Myfanwy, meeting Brum's eyes with sadness.

"The new houses were already built," said Sally, reaching out to touch Brum's hand.

"Thank you," said Brum, acknowledging their comforting words and gestures as if he'd just told them a relative of his had died. Vaguely he knew that his enthusiasm for the planned new houses had been completely taken away from him, but he couldn't understand how. It was Welsh magic – he thought to himself suspiciously and he remembered that book on Northern Ireland entitled *A Problem for Every Solution*. He heard Sally take a deep breath. Oh no, another 'community campaign'!

"There was **another** village," Sally said tentatively. Dafydd looked up from his beer. "Yes" she added, her voice getting stronger. "And they met, the people met together, yes, in the old chapel, and drew up a list. Yes, they would allow each new house to be built, but slowly, and only for someone filling a new job not needed by a local person. The new incomers had to agree to learn the local language, and to learn about the local culture, and there had to be the space and resources in the local school and hospital and so on."

"And no second houses, holiday homes, summer-only residences!" said Myfanwy.

"You can't control all that," said Brum, warming up to his favourite phrase, "It's a free market!"

Myfanwy embarked on another list. "I can't control, you can't control, she can't control, we can't control – but **they** can."

"Who are 'they'?" asked Dafydd, rhetorically. "'They' are the all-powerful gods, but nobody now knows in which office these gods reside – if indeed 'they' exist."

"Supply and demand!" replied Brum. It was his second favourite phrase. "First houses come, then the demand for services or jobs come, then the demand for more houses. But houses are commodities. Houses are bought and sold. You **may** be able to control the **first** new people, but then they sell up and the next buyers…. You can't control them at all!"

Sally began to protest, and Myfanwy turned away. Brum took a deep breath ready to educate his friends into understanding free market economics.

"I knew a village once" said Dafydd quietly.

Brum spluttered. He had just got into his stride. It was time these Welsh people heard a bit more about how the world really operates.

"I knew a village once," said Dafydd again, more slowly and quietly. The Welsh Magic began to work again.

'Freemarket Village'
The oldest name of the village in Welsh could be

translated as 'New Market'. Under the English kings only English people could live and trade in towns in Wales. That was their station in life. The Welsh people had to be rural and poor. That was **their** station in life. That was how free the market was in those days. But there was one soft spot in one of the English kings.

Dafydd saw Myfanwy's and Sally's raised eyebrows.

No, there **was** a soft spot. The village I am telling you about was the ancestral village of his family, though he never spoke of it, the ancestry being more illegitimate than he liked to admit.

So, the king announced he had a whim and he gave the village a royal charter and exempted it from tax. The surprised villagers of 'Newmarket' renamed their village 'Freemarket'.

When they had translated the small calligraphy in the charter into Welsh they realised with much joy and puzzlement that they had complete control over all their own affairs. There was no landowner, no landlord, no owning abbey, no tithes, no tax collector, no fees, no dues. Even better, they were free to make their own rules. 'We will elect a council,' they said, and duly every adult, man and woman, was elected to the council.

When the farmers and craftspeople and entertainers came in as usual to the weekly market to buy and sell, they were very agreeably surprised to find the old tolls and taxes all abolished.

Soon people from the whole area were clamouring to be allowed to build houses and live in Freemarket village.

Almost to a man and woman the council were keen to allow everyone in. 'We will become an important, rich town, and I will become an important, rich, town councillor' was the gist of what most of them said, and the decision had almost been made to make Freemarket village totally open to all. 'It is our destiny to be a town, then a city, as good as any English city!'

Now there was one among them, Iolo, who held up two pieces of good quality vellum, one in each hand….

In the long pause that followed Brum heard himself asking, "What is vellum?" He knew it was almost the right question, certainly enough to enable Dafydd to continue, but the pause continued.

"It's good quality notepaper, like Basildon Bond," said Myfanwy, indicating the top shelf of stationery in the shop part of the pub.

"Actually, it's cured animal skin parted into thin layers," said Sally, suddenly realising as she heard her own words that she'd broken her first golden rule as an integrated newcomer: she'd corrected a local. "Sorry," she added, breaking her second rule: not to patronise.

"And **on** the one sheet of vellum," said Dafydd, raising his voice and flourishing his left hand "was one sentence."

'This,' said Iolo, 'is a bill of sale for my house, whereas this,' said Iolo, lifting the other sheet of vellum, closely written from top to bottom, 'is a lease for my house. The lease is for nine hundred and ninety-nine years. Newcomers,' he announced proudly, 'can buy and sell this lease, generation after generation, but the house will always be mine and the property of my antecedents. In the thousandth year, this lease expires and the house can then be lived in by the children of my children's children's children … and so on to my ten times children's children. And for every moment of the nine hundred and ninety-nine years the inhabitants of my house have to obey all these conditions of this lease.

Sally was laughing. Even Myfanwy chuckled. Brum was thinking fast. The story was over and he had plenty to say.

"That means," said Brum decisively, "that we will build the houses, and only as and when needed, we, the villagers. Sally, you can organise that. We, the villagers will have control because we will set up… a Trust. The Trust will own the houses and lease them. Newcomers will buy and sell, obeying the conditions of the lease and we will make the conditions…"

"I had a condition once," interrupted Dafydd and he began to unbutton his shirt. They all laughed, Myfanwy more than the others, and they all knew that Dafydd was very pleased.

"I could **raise** twenty thousand extra mortgage on my house," said ever-practical Sally, "but I could only afford to **finance** ten thousand. So, if we four each put ten thousand into the Trust that buys a house that costs forty thousand to build. Local labour, community build, and the lease…"

"We sell the lease and the sale of the first lease funds building the next house," announced Brum excitedly. "It's a snowball."

"A pyramid, an accelerator, a multiplier, a domino effect," added Myfanwy helpfully.

"Yes!" exclaimed Sally. "And we can set the price of leasehold to be affordable by local people."

"I knew a house once," said Dafydd, laughing "that had a workshop big enough to work in."

With that shortest short story, a pad of high-quality Basildon Bond was purchased, and a low quality ball-point pen produced from a ball of fluff in Dafydd's pocket, and the housing scheme was roughed out there and then on the bar, with a draft of a leaflet and form in both languages to go to all the houses in the village.

There were three columns on the form. The Welsh speakers, Myfanwy and Dafydd, amused that their names were once again linked, together wrote in Welsh of their pledges of ten thousand pounds each. The English-speaker Brum pledged twenty thousand in his column exclusively in English, and Sally, with help from the other columnists, wrote in both languages of her pledge of ten thousand and requested a gift of land to build on, and offered to be 'the person responsible' to help to set up the Trust.

Their next decision was to join the county-wide protest against the council's plan to build lots of houses for incomers.

It didn't take long to go round the fifty houses with two petitions, one **against** the proposed hundred and fifty more houses, the other **for** the Trust.

SCENE FOUR

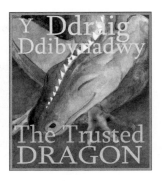

**The Pub – Shop – Honeymoon Hotel
– Post Office – Bank and Chapel
– *The Trusted Dragon*
a month later**

Dafydd didn't like champagne. He particularly didn't like the champagne-perry that Myfanwy had in 'Offa's Offy', the booze section of the pub-shop-post office-bank-honeymoon hotel. However, he filled up the four half-pint glasses with the pink, fizzy liquid and they toasted the successful opening of the post office-counter-with-computer-on-line-banking.

Actually it was a double celebration. The long-deserted lounge bar had been appropriately consecrated and blessed and furnished to be the occasional chapel now the Trust had bought the old chapel and was busy converting the old chapel to two, two-bedroom dwellings, each with a large workshop.

Dafydd raised his glass and toasted 'to the Post Office-bank-occasional chapel' and he found himself looking up at life's story in notices over the bar. **The Honeymoon Hotel. Baby clinic Wednesdays 2 p.m. lounge bar chapel – baptisms, marriages, funerals by arrangement.** Dafydd thought aloud, "Conception, birth, baptism, marriage, booze, death." These lists were infectious. "A One-Stop Shop", he muttered to himself.

There were lots of people in the place tonight, most of the village, young and old. Myfanwy was scrubbed and beaming and Sally, wearing her dog-collar today, was serving behind the bar, but only soft drinks. Birmingham, as usual, Dafydd noticed, was gazing at Sally wistfully. Birmingham had lost weight. Was weight-loss and wistfulness connected?

Sally was explaining earnestly to her three friends, as she poured drinks for three others:

"I'm creating an industrial ministry as well as my on-line ministry" she was saying.

"Industry?" Birmingham was gesturing around him as if to conjure a car factory. "What industry?"

"A ministry of the workplace."

"What workplace?"

Dafydd could see Sally's eyes showing her exasperation, but her lips kept up the smile.

"The pub here."

"Ay, **Myfanwy's** workplace," Birmingham seemed to understand, and Dafydd saw Myfanwy paying more attention having heard her name. "I see," continued Birmingham. "Next to every barmaid there should be a lady vicar!"

"Landlady," corrected Myfanwy.

"Woman priest," corrected Sally.

"Called to the bar," Dafydd's voice boomed over the chatter. "The vernacular confessional. The drinking man's psychiatrist's couch. The drinking woman's counselling service."

Dafydd seldom stood for long at any bar. His great height tended to silence normal chatter. It did so now, and he realised the crowd around him had taken his ironic statements as announcements of yet new services the pub-shop-post office-bank was offering. In an instant he took in the eager faces, liberated yet another pad of Basildon Bond, sat, and releasing his ball-point once more from the fluff, began to sign up people for half-hour sessions with Sally, telling them the first session was free and that the subsequent fees would be based on their ability to pay. "Religious socialism," he murmured to himself, grinning, "Socialist religion," he corrected himself. "God, as working man." No, that was all male, and not politically correct. Quick, add a token woman: "With Mary Magdalene as unionised sex worker," he said aloud ... too loud. The rest of the queue of signees dispersed in embarrassment. Ah well, six names were enough. Word-of-mouth would do the trick from those six onwards. "My big mouth," he complained to himself, and poured into it, with a grimace, the remains of the cheap champagne-perry, with a vague resolution in future to make a cheaper version by mixing cider vinegar with Andrews Liver Salts. He then handed the list of six clients and times to Sally, saying, "Your industrial ministry begins here."

Dafydd's next task was to call each person over and show examples of the objection forms to the county's housing plan. The combination of examples in both languages and Dafydd's great looming shape gave the villagers a new sense of power over their own lives. Yes, perhaps the county's plan **could** be stopped. Perhaps their voices **would** be heard. Perhaps a public enquiry **would** be held.

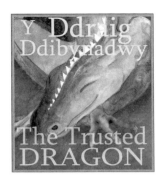

SCENE FIVE

Walking Above the Village,
Seeing *The Trusted Dragon*
autumn, a few weeks later

It was Brum who had planned the autumn walk. Sally had cajoled the others to join, pleased to see Brum's trimmer figure and reduction of breathlessness. The walk was to be the circumnavigation of the U-shaped glacial valley above their village. Wednesday afternoon was half-day closing in the village (which meant simply that one person, Myfanwy, locked one door, and all services in the village shut down).

"See!" said Brum, pointing back as they rose above the village.

They saw the old chapel, where conversions were in concrete now, not lives. The old chapel was flying the Trust's new flag. They all thought of the four local candidates for the accommodation from which only two could be chosen.

They saw the pub, now the heart of the village visited daily by most people for one or other or many services. It too flew the Trust's flag, which Myfanwy had created – a circle of red dragons dancing, holding conversations together.

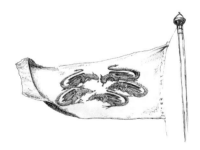

"Well done, all of you!" the joy burst out of Sally. "All of us!" she corrected herself, accepting egoism in place of patronisation. She had grasped the nearest hands, Brum's and Dafydd's.

Brum thrilled to Sally's touch and reached out and took Myfanwy's hand, uniting the circle. Myfanwy, joining her hand with Dafydd's, was looking up shyly into Dafydd's face and blushing.

"Why Myfanwy!" Sally exclaimed, "you look so different in daylight!"

In the embarrassed silence, Sally let go of hands and turned away, and Dafydd said, "To me she looks as beautiful as when she was sweet sixteen." Myfanwy blushed redder.

"Why the walk, Brum?" Sally asked, turning back with a cheerful smile, hoping to repair the situation.

Brum indicated with his hands the head of the valley.

"Dai and Ianto Jenkins told me they both want to sell up. None of their kids want these farms and their kids say the grand-children wouldn't want the farms either. So Dai and Ianto asked me, at least, I think they asked me, not directly, like, but would the Trust be interested in buying the farms and building them a double bungalow in the village to retire to, but the money from selling the farms would need to be at least the market price because they've got no pensions and want to buy new cars."

"You said that all in one breath," Sally said, admiringly. Brum beamed.

"They're my uncles" said Myfanwy. "Why didn't they ask me?"

"I think they asked me", Brum sighed, helpfully, "because they thought I wouldn't understand."

"So it was a hint?" asked Sally.

"It's their dream," said Dafydd, softly and in his story he imitated the farmers' voices as if they too, were there, looking at the village below.

Two Old Farmers

I knew two old farmers once. They worked very hard all their lives to build up their farms for their children. But the children of one farmer said, 'We don't want to do old farming! No on your life, not seven days a week, three hundred and sixty-five days a year, and for what? Peanuts!'

And the children of the other farmer said, 'There's just no future in it, Tad. Remember pigs? You couldn't make pennies out of pigs but you carried on, losing. Remember milk? You carried on losing with milk. Now sheep. That's all you got left, and they cost more than you get for them'

So the two old farmers said, 'Sod it! Our children don't want the farms. The farms are killing us, so, now it's our turn. What do **we** want?' And they decided they would have what everybody else had, a new, dry, warm bungalow with no mice and no jackdaws, a new, quiet, comfortable, fast car, not a slow, noisy old Landrover.

'And a holiday! they said, because they'd never had one, not a real holiday, somewhere foreign, in the sun. 'Oh! And a pension!'

Some of the lads they'd been at school with were on pensions already, at sixty, and fat pensions too. 'Five times what I get to live on in a whole year! And I work every day for my money, and they do nothing!' So they talked to some of their former school friends.

And there was one among their schoolfriends, Iolo, who said 'Stop working now! Sell the land! Even as hill-land for farming, your two hundred acres would give you a good pension. Yes, every year for the rest of your lives!

Ah, but if you sold your land for **building**, it would be worth a **hundred** times as much! You could be millionaires and hand on a tidy bit to your families when you go!'

For several months the two old farmers talked and thought, and talked some more and thought some more. Why had they worked so hard all their lives? They'd nearly died from the sheep-dip organo-phosphates. Their hearts had been broken having to get rid of the pigs, then the milk-cows, then their wives walking out on them, tired of the houses falling down around them and no hope. 'Diversification' was an easy word to say, but bed and breakfast? Pony-trekking? You had to have spare money to start up something like that. Buffalos? Ostriches? What if you get it wrong and they all die? No! They knew sheep. Sheep it was, though nobody wanted the wool nowadays and the meat earned them a tenth of what it sold for in the supermarkets.

Those months of talking and thinking were angry months, and puzzled months, and lost months. They walked their fields and tried to imagine a hundred and fifty new houses instead of tumbling walls and rocky, reedy bogland.

The deciding factor was the influence. They both got the influence but they ignored it and carried on working….

"The influence? What 'influence'?" Brum asked, thinking this was some Welsh secret network he'd never been aware of.

"The truncated word is 'flu', 'influenza', Birmingham."

When they felt at their worst they decided to anticipate their softer, bungalowed, future lives by going to the doctor, especially now that the doctor held a regular clinic once a week in the pub-shop tap room which the village Trust had just refurbished. It was waiting at the doctor's clinic they got the idea. 'The Trust!' they said. 'The Trust will have the answer!'

There was a long pause.

Brum was first to break the silence, "What was the answer?"

Dafydd turned away and began to continue the walk. Myfanwy stepped into the track by his side. Sally turned to Brum and said sadly, "We've raised their hopes but there's no money in the Trust to buy these two farms, nor to build two new bungalows. There is no answer." She touched Brum's arm kindly. His heart and mind both leapt. He hurried after Dafydd and Myfanwy shouting as if on a busy Birmingham street. "Stop! Stop! Sally's given me an idea!"

The sound of shouting was harsh. Dafydd turned aside from the track and leaned on a rusty gate. Myfanwy joined him leaning, their elbows touched, their eyebrows were raised, imagining all too easily the idea Sally had given to Brum.

"Look, all of you!" exclaimed Brum, rushing up, followed by Sally and wishing he was talking to their faces not just their sides and backs. "We'll raise the money to buy these farms…. And build the bungalows. We'll …. We'll make this land into something… something that is the answer…"

"What was the answer?" Dafydd echoed Brum's previous words, quietly. Brum wondered if the question was mocking, but blundered on: "**Our** answer…. Like what we've been doing through the Trust. We see what's needed, get everybody involved… so what have we got?" Brum began to count on his fingers, and Sally, bright-eyed, nodded admiringly. "People round here, they know farming, right? And they even know the farming they've stopped doing. Like pigs and cows, right? And we need lots of jobs, and you can't just make lots more of the same – farm stays, B&B, pony-tracking…"

"Trekking," Sally corrected, but her voice was kind....

"That's what I said. Anyway, not more of the same, but different and pulling in new money, tourists who come just for that...."

"What's 'that'?" Dafydd asked quietly.

"Er... farming, but not the same, ah, and under cover so it's all year round, any weather, and they pay."

Sally encouraged Brum, her voice rising. "Yes, yes, it's not just a farm park or farm museum it's..."

"It's ... different" ended Brum, lamely, his voice falling. A sad silence enveloped them all.

Dafydd took a deep breath and turned, resting his elbows on the gate as he leaned his back against it. "I knew a farm park once," he said, and his three friends looked up at him with new hope.

The Farm Park who was ambitious

This farm park was ambitious. It wanted to be more. It wanted to be bigger and better than all the other farm parks it had ever heard of or had even dreamed about, and one day it saw a child visitor, a little girl called Myfanwy, and Myfanwy was blowing bubbles.

Myfanwy's finger brushed Dafydd's hand.

The farm park watched the bubbles, only partly interested, but suddenly it was fascinated because one bubble landed on an ant-heap, and there the bubble made a clear dome. Within the dome one ant was temporarily trapped and it walked round and round touching the insides of the bubble with its feelers.

Dafydd then made four great gestures with his arms to north, east, west and south.

So the farm park conceived there and then of becoming four enormous bubbles as domes within which there would be four complete working farms, one from the ancient past, one from the not-so-ancient past, one from the nearer past and one from the nearest past, a farm from each period, one powered by oxen, then one by horses, then one by steam, then one by oil. Next to each period farm ...

Here Dafydd made smaller gestures.

... a smaller bubble with the explanations, displays and people to interview to ask, and people doing tasks of the period, and, and a restaurant where you could eat the food of the period, in the style of the period, produced by that period's farm.

"One, ancient, pre-Roman, Iron Age, Celtic, aboriginal," said Myfanwy, seeing onto the landscape the pictures from her school books. "The next, medieval, Middle Ages, peasant economy. The next, eighteenth century, 'improved', enlightened. The next Industrial Revolution, mechanical, Victorian. The next, modern, agri-chemical, contemporary."

"Visitors!" added Brum, "school kids learning; agricultural students studying; the general public, curious; local, national, **inter**national!"

"A four-season 'season'!" Sally said rapidly, laughing with the joy of the air and hills. "Jobs as guides, cooks, waiters, waitresses, farm-workers, display-makers." She seized Brum and kissed him on the forehead. "Oh Brum! And training, **careers**, real, local, village-based, community **careers!**"

Brum was holding Sally's hands and gazing into her smiling eyes. "We must do it!" he urged, though he was ambiguous about what 'it' was.

"I can teach hand-milking," said Myfanwy, "And Dafydd is a wonder with goats, always was."

Brum and Dafydd were now both blushing.

"The climate in Wales was different then, wasn't it?" said Sally. "In a bubble you can control the climate. Then if it looked right, all genuine and historic, film companies might even come to film there…."

"High tech!" Brum exclaimed. "That's my field. We'll make our own DVDs and sell them to the visitors. Virtual Reality Farming."

"We'd have to have lots of special live events," said Sally frowning, "or else they'll visit us only on-line instead of live."

"Festivals," said Myfanwy, "feasts, festivities, festal days, gatherings to mark, celebrate, and honour the passing of the year."

"Performers!" exclaimed Sally with a little, excited jump.

"Mummers, strolling players, folk dancing…" even Myfanwy's list had the music of enthusiasm.

Dafydd was chuckling.

> And the farm park became something the like of which had never been seen before, and people came from all over the world to look and ask and eat.

He paused. "And they called it…." He paused again.

"What did they call it?" Brum's impatience came out as irritation.

"'The Big Farm'?" Sally offered, adding, "'The Four Farms'?"

"'Farming through the Ages'," Myfanwy saw a book title.

"'The Period Farms Experience'," Sally's words were flowing fast. "'Wales at Farming'. 'The Wales Farm Experience'… 'Farms R Us'… 'Farms with Us'… 'Welsh Food Farmed'… 'Fun Farm'…"

"'The Funny Farm'," muttered Dafydd.

"'Fruits of the Earth' … " There was no stopping Sally now … "'Fruitful Farm Experience'."

"'Fecund Fun," muttered Dafydd.

"'Agri-Domes', 'Agro Bubbles'," Myfanwy offered.

"'Aggro-Burst'," muttered Dafydd.

"'The All-Wales Four-Period Agri-Experience'," Brum said, to summarise.

"'Wild Wales Tamed'," muttered Dafydd.

"Oh, but – the title's got to work in both languages" said Sally earnestly.

"IAWN!" said Dafydd. "I knew a title once," and he seized Myfanwy's hand and led the walk along to the bridge over the river.

Brum grabbed Sally's hand and swung it as they followed Dafydd and Myfanwy. "Oh Brum, it's a fantastic idea!" Sally giggled. "All we need now is millions!" she laughed aloud.

"First a business plan with realistic costings," said Brum, "then a marketing plan with realistic figures. Then we'll go for the millions!"

All this realism sobered Sally and she slipped her hand out of Brum's and they completed the walk without touching again. For the first time in his life Brum regretted his realism.

SCENE SIX

**The Pub – Shop –
Honeymoon Hotel – Post Office –
Bank – Chapel –**
The Trusted Dragon
that evening

That evening in the bar Myfanwy dug out some unused rolls of wallpaper and Dafydd drew great, bold drawings and diagrams with a thick, black felt pen. In green pen Sally wrote on words to label the drawings, and Brum wrote columns of figures using the last pad of Basildon Bond. The four half-pints of beer were pushed to the edges of the bar.

Brum looked across at the drawings. "It's too big!" he remarked.

"Big, bold, brilliant," Dafydd chanted, "Think big!"

"'Small is beautiful'," quoted Sally, looking at Brum.

"Believe me," said Brum "I'm an engineer. The cost goes up exponentially the bigger the space you try to enclose in one go – to withstand the wind pressure and the weight of snow for a start."

"What size then?" asked Myfanwy as she waved her new girl assistant to deal with the latest inflow of shop and pub customers.

"Off the peg," said Brum.

"Off the wall," muttered Dafydd.

"Use a well-tried design and make multiples," said Brum.

"Multiples?" asked Sally.

"Yes, twenty, thirty little ones rather than one big one," said Brum.

"Four big ones," Dafydd pointed to the drawings.

" Hundred and twenty little ones," corrected Sally.

"I knew a theatre once," said Dafydd unexpectedly.

His three friends looked up, irritated to be interrupted in their busy-ness, yet the story-magic made them protest only mildly.

"Oh, Dafydd!" said Brum.

"Not now, surely?" said Sally.

"What's a theatre got to do with anything?" asked Myfanwy.

The Theatre

The theatre I once knew was, and is, in the USA. A millionaire built it. Indeed, for the flooring he imported fresh, hot lava from Mount Vesuvius in heated ships and when they poured it onto the floor, it cooled and set.

But the floor isn't the basis of this story. No. The audience, when they enter the theatre have come from the noisy, busy, urban streets that smell of chocolate.

Dafydd reached for his drink, sipped it, and placed it on the sheet of paper Brum was about to write on.

Brum put down his biro and asked "Why chocolate?"

The millions to ship the lava had been made from chocolate-eaters like you and me.

Myfanwy looked hungrily across at the shop's section **Confectionery**. Sally lifted her glass with a far-away look and was surprised when it wasn't a creamy hot cocoa. Dafydd's voice was continuing.

The audience members enter the theatre and they are amazed, transported, enthused, inspired, delighted.

Dafydd cast a doubtful look at Myfanwy. Had holding her hand on the walk infected him with her Thesaurus bug?

They see, above them, the clear, blue sky, with white clouds travelling across it. Yet they know above them is the theatre ceiling. They see before them the outside walls of castle towers between which is a courtyard open to the sky. Yet they know the towers are but the proscenium arch, and the courtyard is the stage.

The lights dim, and the audience gasps. Above them is now the starry sky with each constellation twinkling in place as the clouds, now grey, still pass across as if the theatre air-conditioning is a gentle, rural breeze.

Dafydd paused. Brum looked around him, thinking that the story couldn't possibly stop there. But Dafydd did seem to have stopped. Completely.

"Now there was one among them…" said Brum indignantly, trying to inject a bit of pace and action back into things.

"No, Brum," said Sally, gently, touching his forearm. "That's it."

"What's 'it'?" said Brum, angry now at seeming stupid.

"I'm with Brum," said Myfanwy, surprising everyone with the new energy in her voice. "What's 'it', Dafydd?"

"Well," said Dafydd, amiably, "Brum's correct."

There was one among the audience who said to himself, 'This is not a shopping mall, not a dry museum, not a drive-in morgue. This is not a glitzy, pushy theme park. This is magic and mystery.'

"I've got it now," said Brum, grinning. He wasn't usually irritated for long. "they, Joe and Josephine public, when they wander into our farm idea, they've got to be Welsh-magicked, eh?"

"Yes, Brum," said Sally, again touching his forearm.

"But how, in what way, by what means, in what manner?" asked Myfanwy. She wasn't the village Scrabble champion for nothing.

"The entrance," said Brum, decisively. "It's got to be right, absolutely right."

"I knew an entrance once," said Dafydd in a strange, far-away tone.

The Entrance to the Underworld

I put on a helmet with a light on it. I got into a cage. Great wheels began to spin and we dropped into the darkness. The air was hard and sharp and cold. There was the earth's heart, pumping, pumping. Then the air was warm and old where the cage stopped and I got out and I walked along inside the earth's arteries to where a great bladed parasite was cutting the earth's flesh into shreds to be carted away.

Dafydd's far-away tone was joined by a far-away look. His three friends were silent in the pause. Nobody drank or drew or wrote.

Every collection of stories, every saga has a descent into the Underworld, a death and resurrection, a conquering of the past to be free to create a new future.... The pit of despair when the pits closed...

There was a long pause. Brum didn't ask a question. He spoke, instead, voicing a comment and a statement. Sally noticed a depth in his tone which she'd never noticed before.

"Brilliant, Dafydd! We'll do that – re-open the old ruined lead mine. Time travel. The visitors are taken down into the earth, the darkness, from which they rise into the past."

"Rock paintings!" Sally exclaimed. "They see Middle Stone-Age then Late Stone-Age cave paintings as they descend. They ascend through a hunter-gatherers' settlement into the earliest farming."

"He made his millions in chocolate?" Brum asked, up-to-earth again having risen from his own mystery. "That gives me an idea."

SCENE SEVEN

**The Pub – Shop-
Honeymoon Hotel –
Post Office – Bank –
Chapel – Farm Project HQ
two weeks later**

Myfanwy tapped the newspaper front page crossly as Brum walked in. "You didn't tell us, say, let on, bring us in on your secret, did you?"

"Commercially sensitive information". It was Brum's third favourite phrase. "I was very lucky to time it when I did."

"Lucky," quoted Sally, shaking Brum's hand, her formality at odds with her affection. "It was brilliant and enormously generous!"

Dafydd merely quoted the article from memory, savouring the unintentional alliterations.

'Spectacular Spectacle Coup

Local man sells seeing for a million. Bradley Broad, originally from Birmingham, has sold his patent for self-cleaning lenses to German international glasses manufacturers. Bradley told our reporter, "All the money is going into our local Trust."

" Birmingham," added Dafydd, admiringly, "you are a secretive person! How did you invent such a thing?"

Brum looked away from his three friends. Sally had never seen him shy before. "It's since I lost weight. Now, when I pee, I can ... see myself, see what I'm doing." There was a snort from Myfanwy. Sally's and Dafydd's eyebrows rose simultaneously. "And in a hotel toilet, there were these non-flushing stand-ups and I thought 'How do they do it?' So, being an engineer I went into the internet and read up all this surface chemistry and physics so it all runs away without water and nothing sticks or stinks." Brum sighed.

"Did you pee on your glasses, then?" asked Dafydd, wonderingly.

"No ... no, but there was the technology to make self-cleaning windscreens and car headlights, no wipers needed. The dirt just doesn't stay on, nor the rain, and yet it wasn't yet commercial and mass-produceable. So I just put two and two together…"

"With some brilliance!" interrupted Sally, patting Brum's shoulder.

"And I remembered some treatments we gave to ship's bottoms when I was in the shipyards. They'd probably never connected the two, but… well… I did, and I bought up the old patent, and re-patented it and sold it."

"From peeing to bottoms. 'Where there's muck there's brass'," Dafydd quoted contentedly.

Brum chuckled. "Now you'll be able to buy specs that won't mist, will be clear even when rained on, and will never need cleaning."

"With your name on, credit to you, acknowledgement, fame," said Myfanwy.

"No," said Brum with a sigh of realism. "They've bought me out totally, so nobody will ever know."

"Except us now, and **before** us, all the readers of the paper." Myfanwy tapped the paper less crossly now.

"I'm sorry," said Brum.

There was a sigh of contentment from all four friends. It was partly the beer glasses they'd just silently raised to greet the exciting, funded, new future, it was partly the beer. It was partly the pause before the next busy rush of planning.

"Meanwhile," said Dafydd, slowly, "while you, Birmingham, have been away rescuing all four-eyes from all future rain-blurred vision, we have been making a humbler start in the old coach inn courtyard."

"Oh, yes, Brum, do come and see!" said Sally, excitedly grasping Brum's left hand, causing his beer, in his right, to spill.

All four friends went through the back door of the bar, and there, instead of the familiar battlefield remains of Myfanwy's last three cars, Brum saw a big, clear space with four of the village teenagers working with three retired people of the village restoring concrete patches to cobbles and cleaning out the old stables around the yard. Sally made loud announcements in slow Welsh, and Myfanwy whispered fast translations into English into Brum's ear.

"**Skills sharing**, the old teach the young; **restoration**, retain the character, **utility**, put the old space to use; **workshops**, flexible-use spaces for local people to work in."

"The Trust can't buy the workshops because that would benefit a Trustee," said Dafydd to Brum, "but the Trust will rent the workshops **from** the pub and rent them **to** people to make jobs here."

"I hope you don't mind…" said Sally in a concerned voice.

"Not a bit!" exclaimed Brum, puzzled.

"No, we've set up a trading company while you were away. It covenants its profits to the Trust so the company can sell goods and do the non-charitable things the Trust can't do."

"Ah!" said Brum, grinning, "Now profits, I know about profits. Good work!"

"I knew a prophet once," said Dafydd as Sally guided them around the three future workshops. For his friends, it was strange to be listening to a story as they walked and looked. Their adaptation to the strangeness was to be silent, and point and nod as if suddenly dumb.

The Prophet

This prophet, she was a seer, a soothsayer, a truth-teller who had the second sight. You don't have to be the seventh child of a seventh child. Nowadays you get the sooth by wanting it and waiting. Well, she waited. She didn't try. She didn't push. She just waited. My, how she waited!

Nobody knew, you see. All the while she was at school her father had her working every evening and every weekend.

Sally noticed Myfanwy pulling away as if a wasp was about to sting her. Sally smiled reassuringly but Myfanwy looked right through her at some distant thing.

Dafydd's deep voice was rumbling on. It seemed deeper than usual.

If her Tad caught her starting to read a book or starting to do her homework, he'd say, 'No time for that! There's a barrel needs changing! These glasses need washing! Empty the ashtrays!'

Brum's hands gripped each other and Brum looked long and hard at Dafydd whose voice had gone even deeper.

Oh, she had friends, this prophet, but her Tad sent them away whenever they called by.

There was a pause. They were, all four back at the bar. Brum and Sally both looked at Myfanwy who was suddenly very still and looking down at the counter. Brum's hands ungripped and one hand sought Sally's and gave Sally's hand a comforting squeeze. Dafydd, too, was looking down. Brum and Sally looked at him.

Now there was one among the young woman prophet's friends who said, 'You're bright at school, never mind you can't do any homework. You could go to university.'

But the prophet insisted that she could see all her future only too clearly, and it would all be behind that bar. 'I will tell **you** three things' she said. 'One, **you** will go to university,' she foretold, 'two, you will travel the world, and three, you will come back here.'

Well, every word the prophet foretold came true.

Her friend did go to university, and when he came back from university, she was still behind the bar though her Tad had died.   'Come with me,' her friend said, 'Let's travel.' But she only repeated her prophecy, and he did travel the world.

When he came back after thirty years of travelling the world, she was still behind the bar. 'See!' she said, 'I said you would come back. And here you are.' 'Yes,' he replied 'And here **you** are. All your prophecies have come true. You are a true prophet.'

There was another long pause. Myfanwy served them each a beer on the house and looked at them in turn with a fierce defiance in an equally fierce silence. Her hands were trembling. Nobody interrupted the silence.

Then Dafydd's voice came as a whisper then a cough, then a choked voice, then the voice relaxed.

Now there came the moment when the prophet's friend needed to say 'When we were at school I offered to work for your Tad instead of you, so you could get your homework done and go to university. When I had been to university I offered to work instead of you, so **you** could travel the world. But you insisted you had to fulfil your prophecy.

And the friend then added, 'Now I am back, thirty years later, **I** will tell **you** three things.'

Sally saw Myfanwy was standing rigidly and staring at Dafydd who was looking, comfortably, into Myfanwy's eyes as his voice continued.

'One, going to university is going out to discover things. But the things can come to you equally if you stay still.

'Two, travelling the world is going away to discover yourself. But you can discover yourself equally if you stay still.

'Three, I too am a prophet and I will tell you three more things,' her friend said.

'One, the time you have prophesied for yourself is over. Two, you are free now to go to university **and** to travel the world. Three, I offer, once again, to work instead of you so you can do these things.'

Dafydd and Myfanwy's mutual gaze held through the silence that followed. Sally and Brum watched, fascinated. In Myfanwy's eyes there were tears while her mouth was tense and angry. Dafydd's eyebrows knitted in concern while his mouth opened into a big smile.

"Old fool!" Myfanwy said at last. "I'm supposed to **go**? I'm supposed to go off now you're back, at last? Old fool!"

Dafydd shrugged and looked around him, "Seems logical to me," he said, looking to Sally and Brum for support. "We help the village to self-development. To be true to those principles, we should help one another to self-development too."

"Men and their logic, reason, analysing, quantifying everything," muttered Myfanwy, but Sally could see she was fighting a smile.

"I've developed," said Brum in a quiet voice nobody had ever heard him use before.

"And I've learned so much!" exclaimed Sally with her usual enthusiasm.

Myfanwy was still looking at Dafydd. "You and your 'black and white', 'either or', 'take it or leave it'. Don't you understand? I couldn't be the one to hold you back, with your offers or without them. It had to be you, you old fool! If you'd wanted me that much, you wouldn't have gone to university nor travelled the world, nor done my work for me so I could do those things. If you'd wanted me that much you would have stayed with me ..." Myfanwy was talking faster and faster and was leaning towards Dafydd as she spoke. "It was impossible, go; stay – if you had stayed then who would you have been? The disappointed man who had never been to university and had never travelled the world. I **had** to prophesy. I didn't want you…. with me…. and … disappointed."

Dafydd stood up. To Sally and Brum he seemed to have grown even taller than his great height. He'd lost the slight apologetic stoop and his great chest had filled with air. In a huge voice he said, "Well, I'm not disappointed now!"

Sally beckoned to Brum to come with her. Brum felt Sally grasp his hand and pull it. "Brum, I need you to come and look at some figures!" said Sally, dragging Brum towards the door.

"Oh! Ah?" said Brum in total puzzlement, and he found himself outside the pub-shop and saw Sally had flicked the sign to 'closed'.

"What figures?" said Brum.

"Oh Brum!" said Sally, "Isn't it romantic!"

"Ah, I understand," said Brum, with a beaming smile, and he stood on tip-toe and kissed Sally, much to her surprise.

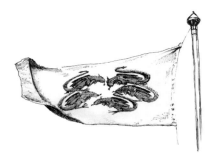

SCENE EIGHT

**The Pub – Shop –
Honeymoon Hotel –
Post Office – Bank –
Chapel – Workshop – Farm
Project HQ
the next evening**

Sally and Brum came into the bar separately the next evening and both were surprised to see Dafydd, in an apron behind the bar, and Myfanwy in a lively orange and green silk suit, sitting very elegantly in front of the bar. "My round," said Myfanwy, and placed the exact change on the bar. Dafydd was humming and smiling to himself as he drew the three half pints.

"Have one yourself," said Myfanwy pointing to the money. Neither Sally nor Brum spoke as they watched Dafydd put the money in the till and draw a half for himself.

Sally laid on the bar the four names of the villagers who had applied to live in the two dwellings the old chapel was being converted to. There were customers in the shop and Myfanwy's assistant was within earshot so Sally tapped the four names and said, "We, the Trustees, must decide. Which two people will get the dwellings?" she said brightly.

"And which two will not," added Dafydd, darkly.

"It's clear," said Myfanwy, tapping the first name with her finger. "She's lived with her father too long. She deserves her own space."

"Ah," said Brum, "But she won't use the workshop." Brum tapped the third name. "But he will, and that makes a house-plus-job." Brum's finger stayed firmly on the third name.

Sally gently nudged his finger aside with her thumb and indicated the second name. "I know she's retired and won't use the workshop, but her grandson might develop his cash-only bike-repairing into a legitimate business, and she's not that happy living with her daughter-in-law." Dafydd's large fingers wandered over the four names and settled on the fourth. "He's just waiting for that dwelling to be able to marry. If he doesn't get it, his girl-friend will have their baby and they may never get married! I vote for a family of three over all these singles!"

All four friends took a breath to say more to support their candidate. All four friends said their first few words simultaneously but somehow Dafydd's words had the magical formula to win out over the others..

The Difficult Decision

I knew a difficult decision once. The difficult decision was fought over hard, behind closed doors, and finally the decision was made, and the decision was posted on the village notice board.

Now there was one among the decision-makers, Iolo the Foolish, who pointed to the decision and said to Lyn, the candidate he favoured, 'Of course, I wanted it to be **you** but, you know..... the others .....' And that candidate told everyone that it was 'the others' who had all, unfairly voted against him.

The other decision-makers, when they each heard this rumour, each went to their favoured candidate and said, 'Of course, I wanted it to be you but, you know... the others...' And all **those** candidates told everyone else that it was 'the others' who had all unfairly voted against him or her.

The winning candidate, Sara, whose name was on the village notice board, listened to all these rumours and put two and two together and understood that **nobody** had really voted for her, so Sara, the winning candidate, felt she'd been voted for only to spite all the other, losing candidates.

Soon all the candidates hated all the other candidates and all the candidates hated all the decision-makers and all the villagers went round saying how totally unfair the difficult decision had been!

There was a pause. As usual Brum asked the question. "What happened next?"

"Ah" said Dafydd, smiling grimly.

All the villagers except the decision-makers got together by torchlight on the village green and they marched in anger to the house that had been made ready for the winning candidate…

"No!" said Sally, instinctively.

And burned it to the ground!

Dafydd's tone was cold with finality.

Brum slapped his hand on the list of names, "We must agree, all of us, to say nothing."

"No, Birmingham," said Dafydd quietly, "we must agree, all of us, to say **everything**." All heads turned to him.

The Difficult Decision – Shared
I knew a difficult decision once. The difficult decision was fought over hard. 'This decision is impossible', said the decision makers, but that was

already after each decision-maker had shouted very loudly at each other decision-maker, 'You are impossible!'

Now there was one among the decision-makers, Iolo the Wise, who said, 'Yes, it is impossible for us to make this decision, so let us allow the decision to make itself.' 'How?' the others asked. 'We draw up a list of the criteria. We award each candidate points, then we give each point a weighting as to how important it is. Then we add up the weighted points and the decision makes itself. Then,' said that decision-maker, 'we publish the criteria, the points, the weighting and the results. Then everybody will know.'

The pause that followed was of a new kind.

"That's not a story!" exclaimed Brum, "that's a proposal. Why didn't you just say so, Dafydd?"

Sally, as usual, tried to quiet any annoyance. "It's a good proposal, Brum, don't you agree, Myfanwy?"

"Is it a proposal?" said Myfanwy in an unusually relaxed voice, "Or a warning?"

"Oh" said Brum, more annoyed, "So you're saying it is a story!"

"If it's a proposal, simply ask, 'What happens next?'" said Myfanwy.

Myfanwy was looking directly at Brum. There was Dafydd standing tall, looming over the bar, and Myfanwy so relaxed on the bar stool. For Brum this new juxtaposition was disturbing. He looked at Sally. Somehow he felt he and Sally should be different, too.

"OK," said Brum decisively, "What happens next?" and he looked aggressively at Dafydd.

Dafydd smiled and leaned forward onto the bar so his eyes were now level with Brum's. "'What happens next?' is a question in the present to be asked after a proposal. 'What happened next?' is the question in the past near the end of a story."

Brum felt mocked, "I was only trying to ask a question!"

"I'm sorry, Birmingham. I'm happy to answer. I only need to know which question."

"This isn't fair!" exclaimed Brum. "If I ask 'what happened?' that makes it a story. If I ask 'what happens..?' that makes it a proposal!"

"That is called 'power', Birmingham, my friend," said Dafydd in an easy tone. Brum spluttered angrily.

Suddenly Sally spoke in a harsh tone they'd never heard her use before "Don't play with Brum! It's not fair!" The three friends were surprised at Sally's strength of feeling.

"And I don't need **you** to defend me, thank you!" said Brum in fury, and he abruptly walked towards the door.

Behind him he heard a great booming voice that seemed to command him to stop in his tracks and turn: "I knew a Birmingham once."

Brum closed his eyes. This was the final humiliation.

Birmingham's Heart

I knew a Birmingham once. It had a wonderful warm heart, but war damaged that heart, and so, for immediate survival that warm heart was replaced by a mechanical heart. There was busy-ness, there was business, there was traffic, the heart of Birmingham lost touch with its warmth. And the people around Birmingham felt vaguely dissatisfied. They couldn't put their finger on why but they didn't approach the heart of Birmingham much any more.

By the time Dafydd had reached this point in his story, Brum had found himself drawn back from the door, as if by magic, and he stood by his usual bar stool, but unable to break the magic by sitting.

Now there was one among the people who began to put her finger on why. She suspected that, under the new, mechanical heart, there was a piece of the old, warm heart, still beating. She gathered friends and they began to talk about **why**, and in what ways, hearts are warm.

When everyone agreed, they took away the mechanical heart, and gradually built up the warm heart again, and the people approached the warm heart of Birmingham again, and rejoiced. And the woman who had put her finger on the piece of the old warm heart was thanked, heartily!

There was a long, calm pause.

In a very small voice Brum said "What happened next?"

Dafydd smiled.

Maybe there was a proposal? We will see... But what happened next in the story was that the reawakened heart of Birmingham began to yearn, as warm hearts do, for another heart to join with. The warm heart of Birmingham saw two other hearts which had joined unexpectedly, and the heart of Birmingham couldn't understand the unexpected new feelings he had of anger and resentment. He wanted to go away, to be mechanical once more instead of having these new things called feelings...

Brum had sat on his bar stool. His shoulders were square, but he was looking down and breathing deeply.

Sally was fiddling agitatedly with the list of candidates' names. "I see!" she said in a nervous voice, "You're saying we should twin up, is that right?"

Myfanwy was rising from her stool towards Sally with arms and mouth opening. With a frown and gesture Dafydd signed Myfanwy to stop. "Twin up, how?" Dafydd asked.

"The village," said Sally, nervously, and Myfanwy settled down deflated onto her stool. "If we twin up with another village, we can help them, and they can help us." Sally seemed to be speaking into emptiness. She had the feeling nobody was listening, even though Brum was looking intently into her face. "Am I talking to myself?" she added, plaintively in a child-like voice.

"We usually are," said Dafydd softly.

"Then we can consider twinning later," she said briskly. "I think we should accept Dafydd's proposal for criteria points and… what was it? 'Weighting'… and publishing all the details of…." She pointed to the list of candidates.

"The decision will make itself," said Brum in a flat voice.

Indeed, in half an hour the decision **had** made itself, and the grandmother and young couple were to be neighbours in the old chapel.

The four friends set off together to call at the four houses and to explain their decisions one by one to each candidate. To the losing candidates they would promise the next places on the waiting list.

The notice detailing the decisions on each name on the list then went up in both languages, with all candidates' permission, on the village notice board.

As they all walked from house to house, Sally and Brum noticed that Dafydd and Myfanwy held hands.

Dafydd and Myfanwy, in their turn, noticed that Sally and Brum were keeping an extra, unusual distance between them. Myfanwy nudged Dafydd meaningfully, but Dafydd shook his head.

SCENE NINE

The Old Chapel
the next morning

"Hey," said Brum, "Dafydd, what are you doing here?"

The four friends were looking around the old chapel, now converted and ready to receive its first households.

"I'm here, like you," said Dafydd, puzzled, "to look round."

"Well, here you are looking **out,** not **round**," and Brum pointed to a fine big photo framed on the wall of Dafydd, young, clean shaven, well-muscled, in his rugby kit looking down on the room with a relaxed satisfaction.

Dafydd glanced at it and looked round at Myfanwy, raising his eyebrows.

"That old thing!" she said. "They should know the history of their village, the hero who played for Wales."

"For Wales!" exclaimed Brum admiringly "And it's signed."

"That was later," Dafydd muttered, still looking at Myfanwy.

Brum was reading. "I know this word, it's 'love', or 'darling', 'cariad', isn't it. You're a handsome lad without your beard. What do you think, Sally?"

Sally and Dafydd were both looking at Myfanwy who was going a deep red.

"Who wants an old photo any more," Myfanwy said, adding, almost inaudibly, "When you've got the real thing."

All of a sudden Dafydd was hugging Myfanwy, "Well, little give-away, where's the photo of you, scrabble champion in two languages?"

Sally was laughing, and the high white ceilings threw back the sound.

"This old place," Dafydd was saying, "it's unrecognisable." His arm was around Myfanwy's shoulder, and she was grinning as the four friends wandered from room to room.

"I could give a cupboard that would just fit there," Sally said, pressing a scriber end to make a note on her little hand-held computer.

"Free-standing cupboards are not 'fixed furnishings'," Brum warned. "By the terms of the lease we can't stop tenants taking away anything that moves."

"Let them!" said Sally with another rippling laugh.

"Even the photos?" added Brum.

"Let them!" said Dafydd, continuing as he sat on the stair looking at the arched windows in the new hallway, "I knew a photo once...."

The others sat close to him on the stairs. A kind of reckless, child-like excitement united them.

Dafydd's story voice was quite different this time. It was an intimate kind of murmur as if he was speaking very privately into each person's ear. His long arms were around all three friends as they sat on the stairs, and his long legs stretched down to one step lower than theirs did. Sally closed her eyes and recalled her grandfather. Brum remembered his grandmother, and Myfanwy could feel Dafydd's warm breath on her skin at last.

The Photo

I knew a photo once. It was a small photo, a candid shot, a snapshot of one moment in time. The photo shows a group of friends. In their twenties they had been in very different places, doing very different things, but this photo was thirty years later. If the photo had been taken the year before, you would have seen them a little distant from one another, a little smug with their situations in life, a little bit trapped, a little bit bored, not living their lives to the full, but not aware, perhaps of how full their lives could be. Oh yes, if the photo had been taken the year before they would all have looked older than they now looked a year later.

Why? Had they discovered the elixir of life? Had they taken ambrosia, the food of the gods? Had they moved to Shangri-la, where you never age? Had they found Tir-na'nOg, the Irish land of perpetual youth? Had the whole-food shop recommended large doses of Royal Jelly?

No. They had discovered only their true selves. They had taken or eaten nothing new. They had moved nowhere. They had found only one another. And only their true selves had reconnected them. So, together... facing new challenges daily together, their lives have become filled and fulfilled, full.

The photo was a quiet moment in their new, full lives...

There was a silence, a comfortable, gentle silence.

"Click!" said Dafydd softly.

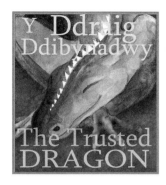

SCENE TEN

The Honeymoon Hotel-in-the-Pub
the next evening

Brum stepped in through the pub door into the shop part. There were three customers and the assistant chatting away in Welsh. Brum waved silently.

At the bar, looking very comfortable on Sally's and his bar stools sat two other locals. They were signalling to the assistant for more beer. Brum frowned and looked around.

He went through another door into the chapel part of the pub. There was a party on. He was welcomed warmly in Welsh but backed out apologetically.

He rushed to the back door of the pub and into the cool air of the courtyard. His three friends were nowhere to be seen, but the workshops were nearly finished. Brum threw a few English words of praise and encouragement into the air and was acknowledged cheerily by the retired and teenage helpers alike. He retreated to the little door leading down to the cellar and up the stairs.

Holding his breath he crept up the stairs following the sign 'Honeymoon Hotel'. On the way up he wondered why he was walking on tip-toe. He remembered warmly that embrace on the old chapel stairs when Dafydd had clicked the imaginary camera and had kissed Sally and Myfanwy and then had kissed him, Brum on his bald patch. "That's the first time I've been kissed by a rugby international," Brum had said at the time, to create laughter to release his knot of feelings.

Standing silently outside the honeymoon door Brum was listening. In his mind Sally was dancing sinuously. Behind the door instead, Sally was talking seriously.

Brum knocked and entered. Sally was still speaking:

"... just not enough. We'll have to choose. Hello Brum, it's decision time. Your money…"

"The Trust's money now…" Brum corrected.

"Quite right, sorry. The Trust's money, we were just saying…."

"You…" said Myfanwy, quietly.

"Quite right. Sorry. I was just saying, … the money's not enough to both buy the farms…"

"Buy both farms?" Brum asked.

"No. Let me finish! To both buy both the farms **and** build the bungalows and do the survey, costing and feasibility for the Farm Fantasia."

"Agri-Dream," corrected Myfanwy.

"Wild Wales Tamed," corrected Dafydd.

"The Farms Project," corrected Brum.

"OK! OK!" said Sally in exasperation. "Never mind the name, there's simply **not enough money!**"

"Buy the farms," said Brum, joining Dafydd sitting on the big four poster. Myfanwy was reclining on the chaise longue and Sally had turned the dressing table chair around so that she sat facing the room. The reflection of the back of her head kept moving strangely in the mirror as she spoke.

"OK," said Sally. "But do we then **work** the farms? My field is theology not agronomy."

"Consider the lilies of the field…" said Dafydd quietly.

"Market gardening, a garden centre?" asked Brum innocently.

Dafydd chuckled. "An arable parable" he laughed.

The reflection of Sally's head bobbed more rapidly.

"Dafydd, this is serious! We are now responsible for a seven figure sum! The farms plus their houses will take all but a quarter of the million!"

Myfanwy eased round onto her elbow. She looked only at Dafydd though she was clearly addressing them all. "Brum is right. If we don't buy the farms we can't build the Agri-Dream and Uncle Ianto and Uncle Dai are relying on us now."

"But we can't build them their bungalows **and** start the Farm Fantasia."

"Step one," said Brum, holding up a finger, "is buy the farms. Now the old chapel is converted, we can borrow against that added value to build the bungalows. The farmers can invest their money from selling the farms and that'll earn them four or five times a year what farming gave them."

"But we've then got over three hundred acres of farm to run or do something with…" Sally pleaded.

"And two run-down old farmhouses and buildings…" added Myfanwy. The farmers were her uncles after all, and she knew how bad the farmhouses had become.

"And hundreds of sheep," added Dafydd, "and sheep are not the birds of the air!"

"Eh?" said Brum.

"Dafydd prefers goats," added Myfanwy, helpfully, this time looking at Brum.

"Eh?" repeated Brum.

Dafydd took a deep breath.

Kids Together

I knew an old farm once. It had had pigs and dairy cattle and sheep. Indeed, there were also always a few hens for eggs, geese for Martinmas and Christmas, and ducks for Sundays. That was in the days when you ate what was in front of you if it was dead, and fed it if it was alive, and sold it only if you had too many of them.

But time went on and in the newer days you only farmed what was in front of you on the computer screen, daily updated with market prices and subsidy data. You ate what was in front of you in the supermarket even though every item had travelled a thousand miles and had passed through seven hands. Each of the seven hands in turn had lowered the nutritional value of that supermarket food while simultaneously raising the price. Likewise you fed your farm livestock from the computer-posted world market prices, ordering material grown in countries you'd never heard of and mixed with items you didn't want to hear about.

Well, in December, the old farmer moved on, and a man, not young – shall I say ... 'newly sprung to the fullness of his middle years' – this new, renewed man took over the farm, sold the sheep and spend January and February making a big playground. It had rocks as castles with paths spirally up and slides to slide down. It had tunnels and narrow walkways and little dens and roundabouts and see-saws, and stepping stones across a stream and a dry hideaway under a waterfall. It was a wonderful playground.

'Why are you building a playground?' the neighbours asked 'you have no kids of your own.'

He replied with a wink 'You will see. In March I will have twenty kids!' The neighbours looked scandalised and locked up their wives and daughters!

Well, March came, and suddenly there were ten fat old nanny goats of all colours and kinds. The nanny goats got fatter and fatter, then one by one, they had kids.

Nine had twins and one had triplets.

It was then that the Easter holiday-makers turned up in response to the adverts for **Kids Together!**, and paid their entrance fees. In the new playground the little playful, multi-coloured goat kids and the little, playful multi-coloured children played and played joyfully for hours in and out of the tunnels, hopping across the stepping stones, playing 'king and queen of the castle', 'hide and seek', and 'let's all run round crazily'.

The parents – nanny goats and human mothers and fathers – were very happy to relax and watch, and the man in his middle years hired out camcorders by the hour so the parents could film the kids together playing and the human kids feeding the goat kids from bottles.

Also on sale was a growing collection of wonderful photos of goat kids and human kids in magical moments of mutual understanding and communication. Before the Easter holidays finished these photos were not only for sale as postcards but as big pictures to frame, and they were also bound into coffee-table souvenir books.

Between Easter and the summer, as expected, no visitors came, and the man of middle years counted his earnings and worked hard improving the playground. It must have gratings so that goat droppings wouldn't be knelt on by the human kids. It must be easily hosed down at the end of each day.

There must be a big covered area for when it rains, and more playground rides.

Meanwhile he bought a further batch of ten in-kid nannys who were reaching retirement age. He also trained the older batch of goat kids in various tricks and skills.

Learning is natural to animals and humans. Natural learning is play. So, when the summer season arrived, the older human children were able to do goat-karting, chariot racing, and even football with older goat kids (who used their heads to move the ball) on a little football pitch, and the new, younger goat kids were reserved to play freely in their discovery games with the younger human kids in the improved playground.

The human parents were amazed to see, sometimes their child, sometimes a goat kid, initiate a new game and develop it together.

There was a little dairy unit now where the parents and the older human kids could see 'cheese-making from tit to tin', start to finish, and they could even have a go at hand-milking the nannys for themselves.

When all the tourists had gone away by the end of the summer loaded with videos, postcards, books, cheeses, and magic memories, the man of middle years counted his earnings again and made a vital decision.

He needed a van.

It would not do, he thought, to serve kid-meat to the visitors to **Kids Together!**

There was a long pause. Myfanwy had stretched languidly on the honeymoon hotel room chaise longue and her eyes were closed. Brum was thinking fast, phasing in the goat entertainment idea with the farm project. It therefore fell to Sally to ask the question "Why a van?"

"Ah, a van," said Dafydd as if it was a completely new thought.

The man of middle years had travelled to many countries. In the poorest countries he'd noticed the people exported very raw materials, for instance aluminium ore, and were paid very little. The less poor countries processed their own very raw materials and exported, for instance aluminium. The richer countries took their own very raw materials one or more steps further, for instance exporting car bodies made out of their own aluminium.

'So,' thought the man of middle years 'I will not export live goat kids. I will not export goat kid carcasses. I will process the goat kids at the end of the season and make tins of traditional goat curry for export to the Indian and Pakistani and Caribbean communities in Birmingham, Bristol and Liverpool.

It took the early autumn, while the goat kids were growing well, for the man of middle years to set up the hygienic kitchens and assemble the ingredients, buy a small canning machine, design the labels, and make contact with grocers' shops in the neighbourhoods in the cities.

Having exemplified natural education, he now exemplified 'Fair Trade'.

Every day through the autumn he cooked and canned and labelled, cooked and canned and labelled. And every evening he treated the goat skins until they were well-cured and soft and supple.

Having exemplified 'Fair Trade', he now exemplified 'Development'.

By the middle of November only the nannys were on the farm and he bought a colourful billy, had the scent glands removed, then let the billy run with half of the nannies for early kidding.

Having exemplified 'Development', he now exemplified 'Self-sufficiency'.

In the days to Christmas he delivered the curry cans to the city shops, and he began to work on the old farmhouse, fixing it to be a perfect example of an eighteenth century Welsh farmhouse. St Fagan's helped a lot.

Having exemplified 'Self-sufficiency', he now exemplified 'Restoration'.

In January the Christmas rush on the curries had given him income and lots of names and addresses from the curry customers asking about '**Kids Together!** As seen on' the can labels. He sent them all discount vouchers and a free postcard, and he went off for a holiday leaving a friend to make a daily visit to check on the goats.

Having exemplified 'Hard Work', he now exemplified 'Having a Holiday'!

Back from his holiday in February he let the billy in with the other twenty nannies for later kidding.

Brum interrupted "You must be kidding! Ha, ha, ha, ha!" Nobody seemed to hear Brum. Dafydd's voice continued.

Having exemplified 'Communication', he now exemplified 'Job Creation'.

He finished the house preparations with displays of information leaflets in both languages for school group visits, and he began to advertise in the village for the two permanent jobs and the four Easter and summer holiday jobs he knew he could now create.

In March and April **Kids Together!** was flat-out with the growing number of holiday-makers, and the first school groups came after the Easter holidays from a radius of two hours' travelling. On a day without school groups the man did his figures and projected the Easter increase of visitors into the summer holidays. It was May, time to bring in the final phase of the enterprise.

Dafydd's pause didn't last long.

"Just a minute!" said Brum, "all those kid skins, fleeces, whatever you call them. You forgot those. What's he going to do with those?"

"Exactly, Birmingham!" said Dafydd encouragingly.

There were various 'under-utilised resources' he didn't, himself, have the time or the skills to exploit – it was the moment to bring in the 'concessions'.

"Discounts?" asked Sally, puzzled.

No, American 'concessions', like who would take up a workshop and stall to craft the kidskins into products and sell them to the visitors? Who would bring in good locally-produced food and drink to sell in a restaurant for the visitors? Who would begin to grow fresh flowers and herbs on the farm to sell to visitors? Who would grow fresh fruit and vegetables on the farm to supply to the restaurant? Who would take on organising special events such as horse-drawn farmwork displays and skills learning?

Having exemplified 'Job Creation', he now exemplified 'Growth'.

The man approached various local people repeating his motto 'I'll bring in the visitors. What can **you** supply which **they'd** like to buy?' He knew it would snowball. The more things there were for visitors to do, the greater the numbers of visitors who would come and the greater the numbers who would return.

Having exemplified 'Growth', he now exemplified 'Service'.

All through May and June he was preparing firm standing for the car and coach parking, putting up signs and building extra toilets. Then June came.

This pause was unbearable.

Brum jumped in: "What happened in June?"

"In June?" Dafydd seemed surprised.

In June the council closed the whole thing down. He'd simply forgotten to apply for planning permission.

"But all those visitors?" Brum was irate "You can't turn away income like that! What did the council think they were doing?"

Sally's hand gripped Brum's shoulder "Brum, it's only a story…"

"But still…." muttered Brum in embarrassment.

Sally covered Brum's embarrassment with, "Dafydd. That's an excellent idea. But remember the planning permission!"

"It stinks!" said Myfanwy, relaxedly opening her eyes. Her three friends turned to her in surprise. "Listen to him! He's working day and night for years. When am I going to see him?"

"You'll see him night and day," replied Dafydd, cheerfully "He does only half the hours because **you** work with him."

"Oh, Myfanwy!" said Sally, clapping her hands together. "I'm so happy for you!"

"You said it was a story!" exclaimed Brum, nettled.

"So, Sally," Myfanwy ignored Brum, "you think it's a good new job for me to be a nanny to an old goat!"

They all laughed at this, then Brum asked "How did you work out all this month by month stuff, Dafydd?"

"On a goat farm in the Snowies in Oz."

"Then call me 'Brum' not 'Birmingham' if it's 'Oz'!"

"Ah, in Oz everything is shortened, even the drinking hours. In my own country I choose to shorten nothing, Birmingham, my friend, except long nonsense Welsh names invented for tourists!"

"Call me whatever you like." said Brum, head down, thinking fast. "But by tomorrow I want that month-by-month development plan over five years developing the farms as they are now to the full Farms Project…."

"Farm Fantasia," corrected Sally.

"Agri-Dream," corrected Myfanwy.

"Wild Wales Tamed," corrected Dafydd.

"Whatever!" said Brum irritatedly. "Then I'll do a rough costing and fund-raising plan."

"It grows!" said Sally "People will come time and time again just to watch it grow!"

"Call it 'Topsy Tamed', then" said Dafydd.

"Eh?" said Brum, as he searched around for pen and paper.

SCENE ELEVEN

Sally's Parlour

Now that the pub-shop etc assistant was trained up, Myfanwy and Dafydd could take time away in the afternoon. This afternoon they walked swiftly through the frosted village to Sally's house for tea. As usual, Myfanwy's short legs took two steps for each of Dafydd's long-legged paces. Their breath steamed as they opened the back door and went in. They were whispering earnestly, "We should have knocked. She's English."

"But she's learned Welsh. That's why we came to the back door."

"True, you'd never knock on a back door."

"Come into the parlour," Sally shouted.

"Oh dear, through the kitchen!" muttered Myfanwy. "And I didn't dress for parlour."

"You're from the last century, my dear," said Dafydd, adding, to mollify his asperity, "but then, so am I."

They stepped into the little parlour of the two-up-two-down semi-detached ex-council house. The parlour seemed already full of Brum, though even slimmer of late. Dafydd and Myfanwy exchanged glances while Sally effusively settled them together on the short, low sofa. Dafydd's legs stretched right across the room.

Suspending criticism, Sally stepped over the long legs and served the tea in mugs bright with red and green Welsh words blaring from them.

Greetings over and tea sipped, the meeting began in earnest.

"I called you here because here we can't be overheard or disturbed," said Sally.

"Even corn has ears!" muttered Dafydd pointing to a corn-dolly above the gas fire. Sally ignored him.

Myfanwy stiffened. She knew Dafydd's punning moods. She got ready to stop his wickedness, but Sally was talking on.

"I know I put that suggestion box up without consulting any of you, and I apologise. In a way it's been useful…"

"In a way?" queried Myfanwy.

"In the way that it didn't get what I expected, but what it got we must address."

"Or re-address – 'return to sender' if we don't like what's written," Dafydd chuckled.

"Don't tease Sally," said Brum with surprising proprietoriality.

Myfanwy stretched to her full height and Dafydd lowered his head towards her.

"It's her house!" she whispered in his ear. "Behave! You're not allowed to criticise an English person in their own house."

"Look," said Sally, briskly "It won't take long, then we can relax. The first letters in Welsh I've translated as best I could for Brum…"

"Birmingham, my friend!" Dafydd's voice rumbled hugely in the tiny room. "You will have to roll our pagan tongue one day since you've become such an institution here." Brum looked a little uncomfortable, but smiled and nodded. Sally sighed impatiently.

"Rather than wait for Brum to attain fluency in Welsh," she said sharply, "here is the gist of the first two letters, Dai and Ianto each write separately but using several phrases in common…"

"But then they are common!" said Dafydd, helpful. "The 'assault of the earth', as any farmers are."

"Dai …" warned Myfanwy, fearful of this irreverent mood.

"Saying," Sally raised her voice as if to quell any future interruptions, "they don't want to rent the bungalows, they want to own them, but they don't want to buy them. Frankly, I'm puzzled."

"Ah, the Celtic mind is more capable than the Saxon one…" Dafydd added his footnote, "… of holding two contradictory beliefs simultaneously, and with equal conviction. They will be masterfully content when the Trust not only buys their farms, but also gives them the bungalows to own for free!"

"But how do they expect us to do that!" Sally almost wailed.

Myfanwy gave Dafydd a strong dig in the ribs. "Myfanwy will talk to them," Dafydd promised.

"I never said that!" Myfanwy protested.

"They're **your** uncles," Dafydd said evenly. "Sally, lover of humanity," Dafydd leant forward gesturing soothingly, "Dai and Ianto have looked into the mirror and have seen only hard-working men. They have looked into the television and they have seen only the idle rich. For them it is all or nothing. When they cease to be hard-working men, they expect to be transformed instantly into the idle rich."

Brum laughed, and Dafydd included Brum into his next statement. "Whereas our friend Birmingham, here, is the ideal combination, the hard-working rich, having chosen fields where civil servants don't interfere."

"And with no sheep!" Brum added, chuckling.

"But Myfanwy," Sally asked exasperatedly "What are you going to say to them? We can't have the bungalows empty and we don't want them to delay selling their farms to the Trust!"

"I'll tell them they're silly old fools, and they can't own and must rent!"

"They can't reap what they haven't sown," added Dafydd.

"I've got an idea," said Brum thoughtfully.

"Anything that doesn't turn them against our plans," urged Sally.

Brum's words came slowly as he thought them out. "Instead of putting into shares what the Trust pays them for the farms, why don't they buy property and live off the rents? Then they **would** be buying **and** owning property, and the rents they **earn** will more than pay for the rents they'll **pay**."

"A Solomon!" exclaimed Dafydd. "A solemn man," he murmured to Myfanwy, hardly changing his pronunciation. "Yes, Myfanwy will tell them that."

"I will not be ordered about by a … a wicked, punning, has-been rugby player!" Myfanwy was laughing.

"Please, Myfanwy," said Sally.

Dafydd mimicked Myfanwy's voice to Sally, "And **I** will not be ordered about by a … church-less vicar!" Myfanwy laughed some more.

"OK! OK!" Myfanwy said "I'll sort out the uncles."

"Thank you," said Sally with a sigh. "And tell us how it goes. Now, the next letters are from the new youth club thing which you've got going in the new workshops, Dafydd. I don't know what subversive ideas you've been stirring up in them…"

"Subversive, socialist, sabotaging? I've just been broadening their perceptions and getting them to say what they want from life."

"Well, **now** they've **written** it! And it's not comforting reading!" Sally was almost in tears. "They don't seem to understand what community is!" She thrust the letter at Brum while she blew her nose sounding a note of vengeance.

"'Dear Trust'," Brum started reading the letter, "'just to set you clear, we don't want to live in our village. It's too small. There's f – all to do, and there's no transport to go anywhere and back. Maybe we'll come back when we're old, but till then, don't go building anything for us. We're off.' Then," said Brum, "there are some very … stylish signatures. These are the teenagers, right?"

In the pause Brum was suddenly aware that Sally was silent. "Say it, Sal," Brum whispered.

"What's the future?" she said with a catch in her voice. "the young people **must** stay in the village. They must have babies. They are our future!"

"The truth is," Dafydd said heavily, "the government and all the education system is trying to educate and equip them **not** to have babies!"

For a moment Dafydd was silent, then his story-voice resonated in the room.

The Outpost

I knew a town once. It was on the frontier of civilisation, or at least what the inhabitants conceived of at the time as 'civilisation', by which they meant only their own way of life. Now, every generation throws up young men and women who are pioneers, adventurers, who rebel against their parents, and that town was no exception. From the town a group of youngsters set off beyond the frontier into the wilderness, and they built a village. They called in 'The Outpost', and, despite government and education, the youngsters had babies, and the babies grew up.

Now babies of pioneers have a great hankering for city lights, and this next generation in the Outpost village in turn rebelled against their parents. 'We will not live here!' they stated, boldly. 'But without you, the Outpost will die!' countered their parents. The Outpost seemed to be in stalemate.

Myfanwy mimicked Dafydd's voice, "Now there was one among them…"

"Indeed" Dafydd laughed.

There was one among them, Iolo, who said 'We are the outpost of the town – let us have an outpost in the town!' And the Outpost villagers built a house in the town where their children could go regularly to experience town life, and the teenagers could live and work, selling the products of the village and buying things the village needed, and having parties and making friends with townspeople.

Dafydd folded his arms with an air of finality.

"And?" urged Brum, "Did it work?"

"Well," said Dafydd "It couldn't be worse than all the youngsters leaving!"

What did happen, of course, was that the friends they made in the town came to visit them in the village, and about an equal number of town people married into the village as village people marrying out.

Myfanwy tapped Dafydd's knee and spoke before anyone else could comment. "I'll tell the uncles, I will. They must buy a house in town and the Trust rents it from them for the use of our village people, youngsters included…"

"The Celtic mind!" said Dafydd admiringly, stroking Myfanwy on the head.

"Like a timeshare," Brum added with enthusiasm.

"I could do with a couple of days in town myself, sometimes," said Sally, smiling broadly.

"I'll come with you!" said Brum tersely, as if protecting her from something.

"I'm sure you're welcome," Sally responded, eyebrows raised at his tone.

"I could write in a cold garret there," Dafydd murmured. "Better than on a wet bar."

"I'll come with you!" This time Myfanwy mimicked Brum.

"You usually do!" said Dafydd with admiration in his voice.

There was an electric silence. Brum felt his skin hot but dared not wipe his forehead. Sally thought the room was too small. Everyone seemed so close. Dafydd and Myfanwy felt exposed, as if their fragile new privacy was open to view.

"What are the other letters, Sal?" asked Brum, breaking the uncomfortable magic.

Gratefully Sally busied herself with the folder before her on the coffee table.

"There's four or five letters or notes from people who don't like the changes to the pub. They're all, more or less, saying 'The pub's not like a pub anymore.'"

"Give me their names!" said Myfanwy reaching forward. She glanced quickly, "Incomers! These bastards never set foot in the pub, ever! They don't even send their guests in or visitors. They've only seen the pub now it's a shop! Ignore them!"

"Myfanwy," said Sally, her tone already breaking her rule on patronising locals, "we can't ignore local opinion. They **feel** that. Their feelings are **valid**. We must do something about it."

Myfanwy was not so fastidious. "I can ban them from the shop!"

Dafydd continued spiritedly "Freeze their bank accounts! Seize their passports! House arrest! Grab their assets!"

"Ouch!" said Brum.

"Oh do be serious!" said Sally. "What are we going to do about it?"

"Sal, you're the only diplomat here," said Brum. "You go and talk to them."

"Better to listen first," said Dafydd.

"Invite them to a pub evening," suggested Brum. "Call their bluff!"

"I think we're talking pride here," Dafydd had drawn back his feet to touch the sofa. One knee was now obscuring his view and the other was hiding Myfanwy. "They liked knowing the pub was there and was 'traditional'. Now they don't know it and therefore can't be proud that it's there."

"Isn't there a story?" Brum's voice was almost plaintive.

"Hmm!" Dafydd stretched his legs out again and Myfanwy reappeared.

The Incomers in his Head

It's true that I did know an incomer family once. They lived in a village. They never went to the pub. They never went to the church. They never went to the shop. But they wrote strong, protesting letters to the press and to their elected representatives when the pub was announced to be closing, the church was sold as a warehouse and the shop became a holiday home. They were the same family who, when they'd originally moved into the village had complained officially to the council about the smells from the cowsheds, and the noise, year round, from the cockerels and from the ewes and lambs in spring.

Soon there wasn't a single other family in the village who didn't have reason to hate the incomers. The problem was, that hatred had no easy possibility to be expressed. You can't shun people who never walk by you, you can't call out names to people who live behind high walls and hedges, so the hatred festered, unexpressed.

Now there was one among the other villages, Iolo, who decided that the real incomer family was not as upsetting (because he never saw them), as that same incomer family were in his head, where they loomed large and were the repository of his whole lifetime of resentments. In fact, the incomers were seldom out of his head, and they were making him kick his cat.

When a man kicks his cat, he knows he's been possessed, and any sensible man, knowing he's possessed, seeks an exorcism.

This man was not uneducated in the subtleties of witchcraft and the violence of religion. Indeed, he considered ceremonial burnings and other seemingly efficacious eliminations of the real family.

However, he was sufficiently aware that it wasn't the real family that were his problem, but the family in his head. Arson and pyromania would simply add guilt and possibly hauntings to the existing possession.

Seeking cures for his bodily misfunctions he had, in the past, found homeopathy to be gentle and effective and he was intrigued how infinitesimally small doses of the seeming stimulant to malfunction could actually cure that malfunction.

He decided, therefore, to call in on the incomer family, reckoning that small doses of the real thing would clear his mind of his obsession.

Wisely, he knocked on the front door rather than walking in through the back. He was welcomed with cool smiles and achieved his first small dose of reality by not being invited in. They answered his question by naming that new exotic bush which they had just planted in the garden, and he thanked them, turned and went away.

That first small dose was quite useful in its effect. The demon family in his mind now had bland smiles.

The next dose was him collecting for the fund to save the village graveyard from being sold for a building plot. He'd thoughtfully brought photos of the graveyard, expecting that the family had never seen it since it wasn't on their weekly car route to the town supermarket. In that, he was right, but he was surprised that they invited him into the house to see a painting of the village as it had been, fifty years before. He duly admired the work of art. Yes, there was the graveyard. Yes, it did look beautiful in the painting. Yes, it would make anyone write to the papers and the elected representatives to protest. Ah, but, no, they would not contribute to the fund because, after all, the painting had cost them a good deal of money, so in a very real sense they had spent money on the graveyard already.

The man had no reply for that, and was ushered out with polite warmth and thanks, but with no refreshment or opportunity to sit.

That second dose had further rescued the hideousness of the family in his mind. The real family were, after all, art lovers, and they truly loved the old village which existed in their painting.

For several weeks Iolo did not return for a further dose. Instead he pondered actively on the phenomenon he had observed. Iolo was an electrician by trade, and a perfumier by inclination. Indeed his familiarity with sparks and volatile oils had made him that pyromaniac in his fantasies. He had, in course of his professional life, fitted many burglar alarms, and his observant eye had missed little when he'd entered the incomers' house.

It was several months before he had all his items ready, then he waited.

There was a short pause. In the tiny parlour all four friends experienced the pause as palpably intense.

"For what?" Brum asked in a whisper. He cleared his throat. "He waited for what?"

Dafydd gave every appearance of having forgotten he was telling a story, but he continued with confident fluency.

He waited for the incomers to go away on their holidays, then he entered their house with care and precaution, and spent three days working hard.

This next pause Brum thought was inexcusable. "But what did he **do**?"

Ah, I had rather tell you what **the family** experienced when they returned.

A third pause was beyond Brum's patience, but as he spluttered into speech Myfanwy reached forward and touched his knee "Brum, don't provoke him!"

"**Me** provoke **him**!" Brum exclaimed. The melody of his four syllables were identical with, "He hit me first!!"

"Just wait," Myfanwy advised, "He can't bear not to finish his story. By asking questions you only provoke him to more pauses!"

"Indeed," said Dafydd, "Birmingham's questions have always given me pleasure. I only sought to increase the rewards. Yes, what **did** he do? You will guess by what the family experienced."

The first thing they noticed was a distinctly porcine odour in the kitchen. Defrosting the fridge and cleaning behind the stove did nothing to remove the smell. The pest control officer, when called in, advised that her trade was in killing **live** rodents – what the family had in the house, she told them, one: was certainly already dead, and it certainly couldn't scamper around; and two: the smell was pig shit, which was about as dead as a smell could be, and was a perfectly natural smell in a country village. The pest officer left, knowing a letter of complaint to her manager would follow.

'Pigs?' The family knew that as a result of their official complaints the only two remaining keepers of pigs in the village had been forbidden to continue.

In sniffing for draughts that might be bringing the smell from some far away village or farm, the family, to their surprise, traced the smell to the traditional craft-paintings of pigs on the kitchen wall.

To cut a long story short...

"Please do, Dafydd. There are more letters to deal with," Sally pleaded.

The family found cockerel crowing sounds at dawn coming from another gilt-framed rural scene, and loud vulgar singing emanating from the painting of a rustic inn at twilight. The Victorian farm family in another painting, so painstakingly portrayed in bucolic harmony were heard to belch and burp, and various silent smells all too human spread from their lower and upper clothing. The paintings of hunting dogs accumulated a wet-hair stink that became quite noxious, and the handsome beasts barked and howled on moonlit nights.

Hurriedly, the family took all the paintings off the walls and sealed them into dustbin bags.

Even their Volvo's air-conditioning couldn't make the drive to the art restorer bearable. With one sniff, the restorer hurried the sealed dustbin bags from the shop to the back room, and then out through the back door.

'These are the culprits,' said the restorer a week later when the family came to her summons, and she showed them a dozen small thick discs each the size of a thumbnail. 'Electronic battery-powered. Timed. Sounds. Smells. You've got a person who is very gifted at making your rural paintings come to life!'

Dafydd's voice became very sad.

It was when they saw the police crying from laughter that the incomer family decided it was time for them to leave the village. Nevertheless, they wrote to the press and their elected representatives about how lightly the police complaints system had treated their grievances. But without a known culprit, a private prosecution was just not possible...

Now if they'd asked anyone in the village, the villagers all knew, as villagers always know, as God always knows all these things. The villagers would have been delighted to tell them who the culprit was. Instead, the family had asked their solicitor, who knew nothing.

'Never mind,' the family members reassured one another, 'even now that we've moved back to town, the village is still with us in the paintings.'

But somehow, whenever they looked at the paintings, the family felt a deep unease as if their two-dimensional village was still alive in all five senses.

And the man (note my lack of pause, Mister Birmingham, except to tell you of my lack of pause, of course), the man found that the incomer family in his mind had moved away too.

There was a final pause then, as Sally opened a tin of exotic biscuits and placed them on a plate saying "Thank you, Dafydd. I think I needed that. A dose of reality. Now to these last two letters. They're anonymous but they must be young kids. Look at the writing. Their Welsh is not exactly perfectly spelt, but the messages are very clear. 'What is the Trust doing for us kids? The **city's** got skateboard parks and adventure playgrounds ...', and I don't know what this is, but some sort of crazy water sports, '... and climbing walls. The town hasn't got it, so to have a good time indoors when it's raining, we have to be driven fifty miles.' So, yes, what **are** we doing for the young kids?"

"Before they become teenagers and want to go away?" added Brum ruefully.

"Perhaps they wouldn't want to go away if we had some things here that they have in the city," suggested Myfanwy.

"But the Cinema Club I started five years ago in the old chapel before the roof leaked – nobody came to the films," said Sally.

"Not exactly the multi-screen, popcorn experience," Dafydd murmured.

"I'll get the teens to research it," Dafydd spoke loudly and began to get up. "When we meet next week I'll have costs and designs and a proposal."

"A story?" asked Brum, rising.

"No question!" exclaimed Dafydd and Myfanwy laughed as she moved to the door.

Sally looked at the plate of untouched biscuits, making a note to have the next meeting in her kitchen.

Myfanwy sighed in relief. Dafydd's punning mood hadn't exploded – **this** time.

SCENE TWELVE

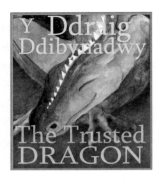

**The First Workshop
in the Pub Courtyard
the next week**

After the celebration of the opening of the the first workshop in the pub courtyard, the four friends stayed on, cleaning up. So far the workshop had no immediate tenant, but the teenagers and Dafydd seemed to be meeting there several times a week, and the sound system, fridge, ashtrays and lurid posters which they had moved in showed they felt this should be a regular use. What other use would be compatible? None of the friends had dared ask that yet. Soon the other two workshops would be finished, so perhaps the question would never need to be raised.

"Put everything down and look at these drawings" exclaimed Dafydd.

"Sci Fi monsters or weird sex?" asked Brum, nodding at the posters.

"Skateboard Park and Adventure Barn," corrected Dafydd and he laid some flip-chart paper on the renovated pool table and pointed to the figures.

"It would cost a year's income from me, but we could have under-cover recreation for kids and teens and the town doesn't have it!"

"Youngsters would come from the other villages," said Sally.

"You bet!" said Dafydd. "That's what our teens are counting on."

"Just a minute," said Brum "That's a drawing of the lambing shed behind the chapel."

"Central," exclaimed Sally.

"Feed my sheep," murmured Dafydd.

"My auntie owns it," said Myfanwy, "but they only bought it for the grants. They never really used it."

"Except for barbeques!" Dafydd reminded Myfanwy wickedly.

"That was only when they were away!" Myfanwy giggled.

"Will they sell?" asked Sally anxiously.

"She says she'll give it away 'to get them skateboarders away from the steps' in front of her house!"

"But how can the Trust afford to develop it?" asked Sally with a sadness in her voice, adding plaintively, "We **must** afford it. We must keep the youngsters in the village."

"Don't hang on so hard," Dafydd advised. "Young people are like soap, hold them too tight… and they slip away."

Myfanwy interrupted, looking very directly at Dafydd. "I held my youngster as loosely as I could, and he still slipped away!"

"But he came back," said Brum, and everyone looked at him.

"Give them more reasons to stay and come back," said Dafydd quietly. "They'll have reasons to slip away, too, so don't resent that, and don't expect gratitude."

Brum laughed, "Yes" he said, "Gratitude wasn't very fashionable even in old God's time when I was a youngster!"

"And we need a minibus," said Dafydd bluntly. The atmosphere changed.

"What? No story?" exclaimed Brum. The tension in his voice anticipated Sally's.

"We can't afford to create the skate park, let alone buy a minibus," Sally whispered, despairingly. "All the Trust money is very tightly allocated. There's no contingency!"

"I knew a contingency once. It was male," said Dafydd very gravely and slowly. The others settled into chairs. Even Sally sighed with a kind of relief.

The small, sad contingency

It was a very small contingency, and all he heard from his parents was 'we need more! We need more!' Soon the suffering of his parents began to obsess the small contingency, but, try as he might, he couldn't, just couldn't grow. 'I'm just the same size!' he used to wail to himself. 'I'll never grow! And my parents will always be unhappy!'

The parents saw how their own unhappiness was oppressing their small contingency, and they felt guilty and became more and more unhappy themselves.

The small contingency saw what they saw, and he tried and tried to hide how unhappy his parents' unhappiness had made him. And they saw him putting on his forced happiness and they felt more and more guilty and unhappy themselves.

It was a hopeless, downward spiral of despair and powerlessness.

Dafydd paused.

"That's a bit much!" exclaimed Brum.

"I am describing communication with teenagers," said Dafydd very quietly.

"Do you mean," said Sally anxiously, "if we don't find the money they'll all hate us?"

Dafydd said nothing.

"But … there… was…," said Myfanwy very slowly as if prompting a senile patient. She continued, "one…among them…who…"

Dafydd was still silent.

"Come on, Dafydd," said Brum cajolingly, "give us a solution."

"I only tell stories," said Dafydd in a whisper, "and some stories don't have happy endings."

Sally was irritated by now, "And some don't have endings at all, so they shouldn't be started if they're not going anywhere!"

"That's your fear, Sally," said Dafydd, gently turning his full attention onto her. "You don't want the young people of our village to go anywhere, but you fear they'll be going nowhere."

"There was one... among... them," prompted Myfanwy more insistently.

"Who?" asked Brum. "The father? The mother? They are the only ones there, apart from the small contingency himself."

"That's just the problem," said Dafydd, now turning to face Brum.

The small contingency's mother and father both tried to reassure him in totally contradictory ways. 'Don't worry that you're small,' said his father privately to him. 'We're all three small. We don't really need you to grow, we just need, all three, to accept less and stop needing more.'

But then his mother, equally privately told him, 'Yes, you are small, but you are young and you **could** grow. You **can** grow. You **will** grow! We are old and cannot grow, so we need you. We absolutely need you to believe in yourself and grow. Grow for us, my son! You are our future! You are our survival!'

The small contingency then told his mother what his father had said, and his mother began to cry, 'You see!' she said, her voice choking, 'your father has already given up hope. It's even more imperative' (yes, she used the word 'imperative') 'for you to grow.'

Next the small contingency told his father what his mother had just said. The father, in his turn, began to cry and said, 'Oh no! You can see she's losing it! She may escape into unreality all together. You are the only one who can help. You must tell her to give up and accept being small.'

Brum's voice broke in quite loudly, "I don't think I want to hear any more!"

"It's only a story," said Dafydd "after all, a hopeless, downward spiral of despair and powerlessness is a hopeless, downward…"

"Yes!" interrupted Sally, "I take your point, but what can we do about it?"

Myfanwy's voice was soothing where Sally's had been hectoring. "There was one among them…"

"But among who?" exclaimed Brum.

"'Whom', not 'who'," corrected Sally.

Dafydd's voice started again, "No, Myfanwy's right. It was the small contingency himself."

Under so much pressure, at the bottom of the spiral he slipped sideways, lateral thinking, the creative solution, 'when you're down and out the only way is up and…'

Dafydd's silence that followed irritated all three of his friends. They looked from one to the other. Who would ask the question?

Then Brum pursed his lips in an expression of surrender to the inevitable. "And what was the creative solution?"

Dafydd's voice continued, softly:

There was one among the three, the small contingency himself, who in his despair thought, 'If you can't get bigger by growing you can get bigger by connecting', and over the next few months he sought out other small, ungrowing contingencies and he lifted their despair with his simple suggestion. 'Let's get together.' At first there were four, then each of the four sought out four more…

"A Mutual Society!" Brum exclaimed.

"A telephone tree!" Sally laughed.

"The old pub Christmas Box!" said Myfanwy, sighing.

Dafydd's voice grew louder through the interruptions.

But when his parents congratulated the small contingency he looked at them severely before they could say anything else. 'Be clear!' he said, firmly, no trace of his or their unhappiness, in his voice, 'this fund is not for your needs. It is only for the agreed needs of the members.' He saw their faces fall and spoke more firmly than ever, 'For a small sacrifice, you two too….

"You too two?" Brum echoed and laughed. Dafydd continued, even louder than before.

'Yes, you two, too,' the small contingency said, 'can become members.'

His parents looked at him. They said 'We have already made our sacrifice. We have lost you,' they said, despairingly, 'now we're left with nothing!'

His mother wagged her finger. 'You have betrayed us. You were our only hope. This will destroy your father!'

His father shrugged and looked down, 'Your mother won't survive this. You were the only hope she was clinging to.'

'Nonsense!' said the small contingency, 'The only sacrifice you have to make, father, is to give up your hopelessness about others and act for yourself. And, mother, the only sacrifice you have to make is to give up your hopefulness in others and act for yourself.'

And, so his parents did, after many tears and recriminations. And when they joined the other members they found they all began to talk about their own secret

hopes about themselves and they found those hopes
were mutual...

"I told you ... A Mutual Society!" said Brum triumphantly, then, when
Dafydd didn't continue Brum looked very concerned, "Sorry, Dafydd, do
go on."

Myfanwy patted Brum's shoulder, "that's not the thing to say, 'Sorry,
Dafydd, do go on'. That doesn't work. It can't work."

"Oh, sorry, Dafydd. Oops" Brum was grinning in embarrassment.
"What should I say? A question? Should I ask a question?"

"You just did," said Dafydd chuckling. "What Myfanwy's hinting at is
that the story's finished. That's the end."

Sally took Dafydd's hand. "Thank you, Dafydd," she said solemnly.
"That was a reprimand, gently delivered."

"Reprimand" echoed Brum, "Who to?"

"To whom?" corrected Myfanwy as she moved across to hug Sally.

"What's happened?" Brum asked, plaintively, "What have I missed?"

"You can't miss the arrow that is not aimed at you," said Dafydd with
mock wisdom, and standing up, he looked down, watching Brum, the
engineer, moving his fingers to try to work out who was firing the arrow at
who.

"At whom," said Dafydd, seemingly out of nowhere, and everyone
looked up at him. "I'll leave Myfanwy to explain it to the teenagers. The
teenagers will get it started. In two weeks I predict...! Well, a thousand
pounds."

"It?" said Brum looking around, lost.

"Oh, Brum! The Mutual Society!"
said Sally, her voice muffled in
Myfanwy's arms.

SCENE THIRTEEN

The Teen Club – Telecottage
two weeks later

The next time the four friends met, with time to sit and talk, was two weeks later, amid the floor-to-ceiling teen culture posters in the 'Teen Club' workshop in the pub courtyard, only now, the room was also called 'Telecottage'.

In the intervening two weeks Brum had been busy looking after the purchase of the two farms. Myfanwy had sorted her uncles into purchasing the property in town to rent to the Trust and had also sorted them into purchasing a holiday, leaving Dafydd to sell their animals and do the research on the design and feasibility of 'Kids Together' now that he had access to both farms. Sally, meanwhile, had been listening to the teenagers and younger children of the village.

"It was a revelation!" she was explaining as the four friends sat among the lurid posters.

"Armageddon? The Beast?" murmured Dafydd. Myfanwy kicked his shin. Sally was going on.

"When they get the bit between the teeth ..."

"Which bit?" Brum chuckled pointing at a sexy, vampire, fantasy poster.

"Brum, please listen!" Sally scolded affectionately, "I'm trying to tell you something. I asked them 'What can you offer the older people in the village...?'"

"I bet they had some suggestions!" Dafydd laughed.

"Well," Sally laughed too, "apart from what might loosely be called 'marriage guidance', they suggested their computer skills and equipment, and, after searching the web they set up this." Sally waved her arms around her indicating the two computers with speakers, phone line and fax, scanner, colour printer, photocopier and price list in both languages, with, so far, **Answer Service, faxes, scans, digital photo developing – any size, use of computer, training in computer layout and design, keying in, instant books, e-mail service, website design, audio and video editing, photocopying.**

Sally also pointed to the notice informing villagers which hours the 'Telecottage' was managed by the teenagers, and the hectoring notice '**Mae teithio'n gachu! Mae canolfannau dinesig yn sbwriel! Gwnewch bopeth o fan hyn! Mae telefythynwyr yn ei wneud yn eu pentref eu hunain! Travelling's crap! City centres suck! Do it all from here! Telecottagers do it in their own village! Chill Out! Skill up! Connect!**'

Dafydd pointed to the two metre high graphic thermometer filling up with red. "That's your touch, the church roof."

Brum frowned, "We haven't got a church! Sally is minister without portfolio. That says 'Skateboard Park' and nearly a thousand."

"As I say," muttered Sally, ignoring Brum's puzzlement, "it was a revelation. The teens organised the younger kids and sent the cutest littlest ones round door-to-door to raise the money and to ask people to pool their spare equipment, hardware and stuff." She pointed again to the machines around them. "And they told me, in very clear terms, that the Skate Park needs table tennis tables, a pool table, and disco equipment. They gave me a list."

"You do too much already," said Brum concernedly. "It's not your field."

"You're damned right!" exclaimed Sally, and even Dafydd raised his eyebrows. "I gave the list right back to them and said, "OK, you do it!""

Dafydd was clapping enthusiastically and Myfanwy offered a toast. "To the teens!"

"To the teens!" the four friends chorused, soprano, alto, tenor and bass. Then they sipped their beers in meditative silence.

"I knew an Attraction once," said Dafydd slowly. Brum looked sharply at Sally. Myfanwy glanced at Brum. Sally frowned.

The Attraction

The Attraction was way, way out in the bush in Oz. "Australia" corrected Brum.

It was like a mirage, no houses, nothing, just the Attraction. The nearest town was hours away. You could do any leisure at the Attraction, any (except gambling), table tennis, tennis, swimming (I don't know where the water came from), billiards, pool, ten-pin bowling. It was extraordinary. Cars converged on it. Cars lay, parked, all around it. There was even an airstrip, but, as I said, not a single house. It was like a powerful magnet drawing wheeled, metal things towards it. Then at a particular time the power stopped, or rather the magnetic poles reversed and all the metal objects were driven away again, scattered, dispersed...

"It had a life of its own," interrupted Myfanwy and she smiled a broad smile.

"It had a power of its own," Dafydd smiled too.

I was young. I was looking for work but also for

somewhere to live. I asked around. There was no vacancy for a rugby coach, or a poet, or a storyteller. There seemed to be no buskers, no street theatre. It was all too hot and dry. All the leisure was indoors, air-conditioned and powered by solar panels and wind turbines and some sort of fuel cells that exploited the sudden temperature drop at night...

"Interesting!" interrupted Brum the engineer.

But there was nobody there at night. Nobody! Most centres of anything in the bush would have a few Abbo...

"Aborigine," corrected Brum

"Native Australian," corrected Sally.

... shacks, but there, nothing. The bus I arrived on was waiting for me at closing time. The air all around was thick with dust from the already dispersing cars. I waved to the bus driver gesturing that I was staying the night at the Attraction. He must have said something to the passengers. They all stared at me and several of them gestured imperiously that I should stop my nonsense and climb on board and not keep them all waiting any longer!

"Hostility!" exclaimed Sally, picturing the scene.

Myfanwy put out a hand and stroked Dafydd's arm.

"You were the one among them!" exclaimed Brum triumphantly. His smile beamed all round "I got there first! Before Dafydd!"

"Yes, my friend Birmingham..."

"Brum," corrected Brum.

...is right. I was the one among them who rejected their 'hostility' and turned away to find a corner to sleep in.

There was a pause.

"Where did you sleep?" asked Brum.

"I never slept there," Dafydd replied thoughtfully.

I was offered at least ten lifts. Nobody could believe I wanted to experience the empty, closed, shut down Attraction! Eventually three vehicles... I suppose they contained the lockers-up ... anyway, these three vehicles cornered me...

"In a triangle," Brum could see it, "you would be in the centre not a corner."

"True, they centred on me," continued Dafydd more loudly.

"They picked on you?" Myfanwy was concerned.

"I don't see the point," said Sally.

Dafydd spoke even more loudly.

At that 'point' they 'picked' on me, and they said that it was impossible that anybody would stay there overnight...

"The vehicles said?" asked Brum.

"Don't interrupt him too much," Myfanwy said anxiously.

"Yes, the vehicles!" said Dafydd irritably.

The pick-ups had darkened windows and PA systems and these darkened vehicles talked to me, or rather shouted at me. They seemed totally unable to conceive of the place being populated at night.

Dafydd's old anger was palpable.

"Magic, mystery, bewitched" murmured Myfanwy her eyes round and large.

"No!" said Dafydd gently, all trace of irritation suddenly gone.

It was the opposite, the soul departed the body when the Attraction closed.

There was a long pause.

Sally said again, "I don't get the point."

Brum uncharacteristically reassured her, "Don't you see? If Dafydd had stayed there the night with all his Welsh mystery and mumbo jumbo…"

"Thank you, Birmingham," muttered Dafydd ironically.

"…the place would have been ruined, haunted."

"Ah!" said Dafydd speculatively, "Yes, I might have attracted Abbo spirits back there to reinhabit the Attraction."

"Aborigine," corrected Brum.

"Native Australian," corrected Sally.

"But I still don't see!" exclaimed Sally. "What's that got to do with us?"

"Sally," said Brum coaxingly, "it's a reminder that our Attraction…" Dafydd and Myfanwy exchanged a significant look, "… needs to retain, hold, keep (I'm talking like Myfanwy) the Welsh magic and mystery. We must build it into our plans. No empty Attractions."

"Well, yes, Birmingham" Dafydd added, looking intently at Sally. "But Sally was finding it difficult to understand because I was really talking about her."

There was a silence within which Sally frowned and Brum looked all around him as if a new Welsh secret had been coded into the fantasy posters.

"I'm sorry," said Sally, slowly shaking her head, "I respect your stories, Dafydd… I respect them very much… They have helped us, and usually I .. this time I don't seem to …" her voice tightened. "And anyway, should your stories be about us, personally, I mean really, should they?"

"An Attraction," Dafydd said very quietly, "needs to be inhabited. Sally, the story is talking about your Attraction. Inhabit it… overnight."

"That's it!" Sally snapped. "That's enough, Dafydd!" She was rising to her feet. Myfanwy's arms were reaching up towards Sally as if to draw her down again. Brum was looking down at his feet but he looked up as Dafydd rose slowly, growing taller and taller until his great figure was looming over Sally like a vast shadow. Brum half rose as if to protect Sally, but he stayed frozen half-way up as Dafydd's huge voice began loud and commanding.

"You're driving away from the Attraction, Sally. Your wheels are raising dust, stop. Park… think … speak… you can trust us."

"Yes," said Myfanwy, earnestly.

For a moment Sally swayed forward towards Dafydd. She took a harsh breath then sighed. There were three pairs of hands reaching towards her.

She reached out to the hands as if being rescued from heavy water. Then, suddenly all four were in an embrace.

It lasted a long minute.

Then, with nobody leading, Sally's three friends stepped back. Sally was standing very still. Her face was flushed. She had been crying a little.

Sally closed her eyes and began to speak.

"Two failed marriages are enough. I'm too bossy. I like to control. I'm a driver, yes, see my dust! You're right. I always want to drive away. Yet, yes, I chose to live here, to commit myself to this community as… as an anchor so I don't drive away… but … I'm so afraid…" Sally's eyes were still closed. She was breathing great breaths.

"Yes, fear," suggested Dafydd gently, "Sally, you fear you will have to leave the village."

Sally nodded vigorously.

"You've done so many things to keep yourself here, to break your pattern of running away. You've learned Welsh. You've read a hundred books on Welsh culture. You've got to know everyone in the village and you've listened to us all."

Sally was nodding and nodding but her lips were tight.

"But…" Dafydd left the word in the air. It floated, then settled.

Sally was shaking her head but her lips were still tight and going white.

"If…" Dafydd let that 'if' settle slowly onto 'but'.

"But… if… strong emotion comes…" Dafydd was watching Sally's breathing. "To this village… to you in this village…" he saw Sally stop breathing and he spoke rapidly now ".. you fear that you will have to leave."

Sally's held breath came out as a great gasp, and she opened her eyes suddenly. The colour came back into her lips as they parted.

To Brum and Myfanwy's surprise Dafydd turned away and sat down, not facing Sally any more. Brum and Myfanwy sat down too. Sally was still standing. Brum saw Sally's eyes close again, but her body was relaxed now, her breathing easy.

"I knew a Sally once," Dafydd said in an amused voice. Myfanwy frowned at his seeming levity, then looked at Sally and saw that Dafydd's warm tone had brought Sally's face, too, into a wide smile. Dafydd's voice was continuing.

A Sally

This Sally divided her self into two. Each of the two parts worked very well, separately. There was her… work-self and that was effective, efficient and public. There was her … personal self and that was romantic, caring and private. Only when this Sally changed out of her working clothes, only when she had closed and locked her front and back doors…

Myfanwy smiled.

Only then, she would settle with a romantic novel or a book about caring, then she curled her body and felt warm and giving.

The irony was, she was alone… there was nobody to care for, nobody to give to in her little house. Oh yes, at work there were plenty of people, but this Sally's giving at work was effective and efficient, not romantic and caring.

Oh yes, behind all the giving that she did through her work, there was a beautiful, romantic and caring vision, but her vision never quite connected, in public, with her personal self.

Yes, the people she worked with liked her, but they couldn't love her.

Dafydd paused. Brum opened his mouth to ask the inevitable question, but Dafydd's pause was short and Brum closed his mouth again.

They wanted to love her, but she forbade it, not in any hard way, she simply slid sideways and avoided their love when they tried to give it to her. After a while they learned not to try.

Now Brum and Myfanwy were smiling and nodding in chorus with Sally. Sally's eyes were still closed, but her arms had begun to wrap themselves around her body while she nodded again.

There was one among them...

This time Dafydd's pause was longer and Brum inevitably asked "Who?" Then he slapped his hand to his mouth and coughed while Myfanwy let out a laugh like a gasp.

Sally's eyes opened at the sudden, harsh sounds and she was looking at Myfanwy who was smiling with the open, open face she normally reserved for Dafydd. Sally's eyes widened with the beginnings of fear and Myfanwy immediately veiled her love into her usual, concerned affection.

There was one among them, among the people in that community...

Dafydd's voice was continuing in a sleepy kind of murmur as if the room was dark and warm and safe...

... who began to dare to love her, but this person didn't realise how, loving this Sally, threatened her whole

new, established, stable, happy, divided life. He was
puzzled at having his good feelings treated by her as
bad. But, luckily, he was thick-skinned and ...

Myfanwy coughed.

   ... he just kept on loving.

The pause was very soft. Brum kept silent. His head was down but
looking up from underneath his brows, his eyes were focused only on
Sally.

"Yes?" said Sally, faintly into the pause.

It was enough of a question.

Dafydd's voice continued, softer and more persuasive, monotonous
and caressing.

   This biggest threat was also Sally's biggest chance.
   She could now, if she chose, be as romantic and caring in
   her work self as in her personal self. She could now be, if
   she chose, as effective and efficient in her personal self
   as in her work self. But ... she had only survived so far..
   or so she thought... by keeping the two selves divided.
   Yet, here was the community ready to love her personal
   self. And here was the one among them, Iolo...

"Iolo?!" snapped Sally and she turned without thinking and pointed to
Brum.

Myfanwy coughed and laughed, then said, "Yes," and Brum and
Dafydd were laughing too. Then Sally was laughing, then sobbing, then
laughing, but just when her knees suddenly gave way, Dafydd was there
and caught her in his arms and lowered her gently into a chair.

"I'm so sorry," Sally kept repeating while her three friends looked at
one another and grinned. Dafydd winked at Brum. Myfanwy kissed Brum
on the cheek. Then Dafydd and Myfanwy quietly left Brum and Sally in the
Telecottage with Sally continually muttering, "I'm sorry."

"It won't work," Myfanwy whispered as she and Dafydd climbed the stairs to the **Honeymoon Hotel**.

"Each wave crashes further up the beach" said Dafydd in mock wisdom.

"Surfers ride only the ninth wave," said Myfanwy, mocking his mockery, and they laughed delightedly as they opened the door together.

SCENE FOURTEEN

Sally's Parlour
the next afternoon

This time Sally and Brum were sitting, hand in hand, on Sally's small sofa. Dafydd loomed large in an upright chair, and Myfanwy was half-curled in another chair next to Dafydd, leaning, cat-like, against him. The four friends were grinning. Dafydd and Myfanwy could see that Brum hadn't shaved and was in the same clothes as yesterday. They could see, too, that Sally's habitual frown had melted into an acceptance of herself which they'd never seen before.

"What are we doing?" asked Sally, gently as she pointed to the plate full of biscuits.

Myfanwy was equally gentle, "What do you mean, Sally?"

"I... things have happened so fast." Sally looked at Brum with tenderness. "The Trust and all the things at the pub, the farms, I've... I've lost the thread. What are we doing?"

"Doing?" Myfanwy questioned "Performing? Achieving?"

"We're doing OK," said Dafydd "You're doing OK, Sal."

"Sally," corrected Brum.

Sally continued, "That's not what I mean, Dafydd. What, overall, looking at it all as a whole... what are we doing?"

"A mission statement," Brum said confidently.

"The meaning of life," murmured Dafydd. Myfanwy turned her stroking of his knee into a pinch. "Are you ready for a long story?" He added, "It is relevant, though it may not seem so at first."

Brum chuckled and swung himself slowly round so his head was in Sally's lap. Unconsciously her soft fingers caressed his bald patch. "Tell away, Dafydd," said Brum.

Myfanwy munched a biscuit thoughtfully. Sally reached up one hand and dimmed the lights. Her hand landed gently back onto Brum's face and rubbed his bristly cheek.

"I knew a little creature once," Dafydd began.

Being

Or rather, it knew me because it was one of my very, very, very distant ancestors. It was furry and striped….

"… like you in your beard and rugby shirt," muttered Myfanwy.

… and it lived among the dinosaurs.

"… that would be Llanelli," Myfanwy smiled.

"… No," said Dafydd, playfully putting his hand over her mouth.

This little creature couldn't compete with them. But one day he stopped in all his frenetic scurrying around, just for a moment, and he had a thought…

"… My name's Iolo!" Brum offered, and laughed.

Dafydd laughed too.

No. This was many, many generations before the first Iolo. No, the thought was a proto-thought, no not in words. The thought was simply an image of his enemy…

"The wing-forward," Myfanwy offered.

"Wing forwards don't eat little creatures!" Dafydd scolded.

"Number eights eat scrum-halves," Myfanwy stated, boldly.

"Only in the season," Brum added helpfully.

"The scrum-halves I played against," said Dafydd, "never came into season!"

"Dafydd," said Sally in mock despair, "ignore their interruptions. What was the little creature's thought?"

> Ah the creature, after seeing, in his mind's eye the image of his enemy, just for a part of that moment, the little striped creature became his enemy.

"Ooh!" said Brum "Jekyll and his furry little Hyde side!"

"Behold. Our dark side," added Sally.

"Not at all," Dafydd corrected them.

> He simply became. He was being, not doing, and in that moment of letting himself be his enemy, he knew where his enemy was.

The pause was quite long. There was an air of lazy contentment in the little front room. Myfanwy helped herself to another biscuit.

"And?" asked Brum cheekily.

The pause continued.

"OK," added Brum, "I'll do it ... and, because he knew where his enemy was, he escaped being eaten, and evolution favoured him and favoured his offspring who inherited his ability to ... become..."

"Well, yes," Dafydd commented admiringly, "but in my story his offspring didn't inherit it. It wasn't a mutation, it was a thought..."

"A meme, not a gene," said Sally, with technical accuracy.

"Hah!" said Brum, "he **taught** it to his offspring!"

"Well, yes," Dafydd echoed his previous response, "but in my story he didn't teach it so much as tell it as a **story**, and the story **enabled** his offspring to learn it."

"That's us," Brum reached up and gently touched the end of Sally's nose.

"You said it was a long story," Myfanwy was puzzled.

"Yes," said Dafydd smiling, "It's the story of the very first story, and there's no story older or longer than that...."

"Just a minute," said Brum, the engineer, "this little striped creature, he can't speak. He only just had the first thought. How can he tell a story?"

Like we all, as very young children, tell our first story before we can speak – he danced it. He acted out being his enemy, and his offspring understood, and when they danced that dance, they too knew where the enemy was.

"I thought you were a pacifist," Brum was very bold today. "You say you don't believe in the concept of 'enemy'."

"I don't," Dafydd smiled, "but the little furry striped creature did, and I have to honour his beliefs. He told the first story."

Sally reached over and very deliberately put a whole biscuit into Brum's mouth to silence him. "I want to hear the story of the first story!" she said with self-mocking severity.

"Generation after generation passed," said Dafydd, gathering the story to himself again.

The dinosaurs died out, and there were mutations. The little, furry, striped creatures grew a bit bigger, but they still danced the dance and knew where the enemy was.

Then one among them...

Brum's muttered "Iolo!" was disguised by his mouthful of biscuit.

Not Iolo ... yet ... She looked around at the growing scarcity of prey, and had a new version of the first story. She saw an image of her prey, and then became the prey, and she knew where her prey was...

"I knew where you were," said Myfanwy contentedly, "even between postcards."

"Dafydd between postcards! Sounds a weird kind of sandwich!" Brum had swallowed his biscuit.

"I knew where you were," repeated Myfanwy, wanting to be heard.

"We're coming to that," whispered Dafydd. Then he continued.

> She taught her offspring, and they prospered because they could find food when others couldn't. They also danced the first version of the story and could still avoid those creatures who preyed on them.

Dafydd's voice was becoming almost dreamlike.

> Many, many more generations passed, and the creatures evolved and evolved until imagining, and becoming and dancing enabled them even to find their offspring when the offspring were lost.

Dafydd leaned now and nuzzled Myfanwy's hair. She leaned into him contentedly. He sniffed her hair, continuing,

> They still found their partners by smell. Ouch!

Myfanwy's fingers had pinched his knee in indignation.

> And in their dancing they began to make the noises of prey, predator and lost offspring and from those sounds-with-the-movements came language. The older, stiffer ones did less dancing and more sounds, and soon, after many, many more generations, language and gestures became the dance, and the dance was danced in the listeners' heads...

"That's beautiful!" exclaimed Sally. "Brum, dance the dance in my head."

"I have," murmured Brum, his next biscuit half-finished. "I did."

"Were the older, stiffer ones, the first storytellers?" asked Myfanwy.

"Oh no, the little furry, striped creature was the first. Stories came before speech..."

"Then how do you know about the first little…" Brum was asking, but Dafydd seemed to ignore the question by continuing to speak.

> Then, one among them saw her friend was ill and sad, and for a moment she had an image of that friend well again and laughing, and she danced those images with her hands, over the friend's body, and laughed, and the friend became well again and laughed too. Others then came to be healed. 'Dance and laugh over me' they begged, and sometimes the healer, in imagining them well would see more, for example, a herb and that herb crushed in boiling water, and would give the infusion as well as the healing dance and the laughter…

"So, comedy was healing," Sally said, smiling.

"Is healing," chuckled Brum.

Dafydd's voice rose louder, but affectionate.

> Then another among them paused in all her busy scurrying and had a thought, an image that was not prey or predator or lost child or healing. Her image was…

Dafydd paused. His head was still, but he looked around at the eyes of his three friends. He saw that each was having their own vision. "What?" he asked his own question almost as a whisper, and they each continued his story.

"An invention," said Brum, "a breakthrough in Stone Age technology."

"God," said Sally, "or love," she leaned down and kissed Brum's lips, "or both!"

"Mystery, mysticism, mythology, spirits, fairies, nymphs," said Myfanwy.

"Yes, any or all of those." said Dafydd, smiling.

> And it was difficult in dance and sounds and words and gestures to communicate something the rest of the people had never seen. But the people watched the

strange dances which she danced. They joined in, hoping
to have the same image, but each had a different image,
though they called it the same, and most of them found
that it was in their dreams at night that these new
images came to life most vividly.

There was a slight pause.

"So, they are 'people' now. Our ancestors," said Brum, the analyser.

"Even the little furry one was our ancestor," said Myfanwy, the niece
of farmers.

"They are paying attention to their dreams," said Sally, the counsellor.
Dafydd's voice became colder.

And there were some among them who began to say
exactly which images and dreams were right, and which
images and dreams were, therefore, wrong.

"Theology," said Sally, the minister.

"Hierarchy," said Brum, the businessman.

"Rules, laws, commands, judicial system, criminal justice," said
Myfanwy, defending the underdog.

"Indeed, justice **was** the criminal," said Dafydd with emphasis.

And the people now knew a new fear, the fear of one
another. The new illness which they feared was the
infection by others of their dreams. The original story,
that first story of becoming was now an instrument of
the Absolutists. What you 'became' was either with them
or against them.

At first, for instance, it was 'with them' to have
images of the dead and to dance and tell of
communication with ancestors. Then the dead ancestors
began to tell their living relatives items which those in
power didn't like, so having images of the dead was then
judged to be 'against them', and forbidden.

> Then there was one among them who had a dream of
> a dream, and on awaking declared joyfully that there was
> a dream dreaming us...

"That's beautiful," interrupted Sally. "that's how I feel, today. Yes, there is a dream, dreaming us."

Dafydd's voice was harsh.

> But that was judged to be heresy and apostasy and
> the work of the enemy and so was forbidden too.

"That's oppressive !" said Sally, disappointed. "I hope there's a happy ending."

"Oppression, repression, suppression, dictatorship," Myfanwy recited thoughtfully.

"Yes," said Dafydd, voice rising in mock admiration.

> The ones who ruled imagined themselves ruling the
> world and had images of becoming greater and greater.
> So they dressed finer and grander, and in the battles
> that ensued, they were the finest and the grandest
> warriors. The lesser people, too, were forced to wear
> uniforms. Those not wearing the right uniforms were
> instantly recognised and eliminated.

"Eliminated?" Brum sat up and held Sally's hand to comfort himself. Dafydd's voice continued.

> All the different rulers quarrelled and fought for
> power until one among them had a different dream.

"Iolo?" asked Myfanwy gently, pointing to Brum.

"Yes, indeed," said Dafydd, smiling.

> The first Iolo took a moment of thought, and in that
> moment he saw an image, not of himself in red, splendid
> robes and in power, but he saw another person, gentle
> and humble, in blue, who possessed not power, but truth.

"Jesus," said Sally, the Protestant.

"The Virgin Mary," said Brum, the Catholic.

"Krishna, Buddha, Mohamed," said Myfanwy, the Thesaurus.

> And Iolo gave up what power and wealth he had, and shared only what truth he dreamed or saw. Ironically, soon, he was called 'The Wise' and had hundreds of followers who didn't obey the people in power. This Iolo the Wise was suddenly a powerful threat to the powerful people.

"But there was one among them" said Brum, triumphantly.

> Indeed, there was one, also called Iolo, but 'Iolo the Great' rather than 'Iolo the Wise'. 'Iolo the Great' could see the writing on the wall. He had a moment where he imagined himself being simultaneously 'Great' **and** 'Wise'. In his mind he would become 'Iolo the Wise' when Iolo the Wise died.

So, Iolo the Great beat all his rivals for power by making the truths of Iolo the Wise into state policy. Now he was irrefutably…

"Irrefutably?" Brum queried.

"Irrefutably, uncontradictably, non-gainsayably…" added Myfanwy

"… Rightly, correctly, justifiably and truthfully," continued Dafydd.

> Under Iolo the Wisely Great the people were content to live quietly, feeling guilty when they transgressed the truths as given from above. Each person knew his or her place, and nobody dared to use the first story anymore. You were born what you were. To 'become' anything else was to be too dangerously different.

"Oh come on!" interrupted Brum "I don't like this. Only by having different ideas have I made my money, my success."

Dafydd grinned and pointed to Brum.

There was one, many generations later, yes, called 'Birmingham' among them who dared to become, dared to use the first story again, and he saw that age-old things could be done differently...

"Absolutely!" Brum was very happy to be at last a character in a story.

...quicker, cheaper, in hundreds, thousands and sold to all. And Birmingham became successful and rich. So did his offspring who dared to become even what Birmingham could not imagine.

"Progress!" Brum smiled.

He and his descendants were able to buy up the castles of the former old powerful rulers, and to give tests to youngsters to select the cleverest, however poor they were, to be helped in their turn to climb to the top of the heap.

"A meritocracy!" Brum laughed, "not society run by old-school-tie and privilege, but by ability, sheer ability and inventiveness."

"Enterprises, entrepreneurs, innovators, explorers, opportunists," added Myfanwy.

"Everything money could buy!" added Dafydd. Brum was enjoying this. But then Dafydd's voice changed to a sadness. His three friends looked at him in concern.

As the generations of successive successful Birminghams went by, there grew in the heart of one of them a longing for ... he knew not what. He looked around at all his material wealth and decided that either it was not enough, or else it was too much. It was never enough... or it was always too much.

"Or it was too much of not enough," suggested Sally, helpfully.

Indeed so. His material wealth did not satisfy. In a moment of thought he experienced a new image of

> himself as a different self, as someone who had nothing
> that money could buy, but everything that he would want.

"That's me!" Brum exclaimed, hugging Sally suddenly and releasing her as suddenly so she laughed aloud. "So, Dafydd" Brum asked "What did he become?"

Dafydd continued very calmly.

> He became a friend, a colleague, an equal in a group.
> He became peaceful, collaborative, co-operative and
> worked for harmony, not competition.

"That's me, lately, the new me!" Brum was practically bouncing with enthusiasm. "Ex-boss, ex-industrial leader. I don't need that any more. No, I don't!"

"You'll sell your big house, the Plas?" Myfanwy asked. Dafydd frowned at Myfanwy but Brum was gazing into Sally's eyes.

"Maybe... now... I can," said Brum, softly.

"The story," Dafydd said, hurriedly.

> The first story ever, had now been used again, and
> that descendant of Birmingham taught others to dream
> of becoming sharers, open, accepting, self-sacrificing.
> For several generations, that's how people were.

"Is that how we are now?" Sally asked, "Is **that** what we're doing?"

Dafydd's voice continued a little louder. It was a tone he had never used before.

> Until one among the descendants of the descendants
> had a new, quite different vision. In his moment of
> imagining, he saw for the first time, the story itself, the
> original story of becoming. He saw that story had been
> growing and changing, being used and abused, favoured
> and forbidden, in different ways by different
> generations. And he saw that the mystery and the power
> and the truth of the story was all in how the story was

told and how the story was used…

"This is you, Dafydd" said Sally with a sudden seriousness. Myfanwy, too was sitting up looking at Dafydd, no longer nestled against him. "You are that storyteller," Sally said in an awed voice.

There was a silence.

Somehow the little parlour seemed suddenly enormously large.

"Becoming," Dafydd's voice was somehow like an echo, as if listening as intently to himself as the others were listening to him now.

'Becoming' became something of itself. It was the power in everyone, the truth all could learn. They could all change and become, change and become, each in his or her own way whenever he or she chose.

Dafydd was almost whispering now.

For days and days this descendant remained completely intrigued with what he had discovered. The dance of it danced and danced inside his head. He thought back over all the stages and changes of his life and was aware how he himself had used and exploited and abused that first-ever story, the becoming…

That's very modern and green!" exclaimed Brum, "Is that what I've become, all alternative and hippy?"

"Is that what we've been doing?" Sally paused, her eyes searching around the room as if for information. "I asked 'what are we doing?' and you're telling me we're not 'doing' we're 'being', or 'becoming'."

"The story," said Dafydd quietly, "the first story is not telling anyone anything. The question is (if there can be a question) the question is, what are you, Sally, doing with the story?"

Sally looked from Dafydd to Myfanwy, to Brum, "I'm not sure I'm doing anything…"

"Yes, Sally," Dafydd said gently "that's where you started this evening. Yes, you are not sure you are doing anything." Dafydd's words were slow and emphasised, as if speaking to an over-simple mind.

"Look!" said Sally, sitting up straighter with a return to her old irritability, "I asked 'what are we doing', and we get a long rambling...."

"Hang on, Sal!" exclaimed Brum.

"...story about a story, and I'm no clearer than when I started."

"But that's the point, Sal," said Brum sitting up matching her straightness, "you need to get an image..."

"...what are you," Sally snapped "some PR image-maker?"

Myfanwy took a sharp intake of breath and tried to speak but had to cough first "Gently, Sally. Brum's only saying 'image' as in 'imagine', 'visualise', 'see in the mind's eye', 'picturing'."

Sally's straightness slackened. "Sorry, Brum. I don't know where I am at the moment."

"That's OK, Sal," said Brum, subdued. "I think the point is that if you take a moment to 'become', you will know.... where you are."

Dafydd said, "I heard your original question as 'What are **we** doing?' so it's not just you – how is each of us using the first story?"

"I'm lost," said Sally pitifully. "Give me an example."

Brum cut in before Dafydd could answer, "I can see me, Sal, in the various stages."

Brum's Inventions

I was a superstitious sort of kid, you know, I used to talk to the trees and lamp posts and things, and I had to do things always the same way. Then I got religious, Catholic, you know, altar boy, all those sermons trying to persuade us to join the priesthood. It was sin and guilt, the whole trip, my first confession, till I had a sort of vision as a teenager that it could be different, and that was when I started inventing things. Do you know what the first thing was?

Dutifully Dafydd asked the question, 'What?' to Brum's story though Brum's whole focus was on Sally. Brum continued.

Thank you, Dafydd, it was a confession box, booth, the confessional, 'Mark One', you know, and I had it electric-powered and automatic. I laugh now, but then I was deadly serious. My confession box responded to key words, each weighted so the worst sins got the highest scores. The machine then added up the scores and the total triggered the correct number of 'Our Fathers' and 'Hail Marys'.

Brum chuckled at Sally's look of amazement.

The Mark Two was for home use and more sophisticated but lower technology. It was purely mechanical, no power required. You pressed in buttons and a spring totalised, then it spun a roller that stopped at the appropriate severity of penance plus one of the parting stock of messages which I'd been collecting from our priests since my first communion. When I presented to the priest the prototype working model at the next confessional he threw me out, bodily and with vim!

"Splendid!" exclaimed Dafydd enthusiastically.

"What did he say?" asked Myfanwy, fascinated.

"He shouted," chuckled Brum, "so all the queue for the confessional could hear, and me tumbling on the stone floor clutching my prototype."

"But what did he shout?" Myfanwy insisted.

"Ex-MACHINA!" Brum shouted in the little room in a bass voice and Irish accent.

I had to ask my physics teacher what it meant. It was quite apt, really. I'd taken the 'deus' out and the priest threw my machine out instead. Well, my physics teacher borrowed my machine, and loved it.

Brum took a pause to smile at Dafydd's obvious enjoyment of his story.

"Confessions of a Physics Teacher," Dafydd coined a film title "Splendid! And then?"

"The teacher gave me lots of books to read on inventions and creative thinking." Brum turned his smile to Sally but saw her expression and frowned..

"You believe God can be replaced by a machine." Sally's voice was quavering with doubt.

"God's mechanical tasks can be done by a machine. Any mechanical tasks can, dish-washing, clothes washing, light switching," answered Brum, his voice full of concern.

"God doesn't have any mechanical tasks," Sally said, her beliefs shaken. She drew away from Brum, but Brum, oblivious, was reciting his own beliefs dogmatically in frank simplicity.

"The modern Luddites are the ones who won't let machines do what machines do best. Yes there is a place for man and woman, but let's liberate humans from the tasks best done by machines!" Then Brum saw, suddenly, that he was in a hole and digging it deeper. Sally was rising slowly and looking down at him in horror.

"You would replace God with a machine! Brum, I don't know you."

That last statement stayed in the air.

Everybody was very still.

Dafydd could see anger, then fear pass through Brum's face, then a puzzlement like a child unjustly chastised.

Sally was looking around as if lost in her own tiny parlour.

Nobody dared to speak.

Myfanwy grimaced and to distract Sally, grabbed the plate of biscuits and pushed it into Sally's hands.

Sally looked down, wondering what her hands were holding and why.

Brum and Myfanwy looked desperately at Dafydd.

Dafydd raised his eyebrows and opened his eyes wide as if the answer to 'what to do?' was not that simple nor ready to hand. Dafydd looked intently at Sally trying to read her thoughts.

"I don't .... know...." Sally said in a flat hoarse voice.

"That's right," said Dafydd very soothingly, "You don't know, and that's right, that's fine. You need ... more time... not knowing is the right state to be in... It's OK not knowing... you don't know. Stick with that... give it space... give it time."

Myfanwy took the biscuit plate from Sally's tight grip and nodded to Brum. Brum took Sally's emptied hands and gently but firmly pulled her down to sit again. He slipped his arms around Sally, and as her head sank against his shoulder he nodded to the others who left almost silently. As they left they could hear Sally starting to sob. Myfanwy sighed as she opened the back door and stepped into the cool air.

"It won't last," she said.

"It has more chance now," said Dafydd.

SCENE FIFTEEN

Sally's Front Room Again
the next day

"Forget the project," said Sally crisply when they met the next day. "Forget the Trust!"

Dafydd was clapping loudly. Brum, subdued, looked up, shocked.

"What did I say?" asked Sally, annoyed.

"It's what you're going to say next that I was applauding" said Dafydd.

Sally Getting Sorted (not quite a story)

"I was going to say, forget all that. I want to get sorted."

"Then say it," challenged Dafydd.

"I said it!" said Sally, angrily. "I've just said it, 'I want to get sorted!'"

Dafydd applauded loudly again. "You do, Sally," he said over his clapping. "You really do!"

"I do," said Sally again, "So shut up and help me!"

Dafydd turned to Myfanwy, "I said it could last."

"Are you trying deliberately to annoy me?" asked Sally very tersely.

"Well, I seem to have succeeded," said Dafydd, smiling.

"You can be a bastard sometimes!" exclaimed Sally. Myfanwy nodded.

"I've legitimised bastardy into a profession," said Dafydd as if commenting favourably on good weather. "So, where do we start?"

"With me," said Sally, neutrally.

"Is that a question or a statement?" asked Dafydd. "Never mind. Instead of sorting out the problems of the world, we're going to sort out the cause of the problems, namely, Sally."

"Bastard!" exclaimed Sally heatedly.

"Hard, cruel, unfeeling, insensitive, heartless ..." Myfanwy spat out the words.

Brum was rising to his feet in alarm, "If there's going to be a fight..." His words tailed off.

"There will be!" exclaimed Dafydd, rubbing his hands, "but nobody will get hurt. All that we're going to fight against – and all four of us will fight it, together – is ... that!" Dafydd pointed dramatically over Sally's right shoulder. All four looked in that direction for a long beat.

"What?" asked Brum.

"The cruel little sprite. Let's call it ... 'George'," said Dafydd.

Sally swung round accusingly, "How did you know that? I never told you."

Dafydd was looking round triumphantly.

Sally's voice continued, "George was my father's name, and my first husband's..."

"And they're still crouched on your shoulder telling you, hissing spitefully in your ear..."Dafydd paused. Sally's right shoulder was hunching and her face twisted. Brum looked on in horror.

It was still Sally's voice, but the words were harsh and cruel. "You'll never make anything of yourself. All this caring, nobody cares about you. Why should they? What is there to care about? You don't care. Deep down you don't care about anybody. You're a selfish little bitch dressed up as Florence bloody Nightingale!"

It was out. The nasty, hateful words seemed to turn and twist in the air. Brum was gazing at Sally's twisted face. Myfanwy was hugging herself protectively. Dafydd's eyes were bright and his voice, hard.

"Is that true?" he asked.

Sally murmured quietly "No." Her face slackened but her shoulder was still hunched.

"I asked, is it true?" Dafydd leaned forward insistently.

Sally's lowered eyes rose to meet his. "No," she said.

"Louder!" said Dafydd.

"No!" Sally said, louder.

"Louder!" shouted Dafydd in his hugest voice. The others flinched.

Sally shouted, **"No!"** and it was twice the volume even of Dafydd's voice. Myfanwy's body was flung back by the force, and Brum's eyes closed as the noise smashed over him.

Dafydd's next words were in a whisper. "Tell George to piss off!"

"You tell him!" snapped Sally.

"He's your George," said Dafydd in rapid fire. "You fed him! You nursed him! You gave him a home! You tell him!"

"Piss off!" said Sally, but at Dafydd.

"Louder!" said Dafydd.

Sally's eyes went white as her neck arched back and she took a great shuddering breath. A tiny voice came out of her. "I can't!"

Gently Dafydd's voice said "Sally, you must. It must be you!"

At the same time Brum was reaching towards Sally. "Sal, love…"

And Myfanwy's eyes were full of tears and her face full of alarm.

Sally's face crumpled into a child's hopeless expression. Both her shoulders hunched and she looked sideways at Dafydd. "I can't," She repeated in a very, very small voice.

"Oh, Sally!" Dafydd gave a great sigh and scooped her into his arms, "not yet, but you will!" He sat her on his knee and began a story.

The Little Frightened Boy
There was once a little, frightened boy…

"Girl!" corrected Sally in her still, small voice.

"No, boy," corrected Dafydd gently.

… and he felt very, very small. The big boys bullied him and nobody defended him. Even his parents told him not to cry but just to hit them back. Well, he tried that, but the big boys just hit him harder, so he said to himself 'I'm on my own,' and it was the loneliest thing he had ever said...

Sally gave a little sob and linked both her arms around Dafydd's large neck.

He knew he couldn't fight, so he practised with his voice and words. First he practised on the dog and soon he had it cringing and whining with just his voice and words. He felt wonderful. Strong at last!

Then he tried his new voice and words on children younger and smaller than him. His satisfaction grew as they ran off, crying to their parents. 'I never touched them,' he said in another, new voice, which was all innocence and reason.

Indeed, this little frightened boy was all politeness to anybody who mattered, anybody in authority, and they all praised him for being so obedient and well-mannered. He was only nasty, indeed deeply, cruelly nasty to the younger, smaller children. To the bullies he was also now polite and obedient, and though they mocked him in simple ways, they left him alone. And strangely, that made him feel more lonely...

Sally was leaning slightly away from Dafydd in order to gaze up into his face, searching for meaning. She still had the rapt expression of a child.

Then a child who was his equal, the same age and height started to try to make friends with him, and his eyes lit up. At last there was someone who cared, who liked him, who wanted to be his friend...

Myfanwy and Brum relaxed slightly from their tense observation of Sally, childlike, listening to Dafydd's voice.

And so the little, frightened boy began to use his special voices, mixing and blending the obedient politeness with his cruel other voice and words.

The results were most rewarding. The friend began to cringe and whine and cry, like the dog, and also come back and back and back for more...

Dafydd's three friends were staring at Dafydd in the silence. Each face had the curled lip of disgust and the wide eyes of horror.

In the silence there was no question.

Sally swallowed and cleared her throat. Her arms dropped from around Dafydd's neck. She shifted awkwardly on his knees.

"Stand up, Sally," Dafydd ordered briskly. "Now, say after me, 'George'."

"George."

"I'm sorry," Dafydd's voice was gentle, his eyes down.

"I'm sorry?" Sally's voice made a question.

"I'm sorry." Dafydd forced the falling intonation and Sally echoed it.

"I'm sorry."

"I couldn't be there to protect you when you needed it."

"I couldn't be there to protect you when you needed it." Sally's head rubbed against her right shoulder.

"But I do care that you were hurt."

"But I do care that you were hurt."

"And I understand why you hurt others."

"And I understand why you hurt others." Sally's eyes were full of tears but there was also a frown of anger. Brum, his eyes fixed on her face was mouthing her words with her. Myfanwy's mouth was simply open in amazement.

"And I understand why you hurt me, again and again, and again."

"And I understand why…" Sally's voice faltered and then went up an octave, again the whimpering child, "why you hurt me!" the last word was a wail.

Myfanwy moved towards Sally but Dafydd's hand urgently motioned her back.

"Again and again and again," prompted Dafydd, gently.

"Yes," said Sally in a tiny voice. "Again and again and again."

"And I want to tell you, George."

"George. George." Sally's voice struggled against disappearing.

"That I loved you through all of it, through everything."

"I did, I did," said Sally, barely audible.

"And I'm sorry my love couldn't heal you then."

"I am. I am." Said Sally, "I'm so sorry, but it didn't work."

"It didn't work then." said Dadfydd. "But now you're showing all your love and all your pain, Sally, little Sally, little girl Sally, adult Sally, it's working now. It's healing George, the George in you… now!"

At the word 'now', Sally let out a great sigh and shuddered deeply. The air in the room seemed thick like thunder-clouds. Then Dafydd stood up, standing Sally up with him. She was standing tall and still and reeling gently as if recovering from giddiness.

"George?" said Dafydd quietly, looking at Sally.

"They're gone!" said Sally, closing her eyes and rotating her head as if enjoying a warm shower.

There was a silence.

"That was a bit drastic, Dafydd!" said Brum, his distress coming out as anger.

"Drastic, but effective," said Dafydd, smiling. "They're gone, Brum. It's the last you'll suffer from them."

"Me?" Brum spluttered.

"Yes, Brum, darling," said Sally in a far-off voice. "I thought you were the same. I'm so sorry."

"Sally!" Brum said, stepping across to her and hugging her.

"Job done! Time to go!" said Dafydd, reaching for Myfanwy's hand.

"You're a butcher, brutal!" Myfanwy murmured.

"No, a dentist. Why prolong the agony? A quick extraction."

Dafydd was opening the door and dragging Myfanwy out.

In the road Myfanwy stepped in front of Dafydd, reached up to his face and turned it and angled it so he looked down into her eyes. She was searching for answers. "I surprise myself, sometimes," Dafydd chuckled. "So don't ask."

"No story?" Myfanwy chuckled.

"An ending with no story," said Dafydd, "except that I need a drink and a bit of loving."

"Just a bit?"

"Plus a bit more for old time's sake. We've got a lot of catching up to do."

"I'd have said we're catching up fast."

"And we've got a start on those two," exclaimed Dafydd, looking over his shoulder.

Myfanwy saw him unconsciously echo Sally's gesture rubbing his raised right shoulder with his head. She shuddered and they strode on, she with two short steps for each of his long ones.

SCENE SIXTEEN

At the Plas
the next afternoon

"I've asked you here," said Brum, solemnly, standing holding hands with Sally, "I've asked you here to say 'goodbye' to this old house…"

"The Plas," murmured Myfanwy looking round at the high ceilings, then at Dafydd who, at last, didn't seem too tall for a room.

"You're selling up?" asked Dafydd sitting on the great settle by the huge fireplace.

"I'm moving out of here and in with Sally," Brum said, beaming.

Sally, still a little pale from the previous day, grinned.

"It's a big, old place," said Myfanwy, sitting next to Dafydd, "you'll be much more comfy at Sally's."

"Tell us the rest," said Dafydd pointing to the vast sofa which Sally and Brum dutifully sank into.

"What do you mean, 'the rest'?" asked Sally.

"Brum knows," said Dafydd. "He's busting to tell us."

"Not yet." said Brum with mock detachment. "First, I'm a bit lost lately on where we all are, and I need rebriefing."

" A progress report, an interim statement, an updating," said Myfanwy.

"The State of the Nation," said Dafydd grandly. "Or is it 'the Nation of the State' in Wales' case?"

"But, background first. What brought us here?" asked Brum.

"Feet," Dafydd offered.

"Your phone call," Myfanwy was helpful.

"No, I mean to be here in our village, and so to be involved in the Trust. It's like … like I'm in the centre of a maze and I don't know how I got here." Brum was cheerful, but genuinely puzzled.

"Safest way with mazes," said Dafydd firmly, "is to be parachuted into the centre, and then cut your way back out with a machete, or a chain-saw, or a flame-thrower."

"Oh, Dafydd," Myfanwy frowned. "You've completely destroyed the maze for everyone else!"

"I'm only quoting the American Way." He put on a Texas drawl, "there ain't no such thing as mazes because I ain't never seen one."

Brum laughed, "I'm the one in the middle and I want to understand."

Myfanwy leaned forward. "Well, Brum, what brought you to Wales in the first place?"

"My Nan," he said, wistfully. "She was Welsh-speaking. They moved to Birmingham for work, then, when my Grandpa died she moved back to Wales…"

"Not here," said Myfanwy, "I'd have known her."

"No, but as a child I was sent to her for holidays. The old farm house, and the dogs, and a donkey, and she kept me really busy. I was, what six or seven when I first went there on my own. 'You're the man of the house,' she said, and had me doing all the practical things…"

"That's you," said Sally, affectionately "very practical, and always busy."

"It gave me confidence," Brum continued. "I wasn't very good at school, but I learned from her to do everything on the little farm. I didn't read till I was seven, and then only to read the manual about the old tractor to get it working."

"Which you did," said Dafydd.

"How did you reach the pedals?" asked Myfanwy.

"Who says I drove it?" asked Brum.

"You drove it!" exclaimed Dafydd and Sally and Myfanwy together and they all laughed.

"I stood to drive it." Said Brum and was silent, thinking and smiling. "For two years I read only manuals…"

"So when you made your money…" Dafydd prompted.

"Yes, I decided to buy somewhere in Wales, reclaiming my roots."

"You've no connection to the Plas or the village," Myfanwy stated. "I'd have known."

"A good property. A good price," said Brum, matter-of-factly.

"I, for one, am very glad you came," said Sally.

"Me too," said Dafydd stretching his long legs towards the log fire. "And then you came drinking."

"Single again. Meet new people. Make new friends. Go to the pub." Brum outlined the simple method.

"But the Trust?" Sally prompted.

"Yes," said Brum, frowning. "I can see how I got to the pub…"

"But the rest is a blur," offered Dafydd "My answer is: you drank too much!"

There were nods, then laughter. They'd only ever had three rounds of one half-pint each.

"It was how **little** you drank that made me decide to close up the pub!" said Myfanwy.

"Which is now so full and busy we don't go there!" exclaimed Sally.

"And you can hire staff and are free of it," said Brum.

"So you can be yourself. Free at last!" said Dafydd.

"Brum, you fancied Sally," said Myfanwy, shyly, "we could all see that."

"Except Sally," Brum smiled.

"Except me," Sally smiled too.

"And here you are," said Dafydd "living in sin with a vicar, and you don't know how on earth you got to that!"

"Dafydd!" exclaimed Sally while Myfanwy laughed aloud and Brum grinned.

"I'm OK on that bit," said Brum.

"So, you're only puzzled on how you came to be a Trustee and have given away your millions…" Dafydd continued.

"Million," corrected Sally.

"… and now are going to sell the Plas and give the money to the Trust." Dafydd made an expansive gesture as if to say 'all of this'.

"How do you know that?" Sally and Brum said simultaneously. Then looked at each other and smiled.

"Minds united already," commented Dafydd. "It's written all over you. Already you're treating it like it's not your home, inviting us here, but not giving us a drink!"

"I'm sorry," said Brum leaping to his feet and heading for the door.

"I should think so!" exclaimed Dafydd in mock shock. "And the best china, mind. The vicar's here!"

"Dafydd!" warned Sally as Brum left the room.

The big door closed.

"Ring for servants," mused Myfanwy to herself, "call, summon, command."

"Ah!" said Dafydd, quietly, "Myfanwy wants to buy the Plas and live as a lady of leisure."

Myfanwy frowned but her reverie wasn't broken. Her fingers were feeling the smooth ancient oak of the settle and the soft, ancient threads of the embroidered cushion beneath her.

"I've a proposal," said Dafydd as Brum came in with four half pints of beer and not in the best china. "The village needs a hotel for visitors to the farm project. So let's all sell up, move in here together and run it as a hotel."

The protests came fast and full and simultaneously.

"Sell the pub!"; "My little house!"; "I hate hotels!"; "The Trust needs the money!'" "We want to live together on our own!"; "You just want a house where you don't hit your head and are too mean to buy one yourself!"

Myfanwy's last remark was heard by all, and they all laughed off the tension.

"This is an interesting moment," said Dafydd. "What has priority, the Trust, or our individual decisions about our own lives?"

There was silence.

"At several points in my life," said Brum ruefully, "I would have said I matter, and nobody else, but now…"

Sally interrupted him gently, "Until recently, I don't think I ever really felt that I mattered. There was always some higher purpose – God, duty, the greater good, the community, but now…"

It was Myfanwy's turn to interrupt, "Yes, I'm like Sally. Now, in **my** life, it's my turn. Yes, I'll work for the village, but I matter too."

The three friends looked at Dafydd. It was his turn in the confessional but he had a faraway look.

"Surely," he said tentatively, "It's a case of win:win…. Let's look for a solution where we all win, we each win … **and** the Trust wins."

There was another silence.

Then Dafydd said, "To do that, we all simply need to look at all sorts of alternatives and then decide."

Myfanwy sighed audibly, "There's only so much of broadening the mind that I can take!" she said, with feeling.

"I'm a bit shaky at the moment. Not too many new things at once, please," said Sally sincerely, but with mock plaintiveness exaggerating her underlying nervousness.

·   "And I'm changing so fast," said Brum in a very contented and relaxed tone, "that I wouldn't trust my own judgement."

"Then I'll just have to tell a story!" said Dafydd with pretended exasperation. Then he raised his fingers like a conductor, and all four chorused as he brought his fingers down … "There was a … once."

The Plas

"A what?" asked Brum obligingly.

"A Plas," said Myfanwy.

Dafydd smiled.

> And the Plas wanted to fulfill the very best possible destiny.

"Was the Plas a lass?" Brum asked.

> OK, **she** wanted to maximise **her** self-expression, **her** self-development.

"A feminist Plas," said Sally, smiling.

> And she thought of all sorts of possibilities and pondered each one for a long time. The lives of Plases are plenty long. She could be a hotel…

"**An** hotel," corrected Sally.

> Or a guest house or a B&B or a youth hostel. But would people come and stay or not? Would she be empty and useless, or worn out fast?

> Then she thought about being an institution, for the mad or the bad or the sick or the wicked or the homeless or the stateless or the mindless or the ones too young to stay with their parents or too old to stay with their children. But would any of them respect her for what she was?

> Then she thought of being an Attraction…

"An Attraction," said Sally, quietly, squeezing Brum's hand.

> … with visitors coming to see her, full in the day, but empty at night.

'No,' she said. 'A house is for living in. But the sort of living I was built for, the grand family and twice their number of servants, that's gone, that's dead and gone and so it should be.'

" A post-modern Plas," said Sally, smiling.

"An anachronism," said Brum.

"Poor old Plas," said Myfanwy.

"Yes," said Dafydd.

She'd heard of other such houses lived in by rich Americans or Arabs, but they weren't homes. The rich fly about so much nowadays, nowhere is a home in the old sense she had known...

"Poor old Plas," said Myfanwy, again.

So what could she be, or rather 'become'? Offices, yes, that was possible, some high-tech services company that, once on-line, could be physically located anywhere in the world. But, again, she'd be empty at night, and, ten to one, it would be nobody connected with her past who would buy her up for offices. And how would they change her? What walls would go? What additions would be made?

The very thought made her itch and creak and moan!

For a while she was in despair. 'I'm from another age,' she cried. 'Nobody wants me for what I really am! Demolish me!' she pleaded. 'Replace me completely with something which this new age really requires!'

Nobody spoke for a full minute.

In that minute, Myfanwy's hands again caressed the old oak and the cushion fabric. Brum looked bleakly around the great room. Sally gazed into the enormous, dying fire, and yearned to stir it into life again. Dafydd's eyes were closed and he breathed very deeply. He seemed to be connecting with something. Soon the others forgot their own thoughts and were all gazing at him.

When Dafydd spoke again it was in his deepest, most echoing voice. It was as if he'd found the exact, deep frequency of the huge room. His voice reverberated and seemed to set everything in the room vibrating. His three friends shivered as the room itself seemed to speak with Dafydd's passion.

'Surely!' the old Plas cried out one day, 'Surely somehow, somewhere, is my perfect destiny! There must be some unknown future plan where I can be a home again, where I can serve the families who have been employer and employed, owners and servants who have had their roots here and have known my soul for generations. I was built by the workers in this community. Surely the community wants what they created? Do I mean nothing to them now? Am I a meaningless, outdated commodity? Am I an out-moded symbol of exploitation?

What is my perfect destiny?'

Those last words seemed to echo up the great stairway to the huge bedrooms, then up the narrow stairs on up to the servants' rooms beneath the eaves. The words seemed then to shatter and float down again with only the question marks surviving.

Brum, when he broke the silence was subdued "A new idea?" he paused "The solution?"

Nobody answered.

"There was one among them," he tried, but his voice was very quiet and seemed not even to reach the walls of the room they were in.

"There can't be 'one among' anything," said Sally, sadly, "there is only 'one' in the story, the Plas."

"Can't we ask Iolo to step into the story?" said Brum looking very directly at Dafydd. But Dafydd was gazing at the floor, his big shoulders hunched over.

"Why can't the old Plas imagine, be, become its own future?" asked Myfanwy, her voice full of concern.

"The future is unknowable," said Sally, blankly. "The poor old Plas only knows her past which is lost and her present which is unwanted. How can she know her own future?" Sally gritted her teeth as if struck by a sudden pain.

"We walk backwards into our futures," said Dafydd in a monotone, "we walk backwards gazing at our past which we can see, blundering blindly, backwards into our futures which we can't see."

"Turn around," said Sally in a sudden, penetrating voice as if tightened in her guts, "turn around!" she repeated more confidently. Her ringing voice seemed to lift the dust in the high corners of the room. In the fire a log rolled and flamed up again with a crackle. "That's what I've done. I can see it now. I've turned my back on my past. I've turned to face the future, and I'm stepping boldly into the unknown!"

Brum's body seemed to lift towards Sally, a vigour entering his face. "I'm with you there, Sal. I don't know what the future holds but we'll step forward, together!"

"Plas!" said Sally, deliberately addressing the house by name. "Plas! Plas!" she said, louder, as if to make it listen. "I'm talking to you now. Hear me!" Sally's three friends were listening intently as if expecting the house to reply. Only the newly blazing log spat and crackled. "Plas! What is your perfect destiny? Turn round! Face the future! Step forward! Know your new purpose!"

There was a long pause. Every ear was alert.

"She knows!" whispered Dafydd. "I can feel it in my feet."

"Your size fourteens!" murmured Myfanwy. "Your big mouth!"

"What is it?" whispered Brum.

"What does she say?" said Sally in a full voice, the loudness of which was a shock in the quietness.

"Feet?" Dafydd questioned. And he stood up and took a few steps. Then he walked in a circle. Then he set off out of the room. "The feet know…" he said and he beckoned to his friends, who followed him, exchanging curious glances.

On up the great stairway they went, Dafydd following his feet, the others following Dafydd.

"Two feet called Iolo!" Brum muttered.

"What?" asked Sally.

"There was one among them," said Brum by way of explanation "and we're following him."

"Is this a story?" asked Sally.

"You spoke to the house," said Brum, "you should know."

"If it's a story," said Myfanwy, "we're in it, and it's happening now." She had a wild look in her eyes and hurried forward following Dafydd through a small door, up the narrow servant's stairs, along a low corridor under the eaves, and there they all stopped. Dafydd's voice was muffled as his bent body turned to speak.

"There must be a door here. My feet have led me as if to a door, Birmingham, my friend, but I can't see it." He coughed at cobwebs and dust.

"There's no door," said Brum squeezing past. "Where?"

"There should be a door!" Dafydd replied, irritably.

"Where?" said Brum feeling foolish and sounding belligerent. Their voices began to argue.

"Here."

"Where?"

"Here."

"Men!" whispered Myfanwy, a normal look replacing the wildness in her eyes.

"No," Sally whispered, "I can feel it too."

"**Here!**" said Dafydd angrily now, and his great fist banged the wall.

144

It opened.

Light and air rushed in.

Dafydd straightened up and stepped up and out. The others followed. They were standing by a narrow parapet over the portico.

"Ah!" said Dafydd in great satisfaction.

"Now what?" said Brum the practical man.

"Pray for guidance," said Sally, the theologian.

"Enjoy the view, panorama, outlook, vista," said Myfanwy reaching for Dafydd's hand.

"What did you say?" said Dafydd urgently.

"What?" Myfanwy asked.

"Say it again, one of those…" Dafydd said quickly.

"I don't know!" said Myfanwy, as if attacked, "view, panorama, vista, perspective. What did I say?"

"It was there before! Again!" Dafydd's voice was commanding.

"Outlook!" said Sally. "You missed out 'outlook'."

"She said 'outlook'" said Brum. "But why…"

"But not the second time," said Sally urgently.

"But why?..." Brum's repeated question was interrupted by Dafydd saying the word 'outlook' very slowly and loudly.

"The Plas has got a great view," said Brum "But a poor outlook, right?"

"Outlook" Dafydd repeated.

"We need perspective?" Sally offered.

"Outlook," Dafydd chanted.

"Viewpoint, beauty spot," Myfanwy tried to be helpful but Dafydd kept repeating the word 'outlook' as if somehow it held a key.

Then Dafydd burst into a flow of words.

"Outlook. Look … out. Look out! Insurance? Alarms? Conning Tower? Air traffic control? Airport? Beacon? Coastguard? Outing?

Excursion? Coming out? Outcomes? No. Outlook. Outlook. Out look! I'm **doing** it! Give me **rest!**"

Earnestly Dafydd turned to Sally, "You ask! What does the house want? What does it mean? What's this 'outlook'?"

Brum coughed, "I've come this far but no further! What the hell am I doing standing on a roof trying to listen to a house?"

Dafydd interrupted Myfanwy's protective protest, "You're right, Birmingham, my friend, but these things are so far beyond the rational, logical mind they are painful of parturition."

"That's childbirth, right?" asked Brum. "Who's having a baby?"

"We all are," said Dafydd, reassuringly "and if you're the father, will you go and pace about in the waiting room while we, doctor and two midwives, will get on with the delivery."

"That's sexist!" protested Sally, "I want the father here! Stay here, Brum, darling, and hold our hands."

"I'll hold yours," said Brum reluctantly, "but this is mumbo jumbo!"

"Your protest is duly noted," said Dafydd, and he closed his eyes and groaned. "I think it's coming. 'Outlook' is … the vision. Look … out … from here," he opened his eyes and gestured around him, "the Plas can see the whole of the Farm Project and the village and the pub. It's all in one and it is the vision none of us has got … and … and …"

The process seemed to be genuinely painful. Dafydd was grimacing. Sally was clutching her stomach and Myfanwy was all tension. Only Brum was gazing around him in a relaxed manner, doing what he did best, evaluating and quantifying.

"And the 'more'," said Dafydd tightly, "Sally, you spoke to the house. Voice the 'more'."

"Oh Dafydd, I don't know how!" Sally wailed.

"Just open your mouth, woman!" Dafydd exclaimed.

All three friends watched Sally's mouth open. They saw her lips quiver, nervously, "It's … 'rotating families'!" Sally said at last.

"And what the hell's 'rotating families'!" said Brum in exasperation.

"I'll take a turn living here!" exclaimed Myfanwy, joyfully, "waited on hand and foot".

"And who will be doing the waiting?" Dafydd asked in wry amusement.

"That's it!" exclaimed Sally. "It would rotate. You wouldn't mind being a servant too, Myfanwy, would you?"

"I'd take my turn, yes," said Myfanwy, "but I'll book being 'Lady Muck' first!"

"What's the point?" asked Brum.

"I think I can see it," said Dafydd. "Not only does the Plas see the whole project, it … sorry, 'she' is wanting to be **part** of the whole project, in fact, brilliantly! Well done old girl!"

Dafydd patted the parapet affectionately. "She's got a more complete vision than any of us. Look … out!" Dafydd turned and leaned his back against the parapet and addressed his listeners.

"She wants to be a home, right? A home like she used to be, the local grand family, the local servants, but that's not how the world is anymore. But if the families rotate their roles, masters and servant, the inequality is voluntary and temporary."

"It could grow on **me**!" said Myfanwy.

"Only because you've had too much of the other," Dafydd reached forward and stroked her cheek. "Don't you see, the Farm Project can't be complete without a real experience of life as it was in the grand house as the landlord of the farms. It's not just the climate and the mechanisms and crops and livestock that we're trying to recreate, but the social structure…"

"The hierarchy, the squirearchy," Myfanwy added.

"Yes, but we are also developing ourselves as well as the project," said Sally.

"I'm with you there," said Brum laughing, "I keep doing things I've never done before!"

"Like me – talking to houses!" said Sally.

"And talking **for** houses, thank you, Sally," added Dafydd. "So we can further develop ourselves by being, in rotation, proper squires and proper servants."

Myfanwy held up her hand for silence. Her eyes were widening. "I've always wanted to know what made people, for hundreds of years, tolerate being downtrodden, and that by a small minority."

"Like you were," said Dafydd, quietly, "by your Tad."

Myfanwy sighed. "I suppose so, and to be a servant, for a while, and then the lady, mistress of the servants I think I would discover more about myself."

"And, Milady, you'd discover about your servants!" exclaimed Brum lasciviously, adding "Lady Chatterley!"

"Oh Brum, this is serious!" exclaimed Sally.

"Brum is serious," Dafydd defended his one friend against the other. "We could **all** explore the potential there is in relationships to be unequal."

Myfanwy, with a sudden very aristocratic English accent said, "Clean this shoe, my man", placing her shoed foot on Dafydd's thigh. They all laughed.

"So do I sell the Plas?" asked Brum, ever practical, "and give the money to the Trust?"

"No," said Sally, "you deed the Plas to the Trust and that will enable the Trust to borrow money on the value of it to restore the Plas… and…"

"The families, in rotation, in the village," Myfanwy continued the vision. "Have the right to a period being the grand family and another period being the servants."

"And outsiders can fill the empty slots as an experience of the Farm Project," added Dafydd.

"And pay for the privilege," added Brum, "and the other visitors to the Farm Project can learn about the experience of being grand, and servant through…through…"

"Dafydd can write more books," offered Myfanwy.

"The teenagers can do video interviews," said Dafydd.

"Can I be Chaplain?" added Sally, seemingly as a non-sequitor.

"Hey, Sally!" said Brum, "Yes, re-open the little old chapel in the grounds! And I can just see you in eighteenth-century vestments, but you'd have to disguise yourself as a man!"

"I'm not sure about that!" protested Sally, laughing.

"Like the woman pope," Myfanwy exclaimed, "they didn't know she was a woman, till she died!"

"I'd rather know sooner," Brum laughed louder.

"Then it's agreed!" said Sally, decisively. "I'm going to enjoy this."

"Thank the house," said Dafydd quietly.

"To the Plas!" said Sally, raising her hand as if with a glass.

"The Plas!" the four friends chorused.

"Iechyd da," said Dafydd.

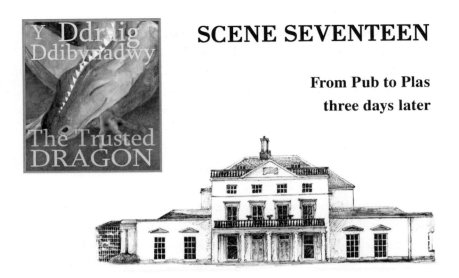

SCENE SEVENTEEN

From Pub to Plas
three days later

Unusually it was Myfanwy who proposed the walk. She explained that she was getting more perspective on her past and present and wanted to look out and see everything again as they had done from the Plas.

Therefore, on the first dry day that winter, the four friends set out, booted and scarfed from the pub courtyard on up to the knoll above the two farms recently bought by the Trust from Myfanwy's uncles.

On the steep and rapid climb east they said little other than enumerating the obvious. The pub was now pub-shop-honeymoon-hotel-post office-bank-chapel-workshops-teen-club-telecottage.

The farms were sold by the uncles, bought by the Trust and the plans were progressing for Kids Together and the first stages were in hand for the Farm Project.

The plans were being costed and put into a practicable schedule.

As they looked across at the Plas at the same height as them but on the north slope of the valley, Brum reported that his solicitors had, that morning, passed the ownership of the Plas by deed of gift to the Trust, with all the elaborate conditions which protected their plans for the future.

"You mean the Plas' own plans for her future," corrected Dafydd, and all four looked across at the sun-lit Plas on the south-facing slope. All four felt somehow that the Plas had changed for ever. Was it (or she) still calling out to them? Certainly there was a warm, welcoming, homely look to her, as if she was smiling out over the village below, knowing her future as a true home was secured.

Now the four friends set to pointing out on the landscape the limits of the Plas' grounds, the boundary of the farms, the roads and tracks and access, and the streams and other important features.

Yes, the Farm Project could embrace the Plas and its grounds, but only with major changes to the project range and location.

They unfolded a map and knelt on its corners on a smooth sheep-grazed bank. Their four frost-steamed breaths mingled as they pointed down at the map and out at the landscape, and changed the previous project plans, by negotiation, to what they all agreed was a greater and more complete vision of 'an experience of farming', now including the social structure, the day-to-day life, the status aspirations and limitations.

"The benefit is also the risk," said Brum. "We're planning lots more labour-intensive projects, interlocking…"

"The jobs!" exclaimed Sally, "It'll create lots of jobs."

"More jobs means more wages, wages are costs, costs need income," Brum said, stopping there, reluctant to say any more.

"So?" asked Myfanwy.

"So," said Dafydd, "what's our 'Plan B' if the visitors and the income don't come in?"

"Precisely!" said Brum, glad that someone else was expressing caution.

Dafydd nodded and continued. "We could have lots of jobs, yes, and the people in those jobs all fired up to do them, and no income to pay them with."

"So, all fired down," added Brum.

"Fired," said Dafydd more bluntly.

"It mustn't happen," said Sally, passionately. "I won't let it happen!"

"OK," said Brum, "I believe you Sal, but how?"

"How what?" asked Sally.

"How will you, or we, not let it happen? What will we do to guarantee it, guarantee a huge annual income enough to pay all those wages as well as the other costs?"

No answers came. They stood up, shook the frost and dew off the map, and began to follow a sheep path above a wall which followed the contour between the upper limits of the fields and the steeper, wilder hill land.

"I pray," said Sally, seriously.

"I drink," said Dafydd, comically.

Brum frowned. "I've sunk all my resources in the Trust. Now all I can offer is my skills and experience," he said, not uncheerfully.

"If I gave my pub to the Trust," said Myfanwy in a quiet voice, "would that help?"

"But it's all you've got!" said Dafydd, protectively.

"Myfanwy!" said Sally admiringly.

"It's not a solution," said Brum dryly.

"Brum!" scolded Sally, "That's a huge sacrifice for Myfanwy."

"OK, I'm sorry to be so factual," Brum raised his eyebrows in appeasement, "but let's say we've got twenty full-time staff at even only the rural Welsh average wage, plus the costs of employing them, National Insurance, pensions etc, every three years we have to find two million. The Trust would have to sell the pub and the Plas and the chapel and the farms just to pay three years' wages and then there'd be nothing."

"Except retired incomers buying all of them, and no local jobs," Myfanwy's tone was back to her gloom before the Trust was formed.

"In our lives so far," said Dafydd sweeping his arms with a great gesture around at the valley, "we have, all four, looked after ourselves, right? We've had the power, the earning power, to feed and house ourselves and to fulfil our immediate wants, right? This year, this busy, exploding year…"

The others nodded at the extraordinariness of their year.

"We have pooled our resources and have been able to do much more, much, **much** more, and have been able to fulfil others' wants, **many** others' wants." Dafydd fell silent.

"And?" said Sally.

"So?" said Myfanwy.

"And, so," said Dafydd after a few more moments of silence "now we've given away our power, we're powerless to stop the whole thing imploding."

"You said a moment ago that it was exploding!" exclaimed Sally, rising panic in her voice.

"Explode, implode. I believe that's one model of the history and future of the universe. We're simply obeying universal laws," Dafydd explained helpfully.

"Oh, Dafydd!" said Sally. "Don't be so cold-blooded. There must be something we can do!"

"Tell us a story," said Myfanwy gently, and she climbed carefully onto the rough wall and settled as if to listen.

The others, having walked on a pace, turned back and gathered around Myfanwy in the winter sunshine. Somehow their moments of pessimism were forgotten as they smiled at one another and at the brightness of the day. Dafydd searched the horizon as if for inspiration.

The Sea Defence

There was a great sea-defence once," said Dafydd pointing west towards the ocean.

And it protected rich farmland and many prosperous villages which, at high tide were below the level of the sea water on the other side of the great dykes.

The defences had always held. Come equinoctial tides, westerly gales, full rivers, come all, the villages and farmland had always remained protected.

But the generations passed. The people forgot the hard work building the sea-defences and draining the land. They began to see the sea-defences as if they had been built by nature, always there, as the hills and mountains. Gradually even the important titles of 'dyke-builder' and 'maintainer' became honorary, then their original meanings faded from consciousness as they became simply traditional family names...

"Nobody was maintaining the defences?" Brum asked.

"Nobody was maintaining the defences," Dafydd echoed, solemnly.

Then one day, when the tide was due to be high, and the westerly winds had blown steadily for a week, the sea rose and rose and rose. The old paths along the top of the dyke which used to be patrolled by sea-watchers in the old days, were over-grown and pitted by animals' burrows. Soon, those overgrown paths were swilling with the push and thrust of the waves and salt wave water was pulsing via animal holes through into the rich farmland. And the tide continued to rise.

Dafydd stopped speaking. The dreamy relaxation of his listeners stiffened. Brum took a sharp intake of breath. He had fallen for it again, set up to be frustrated by silence into asking a question.

He asked. "What happened next?" followed by muttering, "One day I won't ask!"

Dafydd looked around, smiling.

Four friends happened to be walking past the lowest and most neglected part of the sea defences. They yelled. They pointed. They rushed into action.

"Ah!" said Sally as if rescue was in sight.

"There was one among them…" said Myfanwy, optimistically.

"Hang on," said Brum urgently. "What can they possibly do?"

"They did…" said Dafydd, evenly…

…what they possibly could do, and pushed stones and earth into the gushing animal holes. But the water then gushed through other holes and cast out with more and more force whatever obstacles the four friends could lay their hands on. The tide rose higher…

"This is awful!" exclaimed Sally, imagining the desperate struggle.

Soon the surge of the waves was washing over the crest of the wall and slipping and sliding down the landward side, pulling the friends' feet from under them and dragging them down in a flow of pebbles, brambles and mud….

"What can they do!" Myfanwy wailed.

Dafydd's voice rose, relentless.

The four friends mustered all their strength and against the almost overwhelming downrush of water, heaved themselves up by the few not yet uprooted bushes to the top of the dyke, where they knelt in the surf holding on with their cramped fingers. What met their eyes chilled their hearts.

The sea was huge. The sea was massive, powerful. They could feel the great pressure of it shuddering beneath them. They had never felt smaller nor weaker nor nearer to death…

"But there was one among them…" protested Myfanwy, desperately.

"It's too late!" cried Sally.

"Please, Dafydd," said Brum, holding Sally's shoulders, "tell us the tide turned and all the villagers helped to rebuild the defences!"

"They say," said Dafydd in a very flat voice…

    … that, on a clear, still day, when the sea is smooth as glass, you can look into the depths, just out there, and you can see the roofs of those villagers' houses, and you can hear the church bell tolling beneath the water.

Into the cold stillness that followed Sally said, "What could the four friends have done? Dafydd? … Dafydd?"

"When it's too late," said Brum, "it's too late!"

"But even four people, years earlier, couldn't have prevented…" Myfanwy was still struck by despair.

"I've got it," said Sally. "That's what you mean, isn't it? Dafydd?"

Still Dafydd made no reply but just looked down at his feet.

She continued, "Don't you see, Brum, Myfanwy, what Dafydd's trying to tell us is that we will never be enough. Maybe we were enough to get it all started, but we can't, the four of us, ever be sufficient again. It's got to be more people…"

"It **is** more people," said Brum, reassuringly.

"Yes, but it's in us four there has to be a change," continued Sally. "Don't you see, Brum, we must admit we're powerless? We can't take the measures to prevent disaster. We, us four, are never going to be sufficient in ourselves again, not against the huge scale of what we've created."

"Don't worry, Sally," said Brum, trying to calm her.

"No, no, you don't understand. I'm **glad** to be powerless. Then I'll do something about it. I'm glad to know it. Then I can…"

"Acknowledge, accept, adapt, change, prepare," Myfanwy offered, then she added, "but first let's grieve for sufficiency lost."

"Thank you, Dafydd," said Sally, and unexpectedly she started crying.

"You're a brute!" said Myfanwy to Dafydd as she joined Brum to hug Sally.

"Brutal truth is brutal," said Dafydd, "and it hurts me, too."

Myfanwy turned and looked up at Dafydd's face concernedly. "You poor lad, you've been even more self-sufficient than any of us, your whole life, and now…" she wrapped her arms around his waist and pressed her head against his huge chest.

The two couples stood in their embraces in the winter sunlight.

"Have we created a monster?" said Sally, her words muffled in Brum's shoulder.

"A giant," corrected Dafydd, his words high and free. "There's a long tradition of Welsh giants."

"The Big Friendly Giant, BFG," said Myfanwy looking up into Dafydd's face. "He seems gruff, but he has a soft heart."

"The visitors **must** come!" said Sally, determinedly.

"Nobody compels visitors to come," said Brum in a reassuring tone. "Only quality, accessibility, utility…"

"…ity, ity!" mocked Dafydd, "what they want guaranteed is to be dry, fed and experience magic, in that order."

"But first they must be able to get here, and park…" Brum said more aggressively.

"Fair enough!" said Dafydd, backing down.

There then followed a vigorous walk and a vigorous and very specific discussion of main roads, side roads, parking capacity and dry ways of getting from coaches and cars to the covered areas of the Farm Project.

By the time agreement had been reached, the four friends were outside the Plas, and the sunset had turned the world graze-pink and bruise-purple. The temperature was dropping fast.

"I've still got the keys," said Brum, "now I'm a Trustee rather than the former owner, I can show you round."

"Is the heating still on?" asked Myfanwy.

"Is the kettle on?" asked Sally.

"Let's rest awhile," said Dafydd, with mock formality, "and switch off from all this practical thinking." The others nodded in agreement.

"Time for **us**," said Sally, with emphasis. "We give so much time to the Trust…"

"You could tell us a story," said Brum to Dafydd as he opened the great door.

"Try to stop him!" murmured Myfanwy as she rushed through the hall to the radiator in the drawing room.

"Yes," said Sally as she switched the lights on. "But not a helpful story, just a story."

"All stories are helpful," Dafydd laughed, sprawling in the huge settee, "if you are open to the help they contain."

"So, tell us," said Sally, "about you, Dafydd … how did you decide to come back to the village after all your wanderings?… But wait for Brum to come in with the hot drinks!"

As they waited, Myfanwy took a cushion from a chair and made herself comfortable sitting on the low side radiator and she rubbed warmth back into her hands. Sally looked intently round the room, thinking hard, then she shrugged as if to switch off thought. She went over to Myfanwy, kissed her on the forehead, did the same to Dafydd as he lay back, feet up, filling the whole of the length of the huge settee. Dafydd thanked Sally for the kiss and, as he lay, he eased his boots off using only his feet. The boots thumped to the floor. Sally sat on the settle, making space for Brum then sighing, looking at that space as if it was a new thing, and full of meaning.

Brum came in, gave a half-pint glass full of hot chocolate to each person. Then Brum filled the space. Sally kissed his forehead, and Dafydd began to speak.

"I think this is the story of each of us. There is a story within a story…"

"You don't usually comment on stories," said Brum, still at a higher energy level than his three, relaxed friends.

"True!" said Dafydd, chuckling. "Please ignore what I have just said…"

"Don't think of pink elephants!" said Brum laughing.

"Quiet, Brum." said Sally gently. "We're all listening, Dafydd. Go on."

The Shepherd Boy

Dafydd's voice was warm and dark, like the hot chocolate and the winter evening. "I was in New Zealand (they need Welsh rugby coaches in New Zealand) and I was feeling vaguely melancholy, indefinably wistful, full of uncertain longings, searching for the intangible. It was at a gathering of storytellers, and I'd just done my bit, telling a story of an old Chinese man and a mountain. It was a good story and it had gone down well."

Dafydd laughed quietly. "I could see some of my fellow storytellers memorising it to tell it in their turn, with their embellishments. Yes," Dafydd sighed, "the story had been understood in its different ways, but I felt restless, as if nobody had listened to me, as if they hadn't understood me."

So I was only half-listening to the next few stories. I knew those stories already, but from different sources and cultures, so I suppose I was only paying attention to the differences from the versions I knew. Then, at two words at the start of the next story, I woke up to it. 'Welsh hills' the teller had said. My heart began to beat faster. I felt nervous, apprehensive, as if I already knew that this story was for me and I must listen.

The story told of a shepherd boy in the Welsh hills who had wonderful day-dreams and wishes, but he had no money, no skills that he was aware of to bring his ideas to life. He loved the countryside, the wildlife, the changes in the weather, the changes in the seasons, the changes in the year. He knew each sheep and had given each a name and he knew its ways and where it fitted into the flock. Every day he learned new and wonderful things about the interactions of the wild creatures and plants, and he stored all this knowledge away, wondering when and how it could be used. 'Schools' he thought 'colleges', but having never been to school or college, he had little idea what they were or what happened there.

At night and in bad weather he would lead his flock to the old ruined church and shelter beneath what remained of the roof. He had heard tales of ancient monasteries where knowledge of nature had been preserved and kept. Were they 'schools'? Were they 'colleges'? But he had also heard that some king of England who had denied his Welsh blood had destroyed all the monasteries and had given them to his rich friends to make those friends richer.

The young shepherd often puzzled about the contradiction in the tale. 'How could the king **destroy** the monasteries and also give them to his friends?' Sometimes the shepherd would touch the walls of the old ruined church and by touching them he knew the old church hadn't truly been destroyed. Even if the king had battered and burned it, even if there would be not a stone remaining, the church would still be there. Indeed, there was a big old oak growing inside the church. Hundreds of years ago the oak had been a tiny seedling, then a sapling in the shelter of the church. Now the oak was enormous and gave shelter to the boy and his flock which the crumbling church could no longer give.

One night, sleeping, leaning against the old oak, the shepherd boy had a dream. In his dream he went to a far off place called 'London'. In his dream there was a wide river and a bridge over the river, and on the bridge, to

his amazement and disbelief even in his dream, there
were shops and houses! When he woke he was still
laughing at the strangeness of building houses and shops
on a bridge. At his sudden laughter the birds flew up in
alarm from the oak tree, and the boy's sheep gazed
towards him wonderingly.

Then the boy fell silent. He knew, in some deep way,
as if a voice had spoken, that on that strange bridge he
would find the meaning and purpose of his life.

There Dafydd's voice stopped. He yawned and stretched as if getting
ready to sleep. Myfanwy got off her radiator, carried the cushion to the
settee and hit Dafydd with it gently on the head. Turning to Brum she said,
"I'll ask!" and she pushed her hips against Dafydd's knees to make some
room and she sat on the settee, resting her arms along Dafydd's
outstretched legs. "What did he do next? Is that the right question?"

"It'll do," murmured Dafydd, reaching a hand to ruffle Myfanwy's hair
and stroke her cheek. He took a deep breath and continued.

The boy said goodbye to each sheep and lamb
individually. He gave them into another shepherd's care
and would accept no money or payment.

Into his pocket he put a leaf and an acorn and an oak
apple from the oak tree, and a very small piece of stone
from the old church's walls, and he set off towards
where the sun rose.

He had nothing, but by skirting the towns and cities
and thereby being always in the countryside he was able
to use what he had learned, and the wild creatures'
tracks drew him to stores of nuts and roots and berries
and edible flowers and clear, clean water to drink. He
took only part of what he found so there would still be

food for the wild creatures, and he covered the tracks he had made so as not to encourage other raiders.

The countryside changed and changed. From hills that could see the sea, he descended into forested valleys, and deep-grassed water-meadows. He saw great sheep like donkeys that made his little mountain sheep look like rabbits. Yet the countryside, however much it changed, was always the countryside and shared its secrets with him as much as ever...

"Aren't you glad we live in the country?" Sally whispered in Brum's ear, and as he nodded she rested her head against his head. He stopped nodding and made himself into a better headrest by putting his arm around her shoulders. Dafydd was continuing.

At last the shepherd boy could see the smoke of London.

As he got nearer, the smoke grew thicker and the noise grew louder. Everywhere was as noisy and as crowded as the busiest market day he had ever known. He asked the way and asked the way, but was so distracted and buffeted by the crowds that he could hardly hear the answers. Sometimes he clung to a street corner and looked up at the pieces of sky he could see between the crowding roofs just to remind himself that he was still in the same world.

Perhaps it was the same world, but here the ways were so different. In the Welsh hills the red kites gathered on the high air, free as the wind. Here, in London they gathered on waste-heaps picking among the nameless rubbish.

Soon, there was the wide river, and the boy laughed his amazement to see, spanning the river, just as in his dream, a bridge with, on it, houses and shops...

"Old London Bridge!" said Sally, softly against Brum's cheek.

"Is falling down!" murmured Brum in her ear.

Indeed, the bridge had fallen down many times, but had been rebuilt each time.

But the shepherd boy knew none of this.

He just gaped at the wonder of it and walked from one end to the other and back.

Then he shook his head and told himself that he hadn't yet looked for the meaning and purpose of his life on the bridge.

'Perhaps I am to be a shopkeeper, a trader, perhaps I am to live in one of these tall, crumbling houses'.

The boy walked once more from one end to the other and back, this time watching and looking and waiting for some clue as to his destiny.

There were no clues.

All day long and into the evening he walked and watched, walked and watched.

As he had in the countryside, he began to notice the habits of the creatures. Some slyly and almost imperceptibly had slipped their fingers into his pockets while bumping him with their shoulders, but, feeling only the leaf, the acorn and the oak apple and the stone, the fingers had slipped out again.

He saw some creatures speaking loudly, waving one arm threateningly at a shopkeeper, while their other arm, like a completely different animal, was gently and secretly lifting things from the shop counter and dropping them into a secret pocket in a long coat.

But there were no clues to meaning and purpose of his life.

At last, as night fell, he gave up, exhausted by all he had seen and heard and experienced, and, touching with affection the oak wood of a doorpost, he sat down in the doorway, leaned against the doorpost and fell asleep.

He awoke to the opening door pushing against him.

A fierce red face appeared from behind the door and a boot kicked him, 'Get out of my way! I'm opening up. You country bumpkins, you put off my customers. Go away!'

The shepherd boy stood up and apologized and thanked the man for the good night's sleep. The shopkeeper's frown softened. 'Don't think you'll get round me by being polite and all' he said, grumblingly. 'Here! What do you want? Take my advice. Be careful. You can be robbed here. Take my word for it!'

'I can't be robbed' said the shepherd boy. The shopkeeper laughed aloud and called out to his neighbours who were opening up their shop doors too and throwing out rubbish into the street, 'Hey, neighbours, this country bumpkin says he can't be robbed!'

The neighbours gathered round staring and pointing. The shepherd boy greeted each, politely, and each, in turn laughed.

'Why then, tell us,' said the first shopkeeper, 'how is it that you can't be robbed, when we are robbed every day!' The neighbours shouted general agreement.

'I can't be robbed because I have nothing.'

'You'd be surprised! Stay around here much longer' said one old woman, 'and they'll rob you of things you never knew you had!'

Again there was general agreement and some people stepped in closer.

'Why are you here?' asked one, 'I saw you yesterday, you were up and down here, up and down and you never took anything, even what fell on the street.'

Various comments were offered, 'He hasn't learned to steal yet', 'He'll soon learn'.

The shepherd boy reached for comfort behind him to touch the oak doorpost. Was this to be his destiny, to be transformed into a robber? Yes, he could take from these shops and still leave some for others.

'I lied,' he announced, and to a mixture of jeers and curious silence he took from his pocket the crumpled, much-felt oak leaf, the acorn, oak apple and the piece of stone from the old church wall. 'I have these, but those who tried to rob me left them in my pocket.'

Amid the mockery and amusement, the boy's announcement caused the question to come again, 'Why are you here?' and the boy told, frankly about his dream and how he had come there to find the purpose and meaning of his life.

There was a moment of silence from all the listeners to the boy's tale. Some looked sad. Some looked wistful. Some, the first shopkeeper in particular, looked thoroughly irritated by the simple words.

'You take my advice, lad!' the shopkeeper said, his face redder than before, 'dreams are a deceit and a deception. They rob you more than people do. Ignore dreams! Forget them! Don't believe a word of them! Why,' he turned for confirmation to the small crowd around him. 'If I took notice of my dreams, where would I be? Last night, for instance, I dreamed of a tatty, old oak tree in a broken-down church in some cold, wet hills. And there was treasure, think of that, treasure dug under the stupid tree by a one-eyed pirate. Look at me, lad. You don't see my rushing off to some God-forsaken place following my dreams! What would happen to my shop? Are you listening?... Where is that boy! Did he take anything? Did you see him take anything?'

But, smiling, the shepherd boy had slipped away empty-handed into the crowd.

The silence in the drawing room lasted long enough for the four friends, themselves to slip away from their images of London Bridge, the old city, and back, like the shepherd boy, to the Welsh hills.

"I don't want to ask a question," said Brum contentedly to Sally.

"Am I your Welsh hills?" asked Sally, coyly.

"No, my sheep," said Brum solemnly, then he laughed as Sally's hand rose as if to strike him. "My treasure! My treasure!" he cried in protest.

"And you're my one-eyed pirate," said Sally sipping the last of her chocolate, which was, by now, cold.

"So," said Dafydd, lifting Myfanwy into his lap as he swung round from lolling to sitting up on the great settee, "so I came back to the Welsh hills to find my treasure." And he hugged Myfanwy tightly until she protested.

"Squeeze me too hard, and I'll be ruined, devastated, destroyed!" she said.

"All the way from New Zealand?" Brum asked.

"Not in a straight line," Dafydd murmured, burying his face in Myfanwy's hair.

"What did the shepherd boy do with the treasure?" asked Brum.

"You said you didn't want to ask a question," Dafydd challenged him.

"Well, perhaps I'd like to give him some investment advice," Brum said in self-mockery.

"If I'm your treasure," Sally nudged Brum "what are your investment plans for me? What will you put me into?"

"My heart. That's the safest future," said Brum warmly.

"You old romantic!" exclaimed Myfanwy. "Dafydd never says anything like that to me!"

"OK," said Dafydd "But Birmingham's heart is safer only now that he's lost weight and got fitter."

"Oh, Dafydd!" Myfanwy said in exasperation. "You've got no imagination!" and they all laughed.

SCENE EIGHTEEN

Touring the Plas

The tour of the Plas that followed the story was full of detailed discussion of what year to restore it to, how to do that restoration, how to organise the rota of who would live and experience the Plas in rotation as the 'grand family' and the 'servants'.

Then the discussion grew heated as to how to make income from visitors without making the living experience meaningless.

The plan that emerged was for there to be four, salaried, chief servants, as jobs for local people, a butler, a cook, a housekeeper and a head-gardener. Their assistants would be the visitors, suitably chosen and living in and fed, and playing the roles of footmen, boot boy, scullery maids, housemaids and under-gardeners for a week or more's stay. The visitors would pay for the experience and be trained to their tasks by the chief servants.

Those playing the roles of the 'grand family' would be on salary too, and rotate with the chief servants so each had turns at the different experiences of the household.

To the guest rooms would come other paying visitors as 'guests' of the grand family who would mix with them as with friends and to live 'the country house experience'.

Of course, role-playing servants could return on other occasions to role-play being, instead, guests, and vice versa to complete their experience of the lives of the different people in the household.

When compared, as Brum did, systematically, with the economics of a hotel, the projected costs and incomes of the Plas experience looked very good.

"**If** any visitors come!" exclaimed Brum. "If not, then the salaries would be unsupportable. But that's the same for any hotel."

"How about," Myfanwy ventured timidly, "all the people who come as day visitors to the Farm Project – they'll want to tour the Plas and learn about it all."

Myfanwy had, unwittingly lit the blue touch paper. Dafydd's rocket was first to rise.

"Don't be stupid! We can't have real experience with thousands of gawping visitors tramping through the place!"

"It's not a theme park! It's got to be real!" Brum exclaimed.

Sally, trying to be more peaceful said, "Day trippers are out, I'm afraid, Myfanwy." But even Sally managed to sound very irritated.

Myfanwy, under surprise attack hit back, "But I knew this place! There were times when all the village came up here, several times a year, real times, traditions, until the family sold up. Then nothing."

"Ah," said Sally, "before my time."

"Hm!" said Brum, "There were hints to me when I bought this place at the beginning, but I didn't really understand what I was supposed to do."

"Sorry, Myfanwy," said Dafydd in abject apology. "Of course you're right. We've just got to find those… those traditions."

"**You** remember," said Myfanwy, partly mollified, "the summer garden party ..."

"A village summer fete," said Sally, gladly. "we could have several every year, couldn't we?"

"And there was Christmas." Myfanwy continued. "You remember, Dafydd."

"I've had many Christmases in many countries…"

"You broke the greenhouse!"

"Ah, that's why I forgot! Ach! I remember now. We were supposed to sing carols and have mince pies on the lawn and I did a rugby drop goal with my mince pie…"

"It must have been a rock cake to break glass!" commented Brum, sympathetically.

"So there's a Christmas thing. We could have several of those," said Sally eagerly "and what about other times of year? There must be other, traditional festivals we could revive. I've got lots of books at home. I'll make a list."

"It still doesn't mean daily visitors can come ad lib every day," said Brum. And they all looked away from one another as if to gain more inspiration from the walls of the house.

"Walls!" said Dafydd.

"Balls!?" queried Brum.

"Yes, those as well," said Dafydd. "Walls have ears! We make a theatre, no, a cinema, and daily visitors can watch, live, on the screen, the daily doings of the grand family and the servants."

"Why not a series of booths?" Brum proposed excitedly, "where you can pick and choose from the cameras and watch the garden or the kitchen or the butler's pantry or the drawing room."

"And watch as long or short as you like," added Sally.

"Or press a button for video loops of things you'd like to see," suggested Myfanwy, "You know…"

"Boot-blacking," Dafydd suggested ironically, "techniques with the feather duster."

"Let's have no bedroom scenes!" exclaimed Brum with a chuckle.

"No, you thickheads!" Myfanwy spoke over the men "I mean the family at dinner, the servants at dinner, six o'clock in the morning."

"Brilliant, Myfanwy!" said Sally "We could make it into a CD Rom or DVD…"

"Not too virtual!" said Dafydd "or the visitors will all stay at home and only visit us on-line."

"No," said Sally, "you're right, but visitors could have access to a great store of clips to view anything on record in detail, and watch bits live."

"'Voyeur Visits'," Dafydd named the product, or "'Peeping Tom Tours', 'Through the Keyhole Connections' or 'What the Butler Saw'."

"No bedroom scenes!" repeated Brum.

"We'll call them 'Myfanwy's Marvels' since it's all her idea."

"It was your idea, 'Walls'" said Myfanwy.

"And Brum thought of booths" added Sally.

"OK," said Dafydd, "'Myfanwy's marvels in Brum's Booths'."

"What about Sally?" Brum was warming to the names idea now. "'Sally's Sallies'."

"Do be serious!" scolded Sally.

"'Sally's Serious Sallies into Myfanwy's Marvels in Brum's Booths'." Dafydd said with finality.

"What about you, Dafydd?" Sally laughed.

"Dai-oramas," suggested Myfanwy wickedly. They all laughed.

"I'm hungry," said Brum suddenly. "Sally, let's go home."

"Home!" said Sally, delightedly.

"Actually," said Brum shyly, "It's the first time I've called anywhere 'home' since I was a child. Here, Trustee," he added more boldly, chucking the keys to Dafydd, "you lock the old place up," and Sally and Brum left, arm-in-arm into the cold, crisp night.

With lowered head Myfanwy looked up under her eyebrows at Dafydd.

Dafydd raised one eyebrow and grinned broadly. "I'll try not to break any glass, this time," he said, and they tiptoed upstairs in the silence of the grand house, and with a few ladylike airs and some peasant poses, milady Myfanwy was seduced by the tall under-gardener.

SCENE NINETEEN

In the Farmhouse Parlour

This time the four Trustees met in the farmhouse parlour with the local architect, who had been commissioned to draw up the initial plans and costings of the new farm project which now included Kids Together and the Plas as 'Phase One'.

The meeting was frustrating. It was mostly questions from the architect and almost no answers. The frustrations all seemed to be expressed in sports metaphors, 'a level playing field', 'a different ball park', 'don't keep moving the goal posts'.

With a concerted sigh the Trustees thanked the architect and spent another two hours producing consistent working answers to the scores of questions raised. Sally noted all the agreed answers and promised to key them in and e-mail them as an updated brief for a meeting with the architect in a month's time.

"Let me just summarise again," said Brum.

"Oh Birmingham," sighed Dafydd in exaggerated exasperation, "I've been so summarised and précised, I've been reduced to nothing! I'm a dwarf."

"Chance would be a fine thing!" exclaimed Myfanwy.

"We're listening, Brum," said Sally, her patience all used up.

"One, the Plas," Brum counted off on his fingers. "A million to restore it to 1812 as agreed, and to install cameras, viewing booths and systems, and to cover two years' salaries while visitor numbers pick up. Two, Kids Together fifty thousand and cheap at the price as it builds up, and before income comes in. Three, phase one roadways and car and coach parking for Kids Together and the Plas, quarter of a million. Four, for phase one, systems and part-time staff and insurances, another fifty thousand. Then Five, the phase one design and development of the farm project, half a million before it's even been built. Total, one point eight five million we're committed to over the next three years before we can even give the go-ahead for the farm project."

"That's a lot," said Sally, wearily stating the obvious.

"And the Trust's assets?" Dafydd asked.

"The chapel, less the debts, the farms, less the mortgages, the bungalows less their mortgages, the Plas outright, the investment, oh, and the income from the livestock sold off the farms, less the skate park and centre costs, plus their value if they could be sold, total, three million and a bit, and rising each year as the value rises and the mortgages are reduced. Then there's the income from the rents…"

Dafydd interrupted, "That's OK then, borrowing in a proportion eighteen to thirty, about seventy per cent."

"It all seems a lot to me," said Sally neutrally.

"Solvency," said Dafydd "is when you sell all your assets and you can pay all your debts."

"But we must get visitors," Brum said, and then echoed Sally's weary tone. "That's the end of my summary. Thanks, Dafydd for the work you've done on the old farmhouse."

"Myfanwy helped," said Dafydd.

"Thanks to you both," said Brum, "I'd better get Sally home. All these figures make her tired."

"I'm shattered too," said Myfanwy. "I'm going to have figures rattling round my head all night."

"Then I'll tell you all a story, a short, relaxing, figure-banishing story to help you all sleep," said Dafydd, and his three friends felt the tension flow out of them even as he started with his storytelling voice.

The Banker

Once there was a banker and he worked well at the bank, but the figures, the columns, the coins, the notes, the accounts, the projections and the budgets used to go round and round in his head all the way home, all evening at home, and all night in his bed, and even over breakfast and on the way to work and all over every hour, night and day of every weekend and every holiday.

"Was his name Iolo?" interrupted Brum.

"How did you guess?" said Dafydd.

Yes, 'Iolo the Bank', he was called by those who respected him, 'Iolo the Cash' to those who had good security who he lent money to, and 'Iolo No-No' to those who were bad risks and were always rejected.

"I thought you said this would be a **short** story!" said Sally.

"I'll move along a bit faster" said Dafydd contritely.

Iolo tried everything, massage, jogging, mindless TV, cold baths, turning round seven times before he left the bank, self-hypnosis, but still the figures rattled round in his brain. 'I've become a human calculating machine that won't switch off!' he said to himself.

Then at the same time as Iolo happened to be glancing at an article on schizophrenia and on the same page was an advertisement for a Superman movie, one among his friends said, 'Iolo, you're too single-minded'.

And Iolo put two and two, or at least one and one and one together, and he came out with the answer.

The predictable silence was too much for his three friends to bear. They glanced at one another and in chorus said.

"What was the answer?"

"I thought you'd never ask," said Dafydd, chuckling,

> Straight from the bank he went into a telephone box.

Dafydd was silent again.

"Don't tell me!" exclaimed Sally "He put his underpants on over his trousers and flew out as a schizophrenic Superbanker!"

Dafydd was silent still.

"He changed into drag and went round singing in all the pubs," Myfanwy offered as an alternative. Dafydd said nothing.

"He became Mr Hyde and did wicked deeds in the farms of Wales," Brum said with new energy.

"Sleep well," said Dafydd, leading the way to the door.

"But you haven't told us!" Brum cried out in mock petulance.

"He has, Brum," said Sally, warmly.

"What? When?" said Brum.

"We're all in the phone box inventing new futures," said Myfanwy over her shoulder as she trotted out to catch up with Dafydd.

"So we are!" Brum exclaimed gleefully. "The bastard!"

"Well I'm going to change into Mao Tse Tung and drive off for a Chinese take-away and watch the sun set over the sea," said Sally determinedly. "What about you?"

"A hungry Madame Butterfly," said Brum exotically.

SCENE TWENTY

Sally's Parlour
the next evening

After dealing with the incoming mail early the next evening, the four Trustees sat back to share two cans of beer between them. Sally had still not learned how to pour from cans into glasses, so there was a meditative few minutes as they all watched the glassfuls of foam settling to a finger of beer, and they waited to be topped up.

One of the items in the mail had been about grants to help promote or preserve the Welsh language. Myfanwy still looked worried.

She said sadly, "Dai, Dai, sometimes I think it's too late! When we were all poor and we had only our language, we were prepared to die for it. Now we care only for our new car, our new clothes. We'd rather go international shopping than do anything to preserve our national language!"

Dafydd looked, long into Myfanwy's eyes, "You haven't got any car, let alone a new one! You've very few new clothes. You use Welsh whenever possible," he said softly, "and still you are pessimistic about the future."

"I'm one of a few," she said "A dying breed. English has jumped from being the rejected language of the bullying neighbour to the acceptable language of all international communication. The Scots are Scots without a language. In a generation or two we'll have to be Welsh without Welsh."

"I've learned Welsh," Sally protested vehemently. "It only needs the incomers to learn Welsh and…"

"It's not **your** efforts," Myfanwy interrupted Sally. "It's **our** attitudes. So many Welsh-speakers don't seem to care. It's the language they use at home, but if it dies, so what? They can't spare the effort to keep it going. Even in Welsh-medium schools, like our old school is now," Myfanwy looked at Dafydd with a flash of affection in her mournful tale, "the kids mostly speak English in the playground!"

"I'm learning better, now," said Brum encouragingly, "at school French was so difficult, like an obscure code invented to make me fail tests. Instead of 'the' you had 'le', 'la', 'les' 'l apostrophe' **and** you had to know the sex of the word following before you could say the word before! I just thought Welsh would be worse, and I'd feel stupid again. I wasn't avoiding Welsh as Welsh. I was trying to avoid feeling humiliated."

"He's learning well," said Sally in Welsh, looking round to share her praise.

"Oh Sally, Brum," said Myfanwy passionately "what **you** are doing is great, but it's not the point! The point is how do we get our **own** people to care more?"

"Not everyone wants to be a militant campaigner," Dafydd muttered quietly.

"No!" said Myfanwy, sharply. "But even just to keep the language Welsh at home would be a start. You don't have to be a militant to speak your own language to your own children!"

"That won't stop them speaking English in the playground. English is pop, is rock, is cool!" Dafydd offered.

"Then we need to share how much **we** care with the school kids. Then they might care too!" Myfanwy countered.

Sally tried to raise Myfanwy's spirits. "The Farm Project will help. It will help a lot. Welsh will be the staff language of speaking and writing. Visitors will be addressed in Welsh and only if they don't understand will staff speak English. All the notices will be in both languages…"

"But that's been the problem for me," Brum cut in, "Wales being bilingual. I've never **had** to try to understand or learn, and when I've tried a few phrases in bad Welsh, people have replied to me in English. Where's the pressure to learn? Let's do **all** the project **all** in Welsh!"

"You'd be lost!" said Sally.

"Isn't that imposing our ideas on our visitors?" asked Dafydd.

"And we need the non-Welsh-speaking visitors," said Myfanwy.

"Oh, I don't know!" said Brum, annoyed. "You think of a better idea!"

"The March of the Oaks!" said Dafydd, portentously.

"What?" said Brum, asking a question even before the story began.

The March of the Oaks

There was an Ice Age once – actually, several times – and even here, where we're standing was nothing but ice, half a kilometre thick.

Dafydd shuddered and made shivering sounds.

Then the ice melted, the sea rose, and the plants began to come back. The first trees were the birches, the first tree of our tree alphabet, the symbol of new birth and beginnings, trees with light, wind-borne seeds. But the oaks had already started marching from Spain…

"Marching?" queried Brum.

There were no oaks, even in what is now France. From ice-free Spain and Portugal, they began to march north.

"I don't get it," said Brum, puzzled. "How can you march without feet?"

"A 'root' march?" suggested Myfanwy, "or you could just 'stump' along…!"

"Enough!" said Dafydd extravagantly.

Oaks make acorns. Acorns are heavy. They cannot be borne in the wind. When animals eat them they are digested and destroyed. Oak trees produce no suckers or runners, so how do they spread?

"I don't know," said Brum, laughing, "I'm a suave urbanite, not a forester. Perhaps the acorns roll downhill."

"Then how did the first oak get to the top of that hill?" Dafydd asked.

"Boys fired acorns in catapults?" Brum suggested with no great confidence.

"That's sexist," said Sally.

"OK," said Brum, grinning, "girls with big breaths and peashooters."

"Only girlth have big breaths," said Myfanwy.

"That's sexist," laughed Sally.

"And only boys have peashooters!" said Dafydd, "I know, so let me get on with the story."

You do not know how oaks march, so I will tell you. It is by thieving and memory loss...

"Eh?" said Brum.

The murderers and eaters of babies in the spring turn to robbers and buriers in the fall...

"Autumn," corrected Sally.

"Who, in the forest, murders and eats babies?" asked Dafydd.

"Trolls, monsters, giants, infantophages of all types," Myfanwy suggested.

"True, " said Dafydd.

Jays and squirrels. Their spring protein is baby bird flesh. Their fall protein ..."

"Autumn" corrected Sally.

...is acorns, which they steal from the trees and carry off to bury in lots of hiding places in the earth.

"Ah," said Brum "and they forget where they buried them."

Yes, some hiding places they do forget, but those few are enough. A buried acorn has lots of energy. It can support a stout seedling that out-competes the birches and puts them in the shade...

"And so we get oak forest dominating?" said Brum.

Metre by metre, by thieving and memory loss the oaks have marched all the way from Spain to Wales.

"But what does that mean for the language?" protested Myfanwy, usually so patient about Dafydd's seeming irrelevancies.

"Inevitable, irresistible, predictable, pre-destined, pre-ordained, un-preventable," said Dafydd, heavily.

"You sound like me!" Myfanwy exclaimed "and so what?"

"What do oaks represent?... Sally?" asked Dafydd.

"Well," said Sally, thinking aloud, "very big trees, very old, Kings hid in them, they grow hollow. The mighty oak from the little acorn grew. The English oak, a big sort of mother tree."

"Brum?" Dafydd asked.

"Then we, the English, cut them all down to make our navy, the great English navy against the Spanish Armada, the great navy of Nelson, Captain Cook's ships, merchantmen, schooners, tall ships, the world-wide might of the Empire, based on oak ships."

"There speaks the engineer and Englishman," said Dafydd, "but to us Celts, the oak is the tree of the grove, the sacred grove, the oak-knowledge is Druidry. We Celts took the oak and made it a symbol of wisdom passed down from generation to generation..."

"I still don't see what it has to do with our language," Myfanwy interrupted again.

"See the symbolism," said Dafydd, patiently. "The oaks march into Wales from England. We Welsh possess them into magic and mystery. We learn, we understand, we know the oaks. Hence the Romans marched into Ynys Mon and destroyed all the oak groves and the sacred springs they contained. But Romans could not destroy the oak knowledge even though they slaughtered all our bards and druids there among the felled oaks and fouled springs.

"We resisted the Romans for much longer, then became a province, a quite autonomous province, and we possessed many Latin words into our language, into magic and mystery. We learned. We understood, we endured.

"Then the English marched in, and they cut down our oaks to make killing machines. They considered us Welsh as the pigs we herded in the oak forests for the fall crop..."

"Autumn," corrected Sally.

"...of acorns. But, even when you cut down the whole forest, what is forgotten by jays and squirrels grows again." Dafydd lapsed into silence. He watched the faces of his friends, who were trying to understand in what ways oaks and acorns were the Welsh language.

"While there are oaks, there will be Welsh?" Brum offered.

"What is cut down will grow again in unexpected places," Sally added.

"Even if...." Myfanwy was struggling. "Even if ... Welsh dies out as a language, it will ... grow again? I can't bear that, to be the generation that sees it die. Then I would die, not knowing if it will ever come again!"

"In Oz..." said Dafydd.

"Australia," corrected Brum.

"The Abbos..."

"Aborigines," corrected Brum.

"Native Australians," corrected Sally.

"...that I lived with in the bush," Dafydd continued, "they had been suave urbanites, or, more often, unemployed, under-class, slum-dwellers. For two or three generations they had lost their languages, and their culture, and their identity, and their self-respect, and their self-esteem, and their self-confidence..."

"Don't go on!" said Sally. "it's unbearable!"

"...and had embraced English and alcohol..." Dafydd continued.

"Please!" said Sally.

"…and violence…"

"But there was one among them…" Brum proposed.

Dafydd sighed, "A few. Just a few who knew the old ways and the old languages, and that is how my friends started to respect themselves again."

"Ah!" said Sally.

"…and grow again in self-esteem and self-confidence and find their identity and their culture, and let go of alcohol and English…."

"I could let go of English easier than alcohol!" Brum said with a laugh, but he saw Sally's disapproving look, and his laughter died. "Sorry," he said.

"We must keep Welsh alive," said Sally, her full concentration turned to Dafydd, "so it is there when a future generation **wants** to rediscover it?"

"**Needs** to," said Dafydd, softly.

"But will that happen?" Myfanwy asked in a desperate tone.

"The oak forests are back again," said Dafydd.

"But the future is so unpredictable," said Myfanwy.

"Especially when we try to control it," Dafydd added.

There was a pause. Myfanwy's discomfort was clearly not relieved. Sally thought of supportive statements, but kept silent because anything she framed to say sounded in her head too patronising or trite. Brum was trying to invent a scheme, or even a machine to preserve Welsh. Dafydd was breathing deeply, and seemed to be remembering.

"Dafydd, you have faith," said Sally, at last. Did that sound clichéd?

For a moment Dafydd pondered Sally's statement. "No," he said, hesitantly. "but I saw my Abbo friends learning their language, and it was a different phenomenon…"

"Could we use their method here?" asked Brum, ever practical.

"It was more… an attitude, a belief," said Dafydd, wonderingly. "They were told by the old men and women that the language couldn't be 'lost'. Even though the youngsters had never heard the language, nor had their parents, the old people told them 'the language is within you. Your dream spirit knows, and remembers. The language is all there, already, perfectly within you. What we will do is the necessary ceremonies and dreaming to bring it out again'."

"The Aborigines…" said Brum.

"Native Australians," corrected Sally.

"Abbos in Oz," corrected Dafydd.

"…have the largest brains of all humans," Brum concluded, ever technical and factual.

"So," said Myfanwy, "how do they do it? Can we introduce their methods in our classes?"

"Ceremonies to reconnect with the earth," said Dafydd, "to know the rocks, the water, to listen to the air, to hear the clouds, to eat lizards…"

"Ych i fi!" said Myfanwy.

"To dig for water-roots, to be so still and present in the moment that the flies can walk on your eyeballs and you don't blink."

"No!" said Myfanwy.

"To be naked and cover your body with urine and sand to keep out the fifty-degree Celcius sun-heat."

"Not in the classroom!" said Myfanwy.

"And listen for hours to the old people's songs and stories. Then to dance them. Then to dream them."

"No grammar?" Brum questioned ironically. "No, stupid dialogues?"

"No," said Dafydd, simply. "First you go into yourself to **know** that the language is already there, **in you**. Then you go further into yourself for the feel of the language, the resonances within your spirit, the sense that it is in every part of your body…"

"Not just the brain, then?" Brum asked, curiously.

"In your muscles, sinews, tendons, skin, hair, as well as your blood…"

"Did you learn Native Australian languages?" asked Sally.

In reply Dafydd looked deeply and calmly into Sally's eyes for a long minute. The others watched fascinated. Sally trembled.

"What was **that**?" she said, in a small voice, when at the end of the long minute Dafydd had turned his head to one side and had closed his eyes. "I felt all scooped out, then poured into," she added.

"For me," said Dafydd very quietly "the words of the language never came, just the understanding. I could walk in a circle then know the direction to go for food, or water, or shade, or shelter, or human company, or to go to a holy place of wall paintings…" Dafydd's eyes were still closed, and the others felt the presence of something new to them, but somehow very old. They waited, in respect for that presence.

Eventually Dafydd's eyes opened again. He smiled and shrugged. "It was a while ago, yet it's still here."

"I never learned that," said Sally very humbly, "about Welsh, not in any of the classes or courses."

"That was Australia," Brum tried to clarify.

"The equivalent," said Sally, "that should have been my starting point, the equivalent experience of Wales or Welsh."

"A place in the soul," Myfanwy muttered. "And it must be in that place that I'm hurting."

"I haven't got a soul," said Brum, blandly, "or did I sell it early on?" he laughed. "Or perhaps it's only, now, just starting to grow."

"You have a lovely soul, Brum," said Sally, "it's warm and kind and … knowing. It knows more than you realise."

"That's all I need!" said Brum in appreciative self-deprecation, "a soul that's more successful than I am, that's already ahead of me with the woman I love!"

"I'm sure you'll come later," said Sally, reassuringly, then she laughed in embarrassment as she realised what she'd said. At her embarrassment they all laughed, and somehow both couples seemed to agree to go their ways. The evening was over.

SCENE TWENTY ONE

Sally's Parlour Again
two days later

"I'm worried," Sally said when the four friends met next at her house in the parlour, as usual.

"You're always worried," said Dafydd. "I'm not." Myfanwy nudged him. Why was he always so hyper and wicked in Sally's house?

"Well someone has to worry," said Sally, seriously.

"OK," said Dafydd. "Let's specialise and delegate. **You** worry. I'll **not** worry. **I'll** give you my things to worry about. I'll take the things **you** worry about and I'll **not** worry about them. Is that a deal?"

Sally couldn't help herself smiling and the serious tone left her voice. "All right. Let's make it a question then. All the things we're doing for visitors, the visitors who we hope will come, are things about the past, the distant past, the near past, aren't they?"

"That's History," said Dafydd with conviction, adding in a wicked tone, "there's no future in it!"

"Yet we ourselves," Sally said, laughing "have developed our futures. There's the contradiction. I agreed with you, we'd done it for others, via the Trust, giving them insight into their pasts, and plans for the future, then we did it ourselves. We 'lived' the process. So now…"

"Sally wants the Trust to contain some… future things." Brum added.

"It will," Dafydd responded seriously. "In the future," he added, laughing.

"Sally doesn't know how to portray the future but she's concerned," said Brum.

"Thank you, Brum, I can speak for myself," said Sally.

"But you've got nothing to say," Dafydd expounded helpfully, ignoring Myfanwy nudging him.

"Well…yes," said Sally, "but I'm open to ideas."

"But the trouble with the future is…" Dafydd paused.

"What?" Brum asked predictably.

"It dates so quickly!" Dafydd delivered the punch line.

"That's true," said Sally ignoring Myfanwy's spluttering sounds. "So how can we portray a future experience which doesn't date?"

"Open this house as part of the experience" said Dafydd looking round, "'An Incomer's House'," Dafydd said, giving it a title, "full of courses in Welsh and books about Celts! Tastefully converted! To be a cosy piece of England away from home! Myfanwy, will you stop kicking me! I haven't said anything wrong, have I, Sally?"

Sally was looking round the room ruefully. "It's the truth, so it shouldn't hurt, but, yes, that's me, living between two cultures."

"Whereas the genuine hundred per cent Welsh houses in the village are decked up like Costa del Sol with Chinese-made knick-knacks labelled 'Pwllheli'," said Dafydd, "well worth preserving for future generations."

"I was wondering," said Brum in a very level tone trying to cut across Dafydd's frivolity. "Perhaps we could give a vision of the future of farming in Wales."

"What?" said Dafydd undeterred from levity. "Hundred-thousand-acre sheep ranches where the stock is herded and culled by helicopter gunships? Wall-to-wall wind-farms exporting clean energy to all the rest of Europe? Diversification gone mad where every second farm has buffalos, ostriches, lamas, quail, dingoes, alligators, leeches, selling ever more exotic mixtures from farm gates, Welsh honey with Welsh whisky, Welsh mink-milk cheese with pickled leeks, musical Welsh leek liqueur with Welsh chilli peppers in harp-shaped containers! Myfanwy, you've kicked me three times. Are you trying to tell me something?"

"I don't think Dafydd is in the mood to listen," said Sally, severely.

"I'll take him away," offered Myfanwy, "he seems impervious to pain."

"I'm sorry," Dafydd said, apologetically. "I just think we're setting ourselves up to be knocked down if we try to portray the future."

"Aunt Sallys," said Sally.

"You said it!" said Dafydd. "But I will answer."

The Wise Old Woman

"Once there was a wise old woman," Dafydd started, and all the protest and petulance faded from his voice.

> She knew the past. Oh how she knew the past!
>
> She had been midwife and nurse to the village for over seventy years and everyone in the village, in the simplest sense, passed through her hands, many of them from their first breaths to their last.
>
> The years passed, and soon she was the oldest person in the village, indeed, in the whole district, and everyone knew that she knew more than anyone else in their whole, small, world. They came to her, those of every age, for advice and guidance, and because she was so wise, she advised them well, and they followed her advice.
>
> Then suddenly the times began to change. The railway came to the nearby town and brought with it many strangers who, for their holidays, wanted things the villagers had never heard of.

'No, don't grow new things on the farms. Don't make or sew new items. Don't cut new cuts of meat.' The old wise woman's advice was consistent, and the villagers duly followed her advice, and their village was rapidly by-passed by the demands of change and progress, and it was the neighbouring village which changed and thereby prospered.

In the silence which followed Brum reluctantly asked, "Did the village, her village, fade away?"

"No," said Dafydd sadly.

The wise old woman grew older and older and began to babble only about her childhood. Even from these utterances, the people took wisdom, and indeed there was wisdom therein...

"'Therein'?" questioned Sally.

"Yes," said Dafydd, "this is an old story."

But, ever practical in the matters of midwifery and nursing, the people of the village, willing to listen to her advice were now unwilling to have such old and feeble hands deliver their babies, 'you must train an apprentice' they said, and in her lucid moments she agreed and appointed her great-great grand-daughter...

"How old was she?" queried Brum.

She was twelve, and very bright, and she learned quickly. Soon the old, wise woman was calling her 'mother', and when people came for advice and guidance, the old woman pointed to the young girl and said 'ask my mother. She's older and wiser than me.'

And that's how it was. The people obeyed the wise old woman's advice by listening to the young girl, and **she** told them how to change and to try new things and to catch up with the villagers from the other villages around them, and soon their market was flourishing again, and there was even talk of building a branch railway line to the waterfalls in their village.

Dafydd's pause now seemed final, but Brum was, as usual prowling around the edge of the silence. He asked, "How does this help portray the future?"

"Oh, Brum," said Sally, "he's saying we're too old."

"Too old for what?" protested Brum.

"To see the future. We've got to hand that over to the young people," Sally added.

"The teenagers?" Brum asked.

"Younger," said Dafydd tersely, "and the exhibit, display, whatever, should change very regularly."

"Annually?" Myfanwy asked.

"That'll do," said Dafydd "but don't ask me. I'm too old."

"Well, we still act on your babblings – QED," said Myfanwy affectionately.

"But my hands are old and feeble," said Dafydd in a quavering voice showing his huge strong fists.

"Thank you, Dafydd," said Sally in a decisive voice. "So we will ask young people, very young people to keep refreshing an exhibition somewhere in the project called 'our vision of the future'."

"Our future visions," corrected Brum, "er, no, that means we'll never have them, sorry."

"'Possible Futures Through the Eyes of the Young'," Myfanwy offered.

"'Future Shock!'" said Dafydd, "if we survive at all."

"An exhibition," said Sally as if to close the subject "and the other question is, what will we do to… to promote the futures … of our visitors as we have… promoted our own?"

"I've been demoted," said Brum. "And I'm glad of it."

"You know what I'm trying to say," said Sally with a trace of her old irritability. "we should….what is it?… exemplify our development through the Project."

"Have we any right to interfere?" Dafydd challenged.

"'Interfere'? That's ripe coming from you!" Sally snapped, then she said "I'm sorry, Dafydd. I'm glad you interfered, it's just I'm a bit touchy at the moment."

"Worried about your own future," said Dafydd gently. "Aren't you?"

In the following silence Sally spoke, tears in her eyes. "Don't get me wrong, I'm very happy with Brum, I just think, maybe, we've bitten off more than we can chew."

"'We'?" Dafydd questioned softly.

"All right, me, **me, I've** bitten off more than I can chew! I've never even had charge of a whole parish, just a curacy and then counselling and now, suddenly, we're talking millions in money, and millions of visitors, and I'm …"

"Oh, Sally!" exclaimed Myfanwy, "You're the one that's kept us all together, kept us on-track, made us tackle the problems and make proper plans. You've done all the main paperwork. You've…"

Dafydd interrupted her, "You've controlled us because we were willing to be controlled."

"I never said that!" Myfanwy protested. "You put words in my mouth!"

"It's true, Myfanwy," said Sally. "As usual, what Dafydd says is true. I'm fearful of all these other people having to come in on the project and I don't know them. I don't know how they tick. Take the architect…"

"Please take the architect!" interrupted Dafydd wickedly.

"I know what you mean!" said Brum.

"Don't be afraid," said Myfanwy to Sally.

"No, stick with your fear, Sally. It's a real fear. Honour it!" said Dafydd. "Here are your three choices. One, you can conquer your fear and become a raging international executive – let's call that choice 'Imperialism'. Or, two, you take action to guarantee that the thing you fear never happens – let's call that choice 'Avoidance'. Or, three – you can take action to guarantee that if it does happen, you're not around. Let's call that choice 'Escape'. Right? So what will you choose: Imperialism, Avoidance, or Escape?"

"I don't want to become a raging, international executive," said Sally firmly. "Or **any** kind of executive."

"Good on you, Sal!" said Dafydd in an American drawl.

"Sally," corrected Brum.

"What were the other alternatives? Running away, or suicide?" Sally looked grim.

"No, Sally, I said 'Avoidance' – how to guarantee to avoid it happening, 'it' being the thing you fear, or 'Escape', making sure you're not around when it does happen."

"That sounds like resignation and withdrawal." Sally said in a very sober voice. "I've considered that."

"No, Sally!" said Brum and Myfanwy simultaneously.

"Yes, Sally," Dafydd added, "but resignation and withdrawal are both unnecessary. I propose you continue to do what you do best, being co-ordinator of the Trustees, and that we appoint, very soon, an administrator to do the day-to-day executive work, and a secretary to the Trustees to take the extra, growing paperwork, therefore freeing all of us four to do what we do best."

"What's that?" said Brum.

"Drinking," said Dafydd, pointing, pointedly at his empty glass.

"Sorry, Dafydd," said Sally, getting up to refill his drink, "and thank you. I'm so relieved."

"Is that motion passed unanimously?" asked Myfanwy, smiling.

"There are budget implications," said Brum, grinning.

"Sort them!" said Dafydd, laughing, "Which is just another pronunciation of 'sod them'. I'll draw up ads for the two posts. First we'll look locally, eh?"

"They'll have to like working with us," remarked Myfanwy doubtingly.

"And they'll have to like stories," said Brum, frowning.

"We'll select for liking us and liking stories at the interviews," said Sally, light-hearted again.

The Interview

Dafydd took a moment to sip his newly-poured beer.

There was an interview once. There were three interviewers and three interviewees. In strict rotation the interviewers sat in the centre of the table opposite the glass door, to take turns to chair the three interviews.

The interviewees came in, in turn, and each sat in the chair in front of the glass door.

When the three interviews were over, the three interviewers argued endlessly about who had been the best candidate. Funnily enough, each interviewer argued most emphatically for the candidate whose interview he or she had chaired.

Dafydd fell silent, as usual.

"I don't see," said Myfanwy, "Brum, Sally, can you see the point?"

"Is that a question?" asked Brum.

"Not really, but yours is," said Dafydd and he fell silent again.

"There was one among them," suggested Sally.

"Indeed," said Dafydd, "but among the interviewees. This interviewee…"

"Iolo," suggested Brum.

"Iolo the Job," agreed Dafydd...

    ... knocked on the glass door and entered. 'Excuse me,' Iolo said 'I couldn't help overhearing... but you're finding it difficult to choose between us, aren't you?'

    'Difficult?' said the interviewers. 'It's impossible!'

    'May I make a suggestion?' said the interviewee, 'I promise it won't be to my advantage. Yes? All right. Please one of you sit in the chairman's chair. The other two stand directly behind, the tallest at the back. Now, I will sit in the interviewee's chair. The glass door is closed. Now, tell me, chairman, what do you see?'

    'You,' was the reply.

    'And the interviewer standing behind, what do you see?'

    'You,' was the reply.

    'And the tallest interviewer, at the back, what do you see?'

    'You,' was the puzzled answer.

    'Ah,' said the interviewee, 'look more carefully. In the glass door, reflected, what else do you see?'

    'Oh, me!' each of them said.

Dafydd was laughing at the joke, but his three friends frowned.

Brum was the first one to click. "They each saw themselves!"

"They were trying to appoint themselves!" Sally understood too.

"The glass door! We see ourselves in other people!" said Myfanwy "So don't appoint a lookalike."

"Soundalike," added Sally.

"Talkalike," added Brum.

"Better to appoint someone who has the qualities we need, but haven't got." said Sally.

"Like the bloody architect!" exclaimed Brum.

"Exactly," said Dafydd. "If they irritate the hell out of us, they are probably strong in the areas we're weakest in and therefore the areas we feel most threatened by."

"Sounds awful!" exclaimed Sally. "We appoint an absolute pig who gets all our backs up and takes the project in all sorts of directions we don't want to go."

"Disneyland!" said Brum.

"Madame Tussauds!" said Myfanwy.

"A dead museum!" said Sally "with no commitment to the community."

"Look in the glass door again," said Dafydd "we must also be clear not to appoint our darker sides, our four darker sides all rolled into one."

"Which we've just described," said Sally, ruefully.

"Warning heard and noted," said Brum.

The rest of the meeting was taken up with defining the characteristics, the job description, and the criteria for choosing the candidates for Administrator and Secretary.

At last those tasks were complete.

"I've made a little supper," said Sally.

"Not too little, I hope!" said Dafydd.

"I hope we can all squeeze into the kitchen," Sally added.

"I'll leave my legs outside," said Dafydd, stooping as he stepped through the door.

Myfanwy passed piece after piece of bread to Dafydd as they sipped their soup. Sally was in philosophical mood. "I can feel the progress, the relief. We'll get the help we need, but I feel I've also given away something, lost something tonight."

"When God locks the cat flap" said Dafydd in an equally philosophical tone, "He always switches on the extractor."

"Sally's serious," defended Brum.

"I know you and Sally are serious," said Dafydd, admiringly.

"Oh, Dafydd," said Sally, "Whenever you're here in my house you're a…"

"A pain!" said Myfanwy.

"I was going to say 'agent provocateur', 'devil's advocate'."

"Devil himself, more like!" said Myfanwy.

"It's tradition," Dafydd said. "I've only just realised. My Auntie used to live here, you know."

"Mrs Jenkins wasn't your Aunt," said Myfanwy.

"Well, she would have been my Great Aunt if my Great Uncle hadn't have died before they had any children, but they didn't, so she then married out of the family and the children she did have weren't related to me at all. But she was still, strictly speaking, my Auntie."

"What?" said Brum.

"Pay attention!" Dafydd said in a mock-extreme-Welsh accent. "These things are very important in Wales."

"That's true," said Sally, patronisingly, then she looked around to see if anyone had noticed her say it, but Dafydd's voice was rolling on.

Trading Insults

Every time I visited I used to tease her rotten, and she used to tease me. Sometimes we'd just exchange insults. It was great. I was, what, nine, ten when I first visited her on my own, and she called me 'a scraggy beanpole with more lip than wit', and I called her 'a wrinkled jelly bag with more hip than wit' and for a week after every visit I was much easier with all the adults around me because I knew I'd insulted one adult something awful. I saw her, too, being much kinder to her grand-children once she'd called me a dozen devastating names.

We both got better at it. It's an old Welsh tradition I found later, of the bards to trade insults in public competition, only ours were private. So, when I'm in this house I'm...

"Nine years old," interrupted Myfanwy.

"A scraggy beanpole with more lip than wit," said Brum with satisfaction.

"A bit full of yourself, and full of my loaf of bread for tomorrow!" said Sally, laughing. "Well, that explains a lot. I'm forewarned."

"And forearmed," Brum completed the saying.

"I'll save up an insult or two," said Sally, still amused. "For your next visit!"

The One That Stuck

Dafydd told his story between mouthfuls of ham, mashed potatoes and peas.

I knew an insult once. It was told to a little girl at school. The insult came out of the mouth of a teacher and was spat at the little girl, and the insult stuck.

The insult wasn't actually true, not about that little girl, but it stuck because it had been spat so hard, with that teacher's full power and spat from the great height of the teacher looking down on the little girl.

For several weeks the insult stuck there, repeating itself in the little girl's ear. At first the little girl cried whenever she heard it again in her head. Then the little girl, after a few weeks, replied to it each time saying 'It's not true!' But the insult persisted despite all the little girl's tears and protests. Eventually she thought, 'It **must** be true. I've heard it so many times!' and she believed it, and she **made** it true. And all the rest of her life it **was** true.

Dafydd went quiet.

Brum looked across sharply and saw Dafydd was not eating. "Question time," said Brum, "but it's not me, this time, is it?"

"That's a question," said Dafydd.

"No, it isn't," said Brum. "It's someone else's turn, isn't it?"

"That's another question," said Dafydd.

"No, it isn't," said Brum, "Oh, very well, what did the teacher keep saying?"

"You mean, 'what was the insult which kept repeating itself?' The teacher only said it once."

"OK, what was the insult?"

"Myfanwy?" Dafydd asked.

"Mine, was 'You can't sing!', and for twenty years I wouldn't open my mouth to sing."

"But you sing now," said Sally.

"Only since that teacher died," said Myfanwy.

"Oh dear!" said Brum.

"Sally?" Dafydd asked.

"My teachers! One said I was 'a shy little thing with more intelligence than sense', so I became shyer and never trusted myself with anything to do with common sense, only 'intelligent' things." Sally looked sad.

"And the other teacher?" Dafydd asked.

"You're a cold fish!" The words came out in that teacher's voice, and the three friends looked at Sally whose lip quivered.

"It's not true!" said Brum into the silence.

"No," said Sally, closing her eyes, "But I made it true for too long!"

"Brum?" Dafydd asked.

"Oh, lots of teachers told me I was no good at this, no good at that, but then that was true, not an insult, and anyway, I was bloody-minded and I'd just work hard at whatever it was and make it not true, so the teachers had to eat their words. Insults? It was an inner city school. You gave as good as you got. I can't remember a teacher insulting me." But Brum was breathing faster, and he'd been speaking very rapidly when he had suddenly stopped.

"You're a coward!" Dafydd whispered, suddenly, and Brum erupted, almost tipping the little table as he stood up, glaring, then sank back down and put his hand nervously over his mouth, "How did you know?"

"Was it true?"

"No."

"Did you answer the teacher back and give as good as you got?"

"No."

"When did the teacher say it?"

Brum's head hung down. All the life seemed to have gone from his body. Desperately Sally rubbed his back to try to get it to straighten again. Brum's voice was thin and muffled. "The teacher stopped a fight just after it had started. A big boy had just hit me, and in rage I'd hit him back. He was a bully.

"The teacher said, 'Will you fight clean if I watch?' and I said I wouldn't fight." Brum's head came up, defiant. "I'd had a moment to cool down. There was no point in fighting. I would only get beaten in. I didn't even know why the bully had hit me in the first place, so I wasn't defending anything."

"Very sensible, darling" said Sally concernedly.

"'You're a coward.' 'You're a coward'," said Brum flatly, like an endless echo. "Until I believed I was, and that all my reasons for not fighting were only a cloak for my cowardice."

"Poor Brum," said Sally soothingly as Brum's mouth grew tight and narrow, and he fought back tears.

"And so," said Dafydd quietly, "from then on you took risk after risk, often without reasons, and so became a success in life."

"I suppose that's true," said Brum, his tight lips softening into the beginnings of a smile.

"But you've stopped now," said Dafydd. "That's why you don't quite know yourself recently. You've stopped believing deep down that you were a coward. You've accepted yourself turning away from the bully."

"And you've helped to make a giant of a project!" said Sally, "You're not a coward," she laughed. "You took **me** on, and that proves it!"

"I really think that it's true," said Brum, wonderingly, "that I've stopped trying to be a success. That's what's changed."

"It's the real you, not the striving you," said Sally. "You don't have to prove to me that you're not a coward. I know how brave you are to give up success, and the million, and the Plas."

"Aren't those more risks I've taken?" said Brum, doubtfully.

"No, Birmingham, my friend," said Dafydd, "You've only given up the fruits of your risk-taking so now you can live without the compulsion."

"My God!" said Myfanwy. "What idiots we are, spending so much of our lives trying to prove our teachers right, or wrong!" They all looked away, into their pasts. Then Myfanwy looked back at Dafydd.

"And you, Dafydd?"

"That's why I was thinking about insults. It was very helpful for me, trading insults with my Auntie, and none of them stuck, and so I became too slippery, perhaps but I had seen the way my schoolmates would go quiet at insults and I'd seen how they would change."

"From the age of ten," Myfanwy said to Sally, "he was taller than most of the teachers. And from twelve was taller and stronger than any of them."

"It helps," said Dafydd, grinning. "Success or failure were rather meaningless to me. I could run faster and throw further than the other boys of my age just because I was bigger. I could even piss higher" – he laughed – "because I started out with a pisser a foot further off the ground! Success was meaningless, or rather 'relative' as I see it now. And failure? I couldn't climb through small holes in the hedges. I couldn't squeeze through railings like the smaller kids of my age, so I just accepted, in life some can do some things, others can do others."

"And you can tell stories," said Brum, admiringly.

"That's true," said Dafydd and seeing Sally trying to stifle a yawn, Dafydd and Myfanwy gradually made their farewells and eventually stepped out into the cold night.

As usual every light downstairs in the pub was on and every room a-buzz with activity. On climbing the stairs to Myfanwy's living quarters Dafydd and Myfanwy passed joyful noises in the *Honeymoon Hotel*. Then Dafydd and Myfanwy indulged in a recently invented ritual. Having closed the door on the activities around them, they lovingly placed sponge ear plugs into each other's ears.

SCENE TWENTY TWO

Tours for the Candidates three weeks later

The interviews for the new job of 'Trust Administrator' exhausted the four friends. The short-list was six candidates, and Myfanwy, speaking Welsh, took each in turn around the pub-shop-honeymoon hotel-Post Office-bank-chapel-workshops-teen-club-telecottage, then the converted chapel.

Dafydd gave each in turn a guided tour, in Welsh, of the farms and showed his plans for **Kids Together.**

Brum gave each in turn a guided tour, in English, of the Plas and showed the plans for living and filming and viewing.

Sally took each candidate in turn, in Welsh, to see the building site where the bungalows were going up, and the skateboard park, where the teenagers interviewed the candidates, in Welsh, and then she drove them into town, speaking English, to see the rented building.

Then the four friends each shared their impressions of each candidate, read the teenagers' terse reports with great interest, and then interviewed each candidate in turn.

At these interviews Dafydd was volunteered to watch to see they, as interviewers, didn't appoint a look-alike or a dark-side look-alike interviewee, and to spot whose talents balanced those of the Trustees.

The Trustees surprised themselves by agreeing easily on the winning candidate, and they surprised themselves further that it was the local Presbyterian Minister, Ifor.

"Can you detach your religious belief from the job if we give it to you?" Brum had asked, in a hard, challenging voice.

"No," Ifor had replied. "Why should I?"

"Can you detach your political belief?" Sally had added, quickly in a worried tone.

"No. Why should I? Look, if I was a practising homosexual you wouldn't ask 'Will you detach your belief from the job?' Just as long as I don't push it down people's throats."

There had been a pause and Dafydd was first to realise Ifor had made a joke, and laughed. From then on in the interview, all had relaxed and had laughed a lot.

"If I was 'church', not 'chapel'," Ifor had said, "I'd be a bishop!"

Brum didn't get the joke, but the others did. Ifor was in his mid-thirties and was obviously a gifted administrator in the Peace Movement, in promoting Organic farming, in Green Peace, and in Amnesty. He had quite transformed the community that was his chapel's congregation in the town, adding lots of youth activities, work camps, skills exchanges, job fairs, and trips to other communities to see what they did. The adults too he had helped to organise into co-counselling groups, a debt-advice service and 'farming support groups'. He'd led various campaigns against genetically modified crops and products, against various proposed wars, and towards Wales getting a fair share of European Union resources. "I'm a natural networker," he'd said, "or is that 'compulsive communicator'? But come and listen to the silent vigils I organise. You'll hear a different side of me then!"

The four friends thanked the other five candidates, congratulated Ifor, and sighed with exhaustion, bending to collect papers.

"Just a minute!" said Ifor, and they straightened up at his commanding tone, "I'm the administrator now, so I want to interview you for three hours each, in turn, tomorrow. The others can sit in but must remain silent. Here is your homework." He laughed at their aghast faces. "Bring this questionnaire complete for tomorrow please. First interview eight am. Who's first?" He handed each person a four-page questionnaire, Welsh only for Myfanwy and Dafydd, in both languages for Sally and Brum.

Sally muttered, "I get up early."

"Sally at eight am then, and where?"

"My house," said Dafydd. "We've never met there." And he drew a map.

"'Dunrovin'?" Ifor questioned the name of the house.

"It's a pisstake. I rename it every year. Two years ago it was 'The Mortgage', last year 'Dunpayin', next year it'll probably be 'Dunbonkin'." He missed Myfanwy's sceptical expression.

"Speaking of which," said Ifor, laughing as he collected his papers, "I'd be more than happy to officiate at your double wedding," and he left.

The four, weary friends looked at one another with new energy and laughed.

"What have we done?" Brum asked with raised eyebrows.

"We've appointed the right person," said Sally, "and I agree with him."

"Is that a proposal?" Brum grinned.

"Well, at least it's a suggestion," said Sally, and they went out laughing.

Myfanwy looked at Dafydd. "You've met your match there!" she said.

"And here," said Dafydd putting his arm round Myfanwy's shoulders. "Touch the light blue paper," he said, "and retire".

"Isn't it 'light the blue touch paper'?"

"Lightly touch the paper you blew," replied Dafydd, "whatever, you're my box of fireworks, and my match."

SCENE TWENTY THREE

Dafydd's Front Room
the next day

They met in the little two-up-two-down terraced house Dafydd had inherited from his grandmother. Unable to raise the ground-floor ceiling, Dafydd, to cater for his tallness, had dug the floor down a metre, shored up the walls, which were on rubble and earth, and had re-laid the old Welsh slate slabs over underfloor heating. He insisted everyone took their shoes off at the door as they stepped down into the Japanese-style room. The floor-to-ceiling windows looked up the steps to the tiny back garden which was gravel and standing stones, a small druidic circle in Japanese simplicity. 'Shinto-Celtic', he called it.

"The floor's hard," said Sally, "but because it's warm, it feels soft!"

The four friends and their new administrator sat on cushions on the floor, sipped the green tea, from plain bowls and placed the completed questionnaires on the simple, low table.

Ifor interviewed each person in turn, giving the others permission to lie on cushions or sit, and listen. He read aloud the answers to the questionnaires and then through systematic questions built a detailed profile of each person's gifts, strengths, aptitudes, preferences and their useful strategies gained from their various jobs, hobbies and life experiences.

It was a long day. As each three-hour interview was completed, they all went for a short walk together around the village, and returned for a meal during which the next interview started.

"Right," said Ifor at the end of the last interview, "here are my proposals. What the project lacks completely is the participation of the local and wider community." He held up his hand to quiet the started protests. "And that's fine because only now is the project specific and costed and thought-through enough and proven to be working.

"So," Ifor said, decisively, "looking at your profiles here, I see you make a very complementary team, and you have worked out good strategies for coping with your irreconcilable differences." Again Ifor's upheld hand silenced the rising comments.

"I want you to go round as a team, house to house in this village, to meetings called in neighbouring villages, community councils, District Councils, County Councils, Chambers of Commerce, churches, chapels, Merched y Wawr, WI, Rotarians, Lions Clubs, gatherings, societies, everybody, two places per day, six days a week for the next four months. That's about two hundred meetings, and includes ten days off with no meetings. I'll arrange the programme and will equip you with the display material in both languages. We'll also agree leaflets and how to use the radio and TV. It's 'Persuasion Time'!"

"Money raising?" asked Brum.

"If you're sincere and enthusiastic and show you're already making it work well, the money will come in, no need to push for it. I'll handle how we receive money, consulting with you four."

Even at the thought of the two hundred meetings, Sally looked relieved. At last they were all in capable hands.

"Now, when will you advertise for the secretary?" asked Ifor, packing away his full dossier.

SCENE TWENTY FOUR

**The Two Hundred
Meetings
over the next few months**

There were many surprises at the first hundred of the two hundred meetings. The first surprise was that Brum had been secretly learning Welsh from Sally, and, with his various blockages to Welsh removed by Sally's love, example and persuasion, he was progressing well and could answer questions from the floor in his new, rough Welsh.

The second surprise was that at each of the first hundred meetings Dafydd told a story. Well that wasn't the surprise. The surprise was that each story was different and inspired the people at each meeting in different ways.

Carpet Underlay

Dafydd said, for example, at one meeting:

> I was brought up in a two-up-two-down with a tŷ
> bach, and I looked up at the Plas above us as a great

mystery. I was ten years old. What were all those rooms for? So, when I saw the grand family all set off for their holiday in the South of France, and the servants either going with the grand family, or to their own families, I resolved to break into the empty house.

There was a giggle at this admission of crime.

I had no skills as a housebreaker and had never, in our village, met a locked door, even on the tŷ bach (singing's cheaper than locks!) So I went to every door and tried it. One small dark door opened and led me to a cellar, and then by stairs to another door and there was a huge room like an empty butcher's shop. I had no idea what it was for. Then there was a room like a chapel with a long table down the middle. What was that room? There were great stairs and I expected little bedrooms, but there were great rooms like village halls with a big kind of fabric box in each. When I ventured to push aside the fabric walls of these boxes, there were enormous beds inside! I hurried out. It was all too large and strange. Then I saw narrower stairs, still four times as wide as our stairs at home, but a little more familiar. At the top of the stairs was something else familiar, a schoolroom. It was much neglected. There had been no children in the grand family for many years, and I sat down and toyed with a hole in the carpet, and looked round feeling sad.

My finger felt paper. I looked. It was part of a headline peeping through the worn carpet. I rolled back the carpet and sat reading fascinated, for about three hours.

The newspapers were all from late in 1938. Hitler, Mussolini, the Spanish Civil War, renegade outsider Mr Churchill being ridiculed, rumours of movements of Jews, rumours denied, admiration of German roads, reports of Italian empire-building in Albania and Libya and Abyssinia, and all the while I was reading I was saying to myself, 'They didn't know! They didn't know' that the Second World War was on its way.

That's what our project wants to communicate, the real experience of a moment in time, the opening up of cloth-box mysteries. The great kitchen and great dining room explaining themselves in action, and a connection, a connection of souls across the normally impenetrable barriers of time to know, to really know, deep down, what their lives were like. And to confirm that by experiencing those lives, in role, for ourselves, to discover how we would be in those situations. It's a self-discovery project, not a discover-it-yourself, but a discover-yourself-**in**-it project. And we invite you to join us and support it, and see it grow and experience it for yourselves.

Dutch Town, Japan

At another meeting, Dafydd said:

In Japan, where I used to live and work, some enterprising people from the Netherlands had bought some property and built Dutch-style houses. They had Dutch-style shops and food and wore rather traditional, Dutch-style clothes. This picturesque little expat. colony began to attract the local Japanese as visitors, and the word spread, and there was great pressure from

Japanese people to build more Dutch-style houses there so they could live in 'Western style' themselves.

You can go there and see Japanese women in lace bonnets and clogs living what they think is the height of modern, Western lifestyle.

You laugh. I laughed to see their earnest efforts to be 'Western'. But when I returned to Wales what did I see here? English incomers buying up and building, and moving into our Welsh villages and living their own insulated illusions.

I wanted to buy a house in my own, old village. The prices were beyond my means. You nod. Oh yes. I was being excluded from my home, by what, the greed of my fellow Welsh villagers selling up? The greater resources of the incomers?

I looked at houses for sale. I asked, as a Welsh person does 'What about the neighbours?' and English owners would say 'Oh, don't worry about them. They don't bother us at all', and I thought, 'Why not! What's going wrong that neighbours aren't being neighbours?' Welsh owners when asked 'What about the neighbours?' would give me chapter and verse about all the neighbours' flaws and foibles and recent hospital operations, and about those neighbours' relatives and all other connections, the whole oral history of the neighbourhood!

Our project is into making jobs, and we mean full-time, year round, skill-enhancing, career-path, proper, self-respecting jobs for local people. Our project builds houses for local people who want to live in their home village. Our project enables them to live there, and takes each opportunity to buy out incomers and re-establish the community to be Welsh-speaking, welcoming those incomers who want to learn Welsh and become good neighbours.

You, too, can join in and help, for instance by transferring some of your savings away from international banks paying the profits from your savings to their shareholders, to our mutual bonds which still pay you interest and maintain the value of your savings, but your money which you lend through bonds to our project also builds houses and makes jobs for local people, such as yourselves.

Arthur Sleeps!

At another meeting the reception to the Farm Project presentation had been quite hostile. 'All these visitors! All these cars and coaches! Litter! Pollution! Road accidents! Jams! Nowhere for us to park!' The hostile comments came thick and fast. 'We know what it'll be!' 'A few outsiders made rich and us locals doing part-time, poorly-paid, seasonal work with no careers and no prospects!' 'Then someone in London decides to close it down, and even those miserable local jobs are lost, and overnight it's a ghost town, like the pits!'

Dafydd had heard enough, in a thunderous voice he announced "Arthur sleeps!" A hundred frowns swung at him. "Arthur sleeps!" he repeated. "And who will wake him?"

In almost a whisper Dafydd continued:

In a deep, echoing cavern, lit only by the glistening of armour and the jewels on the magic swords, sleeps Arthur, our Celtic king with all his knights. They are waiting for our call, and then they will wake, and ride, and will battle against wickedness and restore justice and goodness. Will you call them? Will you wake them now?

Dafydd spoke louder.

I would not dare to wake them now.

What would they see in me? So far in life I have fended for myself. I have not preserved, let alone enhanced my community. I have looked after number one, not shared my skills and resources to be a good neighbour. I go shopping for myself rather than listen to the woes of the poor living around me. I do nothing to right the wrongs in society other than complain over my beer in the pub.

No! Please do not wake Arthur yet! If he rode out now in his shining armour with his virtuous knights he would cut me down as an evildoer who by my sheer neglect has let my country be invaded and colonised and trivialised and divided and bought up and transformed into a pale, sickly version of what Arthur would want to see.

He would cut me down, and rightly so, and cut you down, too, most likely. So please wait. Give me three years and I will then be able to show a woken Arthur a project that values our history; that gives our ancient strengths and skills recognition; that gives the lie to division and poverty being inevitable; that creates work; that values and shares knowledge; that speaks to the hearts and souls of our people, not their pockets and their wallets, and that sings of our identity as self-respecting, modern, innovative Celts, connected to, but not limited by, our past.

Dafydd spoke quietly again.

Give me three years. Join me. Join us in those three years, and you, too, can show Arthur and his knights what we have made together!

Where is Socialism?

"Where is Socialism?" asked Dafydd at another meeting where the questions and statements had been sympathetic, but pessimistic: 'Aren't you too idealistic?' 'You can't change human nature.' 'When big money gets involved it always turns out different from your high hopes, doesn't it?'

"Where is Socialism?" Dafydd's question cut across the hopeless tone of the gathering.

I asked myself that question, and I went searching. Socialism was there in some households in the Valleys, in the photos of the International Brigades, the books for evening classes, but it was dead, like those old heroes. In some households it was still alive through mutual help and values of solidarity and refusal to assist the galloping growth of capitalism, but in those households it was often an embattled, private socialism like a secret religion.

So I went to a Kibbutz in Israel, and worked as a volunteer for several years, and there I saw socialism alive and well and living in a community.

The Kibbutz members had all things in common. What they earned and made and created they shared equally according to need. The young, the sick, the old were looked after by the labour of those who could work, and every decision was made by the whole community, not some distant power or some internal elite. 'We were treated like shit in Poland' they said, 'but here we are kings and queens. We are all royalty!'

At first I didn't like these monarchist terms, but as I got to know the people I saw that they each oozed self-respect and greeted one another as if each was greatly honoured. It was a monarch's confidence that nobody was superior to you! Likewise, nobody was inferior. The slip into inferiority was prevented by each person's self-pride. That's what preserved their equality.

Oh no, they weren't dinosaurs! They weren't shackled to the past by dogma! Even while I was there, they voted for major changes. The kibbutz children used to be held in common, learning, playing, living and sleeping in The Children's House with properly trained and qualified members looking after them, not parents, not untrained, unqualified parents! But that strong ideal was transformed, and space made for the children to return to their parents' dwellings for the evenings and to sleep.

Other changes were agreed by the gathering of all members, and implemented in ways agreed by all members.

You say we are too 'idealistic' and 'impractical', that 'human nature cannot be changed', but I tell you, **my** nature has changed. These three friends here: **their** natures have changed, and we have met together and agreed together simple ways to bring our ideals into practical realisations.

Those Jews were in Poland in non-ideal circumstances. When they fled from Poland with nothing, they built every building of that Kibbutz from scratch. It is easier for us. You and me, we are not penniless refugees in a strange land. We have resources already. The only transformations required to bring our ideals to life, be they Socialism or whatever, are here, here and now. You can agree. You can act. Nobody is superior to you! Therefore you are very powerful. Stop giving away your power to all and sundry, and join with us to create the society you want!

'They'?

At another meeting, in another village, the mood of those who attended was of discouragement and blame. 'Nobody ever listens to us!' 'You can protest all you want, but nothing happens.' 'They'll impose things on you.' 'They'll block any good you want to do.' 'Big business doesn't allow such things to happen unless they can control it.'

One by one Sally, Brum and Myfanwy became exasperated. The people blamed Brussels, and then London, and then Cardiff. The world the villagers described seemed to be full of malevolent or uncaring 'they, they, they' whose purpose in life was to suppress all good and make everybody feel powerless and miserable.

Dafydd as usual was first to crack, "Who is this 'they'?" he shouted. "'They' seem to be everywhere. You agree? Then 'they' must be **'us'**." Dafydd let that statement hang in the air, then he hammered it in with a series of nails.

Have you ever failed to support a good initiative? You are 'they'! Have you ever discouraged a friend from positive change? You are 'they'! Have you ever failed to protest at an injustice? You are 'they'! have you ever failed to listen to someone's complaint about you, or failed to act on it? You are 'they'!

So, we're in this hall and it's full of the people you all blame and hate, and, lo and behold it is yourselves! Hold

up a mirror. Look at who you are. Look at all that you
have neglected to do all your lives. You are 'they'. You are
the enemy and you know it. **That's** what makes you
powerless and miserable.

Not Brussels nor London nor Cardiff but here in this
village is the unused power that keeps you down and
could lift you up.

Dafydd's hectoring tone changed, and his voice grew soft and warm.
The squirming in seats stopped and the people leaned towards him listening
with lips apart as if to drink in his words.

I was like you, blaming, powerless. In the Middle
East I worked in school after school with the kids. I
suppose I'd despaired of adults. Seeing the kids gave me
hope again. They didn't mind who was Jew or Arab,
Orthodox or Liberal, Islamic, Christian, or Druse. The
kids mixed and made friends. They were human beings.
But not the adults! Oh, in their own, homogenous
communities they were very friendly. Wherever I went,
whatever the religion or culture, I was warmly welcomed
to each house. Like a Welsh house, there'd be drinks
offered, then nibbles, then a full meal, and handshakes
and embraces and laughter and chatter and the adults
and youngsters respected one another very nicely.

But in the schools! A completely different culture!
No handshakes. No welcome. No respect. No courtesy.
No hospitality, and a climate of boredom, alienation and
hostility or indifference between the adults and kids.

I was angry. I asked and asked 'Where does this
cold, disrespectful, discourteous culture come from?'
'Why, for goodness sake, can't you be, in school, like you

are at home?' Nobody could answer me, so I blamed the teachers.

Then one old teacher took me aside and said, 'It was you.' 'Me?' I felt a cold shudder. 'The British' he said 'we were the British Mandate. The British ran our schools. We learned the school culture from you. The British teachers treated us pupils as less than them, a lesser people, not worth bothering to relate to.'

I was dumbstruck. At first I blamed the English. Hadn't they treated us Welsh with the same, cold detachment? I'd heard in Saxon Germany the word 'Welsh' still used, to mean 'foreigner'. Oh yes, I blamed the English.

But then I remembered that some of the teachers in our schools who had imposed the 'Welsh Not' and dismissed our language as fit for home but not for work or for progress in the world, had been Welsh!

Then I began to observe myself. I saw that I, too, had fallen into the cold, Mandate culture. I would stand with teachers watching the pupils, talking about them and pointing to them like they were cattle in a market. I would walk past groups of pupils and not look at them, as if they were trees. I would walk to the head of the school lunch queue with the teachers as if the pupils were some lower kind of humanity with fewer rights than me. I began to blame myself. I was the 'them' I hated.

It wasn't the 'far away them' in Brussels, London or Cardiff or 'the English', it was in me. That was a wonderful realisation. The 'them' was in me and **therefore I could change it**!

I stopped watching and pointing at pupils and instead I talked with them. I greeted them as I passed. I waited my turn in the queue, with the pupils, and gradually some of the teachers, too, began to change towards being 'human'. It was powerful progress, humanising the school by simple, friendly example.

And this is our project. It starts here, as you're listening to us. It starts in your hearts, to believe you can make a difference, together you can create jobs and preserve communities and build houses for our young people. Are you 'them' or 'us'? I suggest that until you admit to yourselves that you **are** 'them' you are not ready to change, to transform the world to be a better place for you as you, and working together, as 'us'.

There was a sigh around the room. Then an intake of breath as if at the start of a race, or of a hymn.

SCENE TWENTY FIVE

Dafydd's Front Room
after two weeks
of meetings

After the first particularly hectic fortnight of meetings, the four friends took two days off from one another, then returned to have the third day off together.

They spend the day lounging in Dafydd's living room/dining room with the patio doors open to the spring weather and the shadows moving round in the miniature stone circle.

"I always feel nervous, Dafydd," said Sally, lazily, "when you attack the audience."

"Challenge, confront, never 'attack'," countered Dafydd.

"I'm always afraid," continued Sally, "that they'll riot and throw us out."

"They've mostly been very positive," said Brum.

"We've raised thousands and thousands, like Ifor said," said Myfanwy, "without even asking for money."

"People recognise a good idea," said Brum, matter-of-factly.

"People are inspired by Dafydd," said Sally.

"First," said Dafydd, "they're persuaded of our sincerity and simplicity by having their questions frankly answered. Then they accept a bit of hwyl. They expect it. That's the nature of meetings and gatherings. That's the thrill of being Celtic."

"You wouldn't do it at an English meeting," said Brum.

"You're right. I wouldn't!" said Dafydd.

"That's not what I meant," said Brum.

"But isn't it a bit one-way?" asked Sally, ever-doubtful of success.

"In what way?" asked Brum, mildly.

"One-way. She just said so," scolded Dafydd.

"Ignore him," said Myfanwy, "everybody does! Sally, what do you mean 'one-way'?"

"Well, we give them our ideas," said Sally "things that are already working well, and the future plans, designs and concepts, and we ask them to join in."

"Yes?" said Brum encouragingly.

"But," said Sally, "we don't invite their ideas."

"Ah!" said Dafydd, "out of the mouths of babes and vicars."

"Couldn't we," said Sally, "ask for their ideas?"

"Surely we've got quite enough ideas of our own," said Myfanwy, dubiously.

"We don't want complications," said Brum.

"Yes," said Dafydd with a mock-diabolic laugh, "we only want their money! Money! Money!"

"That's it!" said Sally. "It's been getting at me, this nagging doubt that we give them an hour of cheap entertainment…"

"Thank you, Sally!" Dafydd acted hurt, "we're not **cheap**." Then he said, in a very satirical tone, "we're absolutely **free**!"

They all laughed, but Sally topped the laughter by recapitulating, "We give them an hour of free entertainment and leave them nothing to do but approve of us and pay up."

"It's one of the most rewarding jobs I've ever done!" admitted Dafydd.

"And me," said Brum.

"And me!" said Myfanwy.

"And you're good at it," said Dafydd proudly.

"Yes, but surely anyone would be good at being approved of and inspiring people to pay up," Sally challenged.

"A vocation," exclaimed Dafydd, "a calling. I am called to be showered with praise and money."

"Isn't that just an ego trip?" said Sally, severely, "I'm serious. I want an answer."

Dafydd hung his head. "Sorry, Sally. What's your answer?"

"Well I think it **is**!" Sally said decisively.

"Is what, Sally?" asked Myfanwy.

"One-way, too much one-way. If we mean what we say, we should listen as well as talk," said Sally.

"If we 'mean what we say', that **is** talk," said Dafydd. "You mean that we should '**mean** what we **hear**'. That's true listening." No-one understood what Dafydd had just said. He saw their blank looks and laughed.

"Oh, Dafydd!" said Sally with her old irritation returning. "Will you listen!"

"I hear what you mean," said Dafydd, "so, we need to clear some space in the plans, in the project, in the meetings, in our heads and in our hearts to bring to actualisation the ideas the audiences put forward."

"Without additional expenditure," Brum cautioned.

"Without giving us any more to do, please," said Myfanwy.

"I don't think we can set too many conditions," said Sally, frowning.

"You say you '**don't** think we can set too **many** conditions'," Dafydd quoted. "Do you mean we can set hundreds of conditions and **no** number will be too many? Or do you mean we mustn't set more than a **small** number of conditions?"

Sally's frown deepened and Dafydd hurried on, "Surely, really good ideas are worth changing the budget for, and giving us a few more things to do?"

"'Clear some space'," Sally quoted Dafydd. "What do you mean?"

"They could write on wet clay tiles what they think is wrong with the world, and we could glaze and fire them and use them to line the walls on the way into the Project," suggested Dafydd.

"'Negatives Alley'," Brum commented.

"'Depression Approach', 'Disheartening Avenue'," Myfanwy added.

"OK," said Dafydd, "alternate the 'what's wrong with the world' with 'solutions'."

"'Answers Arcade'," Brum commented.

"And worksheets. Match the problem with the solution," Dafydd added.

"A problem for every solution?" Brum queried.

"The wrong way round," Dafydd laughed. "A problem for every problem."

"I know!" said Sally, suddenly triumphant. "I'm going to ask them to solve our problems."

"What all of them?" said Dafydd in mock amazement.

"We haven't got any problems," said Brum petulantly.

"That's your problem!" said Dafydd wickedly.

"What?" asked Brum.

"Denial!" said Dafydd dramatically.

"If I'm in denial," said Brum good humouredly, "what are you in?"

"Cloud cuckoo land," suggested Myfanwy, "castles in the air, pie in the sky, over the rainbow, head in the clouds, away with the birds."

"And you're so earthy," said Dafydd through gritted teeth, "there's mud on the back of your neck!"

There followed an unseemly tumble on the underfloor heated slabs, and a brief cushion fight and lots of laughter before normal service was resumed and Myfanwy said, "My neck's not dirty is it, Brum?"

"Don't ask him," said Dafydd, "he's in denial!"

"One day," said Sally evenly, "you'll all stop playing and listen to me."

"But not today," said Dafydd "today's our last day of the holidays!"

"Then Brum will listen!" Sally said, turning a smile to Brum.

"He'll deny it," warned Dafydd, and Myfanwy giggled.

"Then I'll make my own decision which I will here announce," said Sally in self-mocking smugness. "I will collect suggestions for having visitors at the Plas involved in authentic, live events."

"Good on you, Sal!" said Dafydd in his southern drawl.

"Sally," corrected Brum, automatically.

"Thank you, Birmingham," said Dafydd, *falsetto*, in the voice of a shocked duchess. Myfanwy giggled and another cushion fight ensued.

This time, in exasperation, and growing hilarity, Sally and Brum joined in.

Totally relaxed in the shadow of their spent energy, the four friends lay about on the cushions tousled and panting, and occasionally giggling.

"I'm fifty two," said Sally, "this is ridiculous!" and she giggled some more.

"Your best years are inside you," said Dafydd.

"No, behind you," corrected Brum.

"No, before you," corrected Myfanwy.

"No, inside you," recorrected Dafydd, "and you can let your best years out any time you want. Some people never do."

"I nearly never did!" said Sally "Is that grammar?" and she giggled again.

Merlin's Dilemma

"Merlin" Dafydd began quietly, "was born old…"

"I had a teacher like that," said Myfanwy.

"I had a boss like that," Brum chuckled.

But Merlin grew younger as time went on. He lived backwards. Oh he learned, yes and grew wiser, but his body, his face, his appearance grew younger and younger. He was born at the age of one hundred and four, and so, when Merlin was fifty-two, he had lived half his life, and was looking half the age he did when he started. Before him were his forties and thirties and twenties to live, and the teenage years, and childhood, finally to finish as a baby.

'I'm fifty two' he said, joyfully on his birthday 'I've never felt younger!' (which he said every birthday, because it's always true when you live backwards!) 'I'm strong, fit, I can move freely, I can see well, I almost don't need any reading glasses, and I'm at an age when people, generally, respect me.' And, as at every birthday, he had a great conflict within himself whether to do a great magic and stay for ever at that age. 'I've finally got rid of all my old age aches and pains. My teeth are nearly all there. This is a good age, fifty two, to stop at.'

But then he got to thinking of fifty one. What would that be like? He'd feel just a little younger and more carefree, or would he?

It was a difficult decision, at birthday time, to let go, and get younger. 'Each year I gain wisdom. Each year I learn more knowledge, take on new skills, become a more powerful magician. When I was new-born, a hundred and four, people expected me to be somewhat incapable, at a hundred, too, so they gave me the benefit of the doubt in the first four years as I learned my first magic powers.

'At ninety they expected me to be a very wise old man, but I'd only lived fourteen years, and was clumsy with my powers and somewhat inept.

'Ah, eighty! They still respected me as a wonderfully old and wonderfully wise man, and by then I was pretty good, although I say it myself, after twenty-four years at the job.

'At seventy there were wise men and wise women older than me, but I was easily able to out-magic them. I was in my full vigour of thirty-four years' experience.

'Then – oh dear! At sixty they said, 'He's not so old. He's too young to be so wise.' So they ignored me. Even when I was ready to give my best wisdom, they passed me by and went to 'older' people. 'I've never been so wise, so powerful!' I wanted to tell them. But they were never there to tell.

'Ah, my fifties, what a decade of independence so far! Fewer and fewer people have beaten a path to my door. There have been fewer and fewer expectations. I have been able to develop myself, high and free and I have had time to entertain doubts rather than certainties, and doubts are always more entertaining than certainties.

'Hm! Fifty-two. Am I fed up with being ignored? Have these last ten years of self-knowledge been wasted? Who benefits but me from the wisdom I have gained?'

The three listening friends had lain back, eyes closed.

For a while Merlin pondered on being fifty-two. There were advantages and disadvantages. It was a time to be private or public. He could choose as he had never been able to choose before.

'I could challenge all the wise men and wise women and have a competition to show I am wiser than all who look older than me. Or I could just be a private person. I am now young enough to marry, and to develop my further powers solely in my head.

'Yes, I could marry and get younger and younger every year within my marriage ... Or, I could stay at fifty two and stay single ...'

Dafydd's own voice replaced the Merlin-voice once again, "What would you advise?"

"Marry," said Myfanwy. "It'll be fun getting younger with someone."

"Yes, don't stay single," said Brum, "there's all that wisdom to share."

"Private, yes, but together with someone. Marry, yes. Is that unanimous?" said Sally. "What about **you**, Dafydd?"

"No insult to you, Sally," said Dafydd, deliberately misunderstanding her, "thanks for the offer, but I'd rather marry Myfanwy!"

"You bugger!" said Myfanwy sitting up, "you fooled us all!"

"That's no way to speak to your fiancé" said Dafydd evenly.

There was a pause. The importance of it all filled the room with a strong silence. Into the silence, as usual, Brum put a question but it was not to the storyteller.

"Sally ...?" said Brum, slowly.

"...Yes..." said Sally, equally slowly, her eyes bright with tears rolling down her cheeks.

Sally and Brum sat very still looking into each other's eyes.

Myfanwy hit Dafydd with a pillow so hard and so many times he lost count. Then she fell onto him and held him as if he or she would drown. Then she said "Yes!" in the voice she used to shout 'time!' when the pub was full on a rugby night. 'Perhaps,' Dafydd thought, 'she has at last taken revenge for all the times I wasn't with her.'

"I won't leave you," he murmured.

"I know you bloody won't!" said Myfanwy, and she snuggled, like a baby, into his arms.

SCENE TWENTY SIX

In Sally's Parlour Again
after two more weeks
of meetings

The next few weeks were particularly hectic. The four friends were preparing with Ifor not only for the hundred more meetings, but also for their double wedding. However, the self-development they had done had taught them to be relaxed under stress – most of the time – and to find warm resources and positive energy however busy they were.

It was in the week before the weddings that Dafydd said to his three friends, "It's time for you to tell **your** stories now," and, despite his friends' protests, Dafydd said he would refuse to tell another story at a meeting until they had each told one.

"But what story?" all three friends asked, each in their own way.

"The easiest story, the best story, the most powerful story," Dafydd replied.

"But what's that?"

"You!"

Y Ddraig Sy'n Cysgu

The Sleeping Dragon

Sally's Story

And so it was, at the next public meeting, after the audience's questions had been answered, Sally stood up, cleared her throat and said:

What has happened to me, lately, is a kind of miniature of the project. Yes, we are helping to create not a visitors' centre or theme park, but a set of environments where each person can develop at their own pace.

Sally's voice gained strength.

I know that sounds vague and pretentious, so let me share with you my personal story of how that has worked for me. I feel as if a dragon has woken inside me. That's the name of our pub, the new name – *The Dragon Wakes*.

All my life I was not a dragon. I was a mouse, diminished by negative messages I received from other people 'you're only a girl', 'you're a shy little thing with more intelligence than sense', 'you're a cold fish'.

Those negative messages had no power except the power I chose to give them. Because I believed them, I made them true.

At the murmur of sympathy from the audience Sally smiled.

While working on this project, **by** working on this project, I have, step by step, worked through these negative messages. That was tough! They had been my outer skin, what the world saw, my outer clothing. Suddenly I felt very naked, and vulnerable. I didn't know myself. Who was this person who had got rid of the negatives I'd held onto for so long?

Once I'd accepted that it was still me, I had to get used to facing up to my potential, my enormous potential! You see, I'd got rid of all my excuses for failure. Now there was nothing in the way.

Sally shrugged as if casting off all limitations.

My three friends here helped me to have the courage to say what was good about me. Oh! I could never had dared say I was good at anything! Now I can. It's not boasting. It's not showing off. What I say is true.

Sally laughed delightedly. Then she grew sad.

The other thing I couldn't do was to be truly loved. Do you know that one? I can see some of you nodding. Yes, I was 'bad', therefore nobody could really love me. Anybody who tried to love me must be 'bad' too, because I was 'bad'. Therefore anybody who tried to love me ... their love was worthless because I was worthless!

What a trap! But I had made the trap myself, and had stuck myself in it.

I served. That was my role, to help and serve, oh and to avoid being loved. All this helping other people was doing, doing, doing good. I was so busy I was exhausted. I never took time off from **doing** good to actually **be** good! You laugh! I can laugh now, but then I really didn't believe I had a right to be good!

I realise now that I was so attached to the past, tied to it by negative ropes, that I had no future.

I trained as a vicar, yes, you're looking at 'an ordained woman priest'! But I never had the courage to take over a parish. 'Anyway,' I told myself 'the church is going out of fashion. I'll do it all on internet, the modern way.'

But I tell you, now, this project is far more the true work of any church than anything I've seen churches doing today. We're making jobs. We're restoring and preserving communities. We're working within communities, promoting mutual help and co-operation. We're getting all ages and generations working together, and we're helping others to grow, like I have grown, in my own way and in my own time.

Sally took a deep breath and stood tall.

The dragon has woken in me. Are you prepared for your dragon in you, your best dragon to wake in you? If so, join us for a gentle, widespread awakening!

The loud applause that followed the moment of impressed silence surprised Sally. "I could be a vicar now!" she whispered to Brum,. And when she smiled at the audience she felt the tears coming, and she let them come.

SCENE TWENTY SEVEN

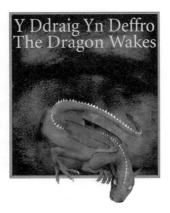

Y Ddraig Yn Deffro
The Dragon Wakes

At Another Public Meeting

Brum's turn came at the next meeting. He was very nervous. He gripped Sally's hand as the questions and answers finished. "Share it!" Sally prompted. "Be honest."

Brum's Story

"I'm scared," said Brum to the audience and they listened all the more intently.

You see, I've been a very successful businessman, engineer, innovator. I've often given professional presentations in front of audiences, but that was always about a product, an invention, a machine.

Is anybody here like me? You can talk about anything, except yourself? Ah, I'm not alone, then! Thank you. I don't feel quite so scared if you're as bad as me. Oops, sorry. I shouldn't insult you.

But isn't it a man's job to work hard and to have no emotions? Oh yes, I was the specialist, ideal man, a workaholic with no feelings!

I lost my wife. She left me. I didn't notice for three days! You can laugh! I didn't laugh at the time. I didn't have any feelings, I just recorded her leaving me as a fact. In her note, when I found it, she'd said, 'You're never at home for the children. They don't know you. You don't know them'. I remember saying to myself 'That's true', and carrying on working. Oh yes, feelings were a waste of energy and a waste of time. I'd often told my wife that, as helpful advice.

Well, she decided to waste her energy and time with someone else, and I'm glad to say he **did** spend time with her and the children, and they've been very happy.

But what a cost to me!! No, I hadn't wasted time or energy, but I'd wasted my marriage and my children!

It only gradually dawned on me how lonely I was.

When life is all logic and no experience, there's not much space for realisations, but the signs were all there. Symbolically I bought myself a big, empty house, here. In my dreams I yearned for my childhood again, and my grandmother. I yearned to play but I ate for comfort and became too fat and immobile to play. I was never content with the past or the present. In work I was always moving on, pushing on. They called me 'Mister Future' because of my inventiveness.

So I tried to remember what friends were.

Vaguely I recalled that they were idle, lazy people who chatted in pubs.

I went to the pub, our village pub, then called *The Sleeping Dragon*, and slowly, gradually, I learned to take time, to take all evening to drink three half-pints of beer, and to slow down, slow down and chat.

Now I understand that I was letting the future rush on ahead of me where it belongs. I was reclaiming the present, the moment, moments of contentment idly chatting with friends in the pub, savouring each sip of beer.

Oops! Sorry I'm making you thirsty! I can see some of you dribbling already! So I'll close with my personal vision of the project we've been presenting to you at this meeting. By the way, we've renamed the pub *The Dragon Wakes*. This project...

Yes, this project has not only developed itself, it has developed me. Call me 'Mister Now', not 'Mister Future'. The project, for me, is all about savouring the moment, letting yourself be in that experience, to let the experience, each experience, seep deeper and deeper into you until you **are** that experience. **Then** you learn. Certainly then **I** learned!

And you can help us to help countless others to learn too, to learn what they need to learn, in their own way, when they are ready for it.

Thank you. I don't feel quite so scared now. In fact I rather savoured sharing all that with you! Can I do it again soon?

Sally raised her eyebrows at Brum as he sat down. She was amazed. As he had talked about seeking out the pub, she had remembered him as he was then, unfit, fat, puzzled, driven, seldom understanding anything that required feelings. She'd felt pity for him then, the wish to help him. At the same time she'd despised his unwillingness to integrate with Welsh culture. She'd despised the block he seemed to have towards learning the Welsh language. What a mess he had been! And now he was smiling broadly at her. No, he was grinning, and so was she.

In the middle of grinning, Sally frowned. How on earth did it come about that they had fallen in love, and were about to marry? She blinked. Yes, there was the new Brum, slim, fit, full of feelings and with such loving

understanding for her! 'Why puzzle over the past?' she told herself.
'I'm in love in the present!' Her frown faded and she blew Brum a
kiss.

Myfanwy's Doubts – not quite a story

"It's all very well for you!" said Myfanwy when the friends met after
Brum's story. "All three of you are professional speech-makers. All I've
ever said in public is 'Last Orders!', 'Time!' or 'Out! You're banned!'"

"Hold that," said Dafydd. "Start with that. In that, you're confident, in
charge, in control – indeed , loud!" All four laughed, but Myfanwy
persisted.

"So, I start with 'Last orders', but what do I say then? My mind will
go blank. '**Will** go blank?' What am I saying? My mind's **already** blank."

"You're very good at definitions," said Brum helpfully.

"Synonyms," corrected Sally.

"You're scrabble champion," said Dafydd.

"Oh yes!" exclaimed Myfanwy sarcastically, "a twenty-minute string
of obscure words, exotic phrases, curious sentences will have them **very**
interested! I don't think so!"

"I have faith in you," said Dafydd softly.

"Thank you!" said Myfanwy sceptically, "but your faith won't pump
air up out my lungs and work my lips to speak."

"It could," said Dafydd archly, "but in public…?" he left the question
hanging amid the laughter.

"Sally…you were stuck…in the past," Myfanwy had her thinking cap
on. "Brum, you were 'Mister Future'. You both had to…reclaim the
present…Where am I, then?"

"'Then' or 'now'?" asked Dafydd.

"'Then'!" said Myfanwy decisively. "I was stuck in the past… and
waiting for 'Mister Future'."

"I thought I was 'Mister Right'." claimed Dafydd, in mock romance.

"I **know** you thought you were 'Mister Right'!" said Myfanwy. "A 'right' long way away in the Antipodes!"

"Antipodes?" queried Brum.

"Oz," said Dafydd.

"Australia," corrected Sally.

"I think I've got it!" said Myfanwy.

"I hope it's not catching, then," said Dafydd, adding "Ouch!" as Myfanwy kicked him.

SCENE TWENTY EIGHT

At the Next Public Meeting

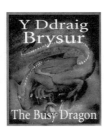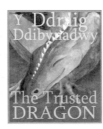

At the next public meeting Myfanwy didn't step forward as her time came to speak. She was bending, rummaging in a large bag.

Myfanwy's Story

Her three friends looked anxiously on as they heard a muffled clanking sound. Then they were startled as she stood up and rang a handbell. 'Dong!'

The audience jumped.

"Last orders, please!" Myfanwy yelled.

"That was me," she said. "And, until now, the full extent of my experience as a public speaker." The audience laughed.

> I was the barmaid at my father's pub. That's it, the barmaid. What is a barmaid? A whole bundle of other people's expectations. That was me. My father's expectations, work every day, no day off, no time off, no studies, no career. The customers' expectations – listen, be jolly, listen, laugh at their jokes, even when I'd heard

them a hundred times before. I let them define me. Yes, I let them define me.

I was bright. I knew that. I knew that much. I was bright enough to know I was bright! But I couldn't sing. That's the only thing the customers could criticise me for. Why couldn't I sing? Because an old witch had put a curse on me. Don't look so startled! I'll translate that sentence for you. 'An old witch had put a curse on me' means 'a teacher told me 'you can't sing'.

The audience laughed again, and Dafydd, watching Myfanwy with enormous concentration saw her rise to the laughter and fill her chest with more air and speak more confidently. His anxious frown melted into a smile.

I was miserable. You know what kids say nowadays 'Get a life!' I would have loved a life, any life except the one I had, stuck behind the bar as my dad's slave and the customers' dreams. Oh yes, I can laugh now! I was young then. And being short, the customers could only see me from the nose up, so they could be pretty free with their dreams!

The audience laughed loudly, and Dafydd grinned.

So here was I, miserable about my life, and my past seemed like it would go on and on and never change. Do you know what I mean? You look into your future, and it's identical with your past, only more of it!

Even when my dad died and the pub was mine, I was still trapped. The customers told me I mustn't sell up, and they didn't spend enough to let me employ anybody... have you been there? I couldn't blame my dad any more. I was now my own slave!

> Ah, but I had a secret. At the age of fifteen I'd made the mistake of falling in love with that great llwdwn over there.

Myfanwy pointed the bell at Dafydd, and it rang, and he held his heart and gave her the sweetest smile. Myfanwy laughed aloud, and the audience laughed with her.

> But he was all over the place. Oh no! Not all over me, but all over the world.
>
> So I had no hopes. I was gloomy about the past, gloomy about the present and gloomy about the future. Have you ever been to a pub with a very gloomy landlady? Ah! You came to my pub? I bet you only came once! I knew I was driving custom away with my gloom, but I felt I had a right to be gloomy. It was 'all their fault', so 'they' could suffer!

Myfanwy paused, looked at the bell, and seemed to falter. Dafydd half-rose, but then sat back down as Myfanwy had the audience laughing again with:

> I'll call 'time' in a minute... you're probably wondering what all this is leading to, my autobiography and all. No? Well if you're not wondering, you're not as bright as I am, I'll tell you that!

The audience laughed again.

> What I'm wanting to say is that we don't need to be trapped in the gloom. That's what this project is about, taking action, not to escape, like llwdwn there, but taking action together to change things for the better.
>
> The *Sleeping Dragon* pub, my pub, has gone through various names, *The Busy Dragon*, *The Trusted Dragon* – and it is now *The Dragon Wakes*.

Are you sleeping dragons too? Then wake up. It's
        TIME!

Myfanwy clanged the bell to accompany her great shout, but even her loudest shout was drowned by audience laughter and applause.

Myfanwy looked round in glowing pride at Dafydd, and was surprised to see proud tears streaming down his face. She laughed with a full-bodied laugh that Brum and Sally had never heard before. This was a new, very powerful Myfanwy.

SCENE TWENTY NINE

Y Ddraig Yn Deffro
The Dragon Wakes

The Butler's Pantry, the Plas
five days before the weddings

Ifor was temporarily installed in the butler's pantry at the Plas. The new Trust secretary was in the Housekeeper's sitting room next door. Ifor had summoned the four friends there, and they entered, chatting amicably.

"More marriage preparation, Ifor?" asked Brum. The preparation workshop Ifor had led with them had been hilarious and insightful.

"How many more marriages do you want?" Ifor replied as usual playing on words. "No, you're here to hear my decision for the name of the whole project."

"You can't decide that!" said Sally.

"We haven't even discussed it with you," said Brum.

"It's the 'Agri-Dream'," said Myfanwy

"'Wild Wales Tamed'," countered Dafydd.

"'The Farms Project'," corrected Brum.

"No, it's 'Wales' Farm Fantasia'," Sally said, with finality.

"Precisely!" said Ifor "You can't decide and you can't agree, and you hired me to do what you can't do. So, it's … *The Dragon Wakes, Y Ddraig yn Deffro.*"

There was a stunned silence.

"That's got nothing to do with farms," said Brum, puzzled.

"You can't name a project for a pub," said Myfanwy, worried. "**My** pub," she added.

"The name needs to contain 'Wales' or 'Welsh' and 'Community'," said Sally pleadingly.

"And 'solidarity'," offered Dafydd "and 'co-operation' and 'collaboration', oh and 'disestablishmentarianism'," he added as an afterthought.

"I think Dafydd has got my point," said Ifor, laughing.

"The Dragon Wakes…." said Sally, testing it.

"The Dragon Wakes…" said Brum, savouring it.

"It's different," said Myfanwy, "no different from my pub, but… 'different'."

"Dafydd?" Ifor turned, insisting on a comment.

"We've all said 'The Dragon Wakes' recently," said Dafydd.

"I know. And with passion. I was there," said Ifor.

"It certainly says more than 'farm project'. It's more what we're all about…" Dafydd added.

"But?" Ifor demanded.

Dafydd shrugged. "But we'll have to live up to it."

There was another silence, not stunned, but there were several deep breaths.

The five looked round from one to another. It was like a quiet bond, a silent determination, a sensing of the power each had released.

Dafydd closed his eyes, then "GrraOOR!" he roared, in his biggest, deepest voice, and the new secretary came rushing in, alarmed.

The five friends laughed.

SCENE THIRTY

In the Butler's Pantry
three days before the weddings

It was three days before the double wedding.

At the previous public meeting Dafydd had still refused to tell a story. Each of his three friends had now told their story. All three then tried to insist it would be Dafydd's turn again at the next meeting. He refused.

The argument was now happening in the butler's pantry with Ifor as 'Chair', they all looked at Ifor to cast a deciding vote.

"Three against one is not enough against Dafydd," said Brum, chuckling. "Ifor, we need your help."

Ifor raised his eyebrows at Dafydd and Dafydd nodded. "It's agreed then," said Dafydd, and there was a murmur of approval. "**Ifor** will tell his story at the next meeting!"

"Ifor!" was the general exclamation. The protests dissolved into laughter as each saw the sense of it.

In the laughter Ifor was accepted even further as the fifth friend.

"My turn, then," Ifor agreed, and he cleared his throat. "Mind you," he warned "I haven't made any public speech recently that wasn't either political, or religious, or both."

"Both!" was Dafydd's request.

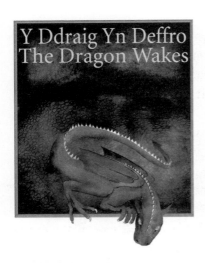

Y Ddraig Yn Deffro
The Dragon Wakes

SCENE
THIRTY ONE

The Next Public Meeting
Ifor's Turn

Ifor Speaks

"The next hymn is…" Ifor started, and he joined in the laughter.

> Yes, most of you know me, as a parch in pulpits or a protestor on platforms. Now I'm a new animal, an administrator-in-action. What's that? I'll listen to myself now and I may find out!

Ifor joined in the laughter again.

> In essence, the Public Sector has failed! And, the Voluntary Sector has failed! The Voluntary Sector has imitated the Public Sector, and has become its slave. The Voluntary Sector now consists mostly of committees applying for grants from the Public Sector.

Ifor looked around the hall, waiting for the nodding to die down.

> Where is the action? Where is the independent action that is not tainted or corrupted by the Public Sector or the Voluntary Sector? I tell you this, the rule of life that I have learned is 'Money follows ideas', not the other way round.

Don't sit in committee rooms filling in forms for grants. Don't wait for Westminster, the Welsh Office, The Assembly, local government to give you back your taxes in the way they see fit. Take action yourselves!

Then Ifor's tone became more gentle.

You know what your community here needs. **You** are the experts. **You** live here every day. No matter what high-tech equipment and qualifications some visiting specialist has, she or he doesn't know, can't **possibly** know what you know!

Our experience in 'The Dragon Wakes' is this: ask yourselves what you want and need. Listen to one another. Take responsibility. Take action, and the things you want to happen will happen.

The latest development in our project may amuse you. It quite shocked me!

I went round the project village listening to each family (and each member of each family) in turn.

What surprised me is that they want to have visitors.

They want to have their houses open to the public!

They have decided to be open one day per month each. 'It'll make us tidy and clean,' most of them said first. 'And it'll be handy income'. 'At five pounds per visitor the visitors can stay as long as they like between 8 a.m. and 9 p.m. and ask whatever questions they like.'

'Famous for a day', I suggested they call the scheme.

'Fly on the Wall', someone else suggested.

Another said, 'Space Invaders'.

They've decided on 'Being in the Village'. They want the visitors to really experience their households and for the visited to learn from the visitors. The experience will be in Welsh, so non-Welsh speakers will have to watch the body language and voice tone and work things out for themselves. We've already had bookings from learners of Welsh who see it as cheap, effective practice!

This made me realise that I, myself, have been seeing the prospective visitors to our project in too narrow a light, as interlopers, or colonists or imperialists, or interrupters of my work, or takers of our jobs, buyers up of our houses, diluters of our culture, destroyers of our language, users up of our hospital beds, cloggers of our roads, litterers of our beaches. That's not to say that I have ever resented visitors!

Ifor waited for the laughter to die down.

The **other** side of the coin **is** the coin – the summer money that keeps many of us going through the year, though sometimes 'keeping us going' sounds rather like a laxative!

But now I've changed. I see visitors as people who can learn about themselves through us, and when we observe them learning, that teaches us about ourselves.

Ifor paused, looking around at the faces.

I can see that I've lost some of you there, so let me give you an example. A visitor attended a Sunday chapel where I was preaching. She cornered me afterwards. 'What does it mean to be Welsh?' she asked. Now that's a simple enough question, but what would you answer? Think about it. 'What **does** it mean to be Welsh?' What would **you** say?

Ifor nodded and smiled as if accepting everyone's thoughts with approval. He gave them time to think some more, then continued:

To me there were two questions. One, what did she **expect** me to say? 'Welsh cakes, laver bread, male voice choirs, rugby? Owain Glyndwr, Prince Llywelyn, Dewi Sant? Coal tips, rain and unemployment?' The second question was, what did I **want** to say?

What I said first was 'We are not human beings.... We are human becomings. I don't look into the past, I look to how much I can be transformed for the future.' Then, having heard myself sounding pompous again, I told her a story. I'll come to the story in a minute, but that visitor's question is my example. From her question I learned what I thought at that moment, that moment's idea, the meaning to me of being Welsh. In her responses, part-positive, part-negative and part-uncomprehending, I learned how much she, as a typical visitor could or couldn't understand or accept from what I was sharing.

Do you see now? That visitor was not just a source of income, nor just a source of annoyance, but a source of insight and clarification.

All right then, the story!

Sweden has many islands. The people on those islands are like the people in many of our rural communities, an ageing population becoming progressively more of a burden on the state; difficult to reach with increasingly needed medical services; young people off and away as soon as they can; and no new young people wanting to go and live there; facilities closing, post offices, shops, schools. So, what did the Swedish government do? They dropped in one thing onto each island... No, not a Red Cross parcel to prolong the problem... No, not bubonic plague to finish the problem... simply ... a teacher. So each island suddenly had a school, even if there was only one pupil.

The result? Young people with kids moved to the islands. The island communities became younger, more lively. More people stayed. Having the teacher as an articulate, educated person on each island meant more of the people's due benefits got claimed. The teacher was like the services of an independent Citizen's Advice Bureau. Also, each community began to solve its own problems in creative ways. No post office? So the kids in one school trained up to run a post office in their school in the lunch hour. Falling prices for raw materials the islanders could sell? So the teacher helped create value-added processing, you know, raw mackerel becomes smoked mackerel. Smoked mackerel becomes smoked mackerel pate. Smoked mackerel pate becomes smoked mackerel pate terrine -high value products sold direct to mainland hotels where all the income from the product and the processing comes back to the island. 'Fair Trade'.

She, my visitor, said 'Hey, I asked you about Wales. You're telling me about Sweden!' So I said, 'You asked me not about Wales, but about being Welsh. My answer is this – being Welsh I reach out internationally to find creative solutions to our problems, not to copy, but to be inspired by, and I know we will transform those solutions into something uniquely Welsh.'

That was a bit pompous, too, but I'm allergic to this narrow view of Wales and being Welsh. We are a nation not just in relation (or opposition) to England, but in relation to the world. We can reach out to all other nations and hold our heads up high and contribute our ideas on the world stage, as well as learn from others.

In the project village, inspired by the Swedish model, we, the Trust, have just employed a full-time teacher of Welsh. Why? We all speak Welsh (or most of us). She runs a daily playgroup all in Welsh. She is in the playground at the primary school in breaktimes doing interesting things, storytelling in Welsh, teaching Welsh playground games. In the lunchtimes at the primary she sings in Welsh while the kids eat. Then she provides a counselling-listening service. In the evenings in the pub workshops she has clubs for the different ages, and there she does Welsh crafts, cooking and Welsh history in very practical ways in the medium of Welsh. All those things were in her brief, but she is also, now organising excursions and exchanges to other Welsh-speaking communities and developing projects and teaching materials in Welsh about our own community.

How can our small village afford to employ an extra teacher?

Ask the question another way: how can we afford not to?

In purely financial terms her extra encouragement and involvement will increase our children's lifetime earnings by enabling them to get better exam results and to achieve higher and higher qualifications. The playgroup she runs already has enabled several housewives in the village to get first jobs or get better jobs. The materials she has created are on sale for visitors and for other schools. The website she has created will also bring in new opportunities. I'm confident her salary will be justified purely financially in the increased prosperity of the village.

But she is justified much more broadly than just financially. In preparing us for *The Dragon Wakes* Project, she is invaluable. She is helping us to reinterpret our Welshness as partly an outgoingness, rather than wholly an insularity.

Yes, our Welshness expresses ourselves to ourselves. It will also, thanks to her, express our Welshness to others.

In these ways, through our language and culture, her presence will pay for itself ten times over.

Ifor then took hold of his lapels in a mock-preaching way and in a mock -preaching tone said,

This reminds me of Jesus...

Yes, it makes me laugh too. This is the sermon bit! Greeting me as you came in, many of you asked me, had I lost my religion, or why had I left preaching. I promised to answer you, so here it is, my story.

Jesus, while He was in His ministry, sent His disciples out, to go into the villages. He gave them His own powers to heal and so on. They had nothing else, no money, no status, no titles, no training, no authority.

When I saw this job of administrator advertised, I thought of that lonely time of Jesus' disciples leaving all their securities and support systems and having to live only by the power of ... of what? We each can name it in our own ways for ourselves: love; God; the Inner Light. To live that way, it's all very well being **given** the powers

> of Jesus, you also need to **take** those powers, to possess them, to grow into them, to expand to your full potential, or you can't use them.

Some of the audience gasped as Ifor, in a few silent seconds, seemed to grow taller and stronger and a new light shone in his eyes. His voice when he spoke was larger, fuller, yet very, very gentle.

> It was time for me to set out on the road, and to grow. As a Parch I was protected in many ways, by your expectations of me, for instance. The work I am now doing is as directly chapel work as I have ever done, but it is more powerful, more loving, more complete.

Ifor paused, smiling. "Join us!" he said. He sighed, as if in great satisfaction.

> So my last thought to share with you is this: when I say 'join us', you can ask the question, 'How can we possibly do that?'
>
> Listen to the question again: 'How can we possibly do that?'
>
> It's an exclamation, a rejection.
>
> Let's reframe the question as: 'It's possible. Now, how can we do it?' Say it with me, if you wish: 'It's possible. Now, how can we do it?'

Before the applause, there was an interested silence as various members of the audience looked around at one another beginning to seek out equally inspired individuals to meet and explore potentials together.

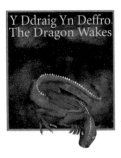
Y Ddraig Yn Deffro
The Dragon Wakes

Afterword

You'd like to know what happened next, wouldn't you?

Well, the double wedding went well, and **Kids Together** started the next day with the arrival of the nanny-goats heavily in-kid. Dafydd and Myfanwy's honeymoon started with them moving into the old farmhouse and, in the new goat yard, getting acquainted with the nannies. The honeymoon ended with the kidding one after the other, or rather twins after twins, and Myfanwy quite fell in love with the little soft, playful creatures.

The TV news magazine couldn't decide which was most interesting, Ifor's words at the Opening of **Kids Together,** or the antics of the tiny goat kids with the young children. The resulting edit was a weird mixture of both; Ifor's voice over young creatures playing.

"We are talking farms or workshops," said Ifor's voice as goat kids play-fought with little butting charges, and as they shook their soft heads in surprise at how hard they had hit each other.

"Do we make things people want? That's production."

A child and goat-kid were nose to nose, getting acquainted.

"Or do we make people want things? That's marketing."

A goat-kid's tiny hooves were on a kneeling toddler's thighs. The toddler was feeding the goat-kid from a bottle and the goat-kid's tail was wagging.

"Or do we make people who want things? That's consumerism."

A child on all fours was looking back at the goat-kid standing on the child's back. Both seemed to be laughing.

"Or do we make people into things? That's capitalism."

A child and goat-kid were playing hide and seek behind two rocks.

"The paradigm of the last century was the assembly line. We made ourselves or allowed ourselves to be made into endless makers and endless consumers of endless uniformity.

"What is the new paradigm that Wales offers in the new century?"

A child and a goat-kid were playing 'chase me' around a miniature castle while two more goat-kids were playing 'king of the castle'.

"Here," Ifor's voice continued, "is a new paradigm. Animals and humans on a basis of freedom, equality and individuality are interacting creatively and learning from one another. Neither child nor goat-kid will be unaltered by these encounters, but also, neither will be diminished. Let us apply this to our own lives."

The closing shot was of a bright-eyed child and a bright-eyed goat-kid each equally curiously looking into the camera, one to touch it with a pink nose, the other with a pink finger.

'Film us?' said a caption 'you must be kidding!'

Sally and Brum's honeymoon was spent on a very intensive butler and housekeeper course at a catering college.

Ifor's daily e-mails to the honeymooning couples were very encouraging. The money was coming flooding in, lent as bonds, and given as donations. 'Friends of the Dragon Wakes' soon numbered hundreds and the radio interviews and TV coverage were repeated several times nationwide in Wales and Ifor was having to schedule in a TV documentary team come to shoot the progress of the whole scheme.

The big money followed, encouraged by the flood of small money and the projected visitor figures, and reassured by the solid assets of the Trust properties which the big money people were happy to cover, so the big money people effectively took no risks at all.

As the months went by, the project grew. Yes, **Kids Together** led in the visitors who soon got interested in the exhibition about the farm domes being built.

The project in construction rapidly became a thing to view in its own right, and visitors came again and again to see the latest stages in its progress.

Often Dafydd was to be seen striding about on the great blocks of stone hailing the visitors in his greatest voice, telling them how the building work they were seeing was a symbol and parallel to a constructing of their own new lives.

Myfanwy, having discovered her comic talents at that public meeting, found a new vocation making very entertaining running commentaries on the visitors' children playing with the goat-kids in the **Kids Together** playgrounds. An unexpected new product was tapes and CDs of her hilarious monologues, in both languages. The Welsh TV channel S4C asked her to help make a series for children about goat-kids and human kids, and Myfanwy's voice – self-deprecating, ironic and characterful – became famous and in demand for voice-overs.

The Plas, meanwhile was up and running. In the winter season Dafydd and Myfanwy went off to train as head gardener and cook, so that, with Brum as butler and Sally as housekeeper, all four friends were able to take the first visitors to train as servants to serve Ifor, who moved in with his family to be 'grand'.

The initial fear was that, like role-plays of prisoners and guards, they would find themselves drawn into abuse of power. That didn't happen, though the temptations were an education in themselves.

For socialist Ifor, this was an experiential insight into history and a wonderful learning experience, and his Trustees serving him taught the four friends new forms of patience!

When spring arrived, the roles rotated, and a number of little tricks were played by way of vengeance, but that, dear reader, plus what they all learned from being 'grand' and from being 'servants' will have to wait for the next book.

At last the opening came, the grand opening of *The Dragon Wakes* in all its working parts.

Five years of hard work had gone into this, and there were now a hundred-and-five full time, self-respecting jobs for local people, plus lots of seasonal work with training included in the school holidays to keep the teenagers involved, contributing, and in sight of decent careers in the project if they wanted them, oh, and with salaries enough to buy houses in their own villages.

The Plas, much to her surprise, was awarded a prize for the teaching of Welsh. "Well," said the judges to the Trustees, "you didn't set out to teach Welsh, but the immersion in Welsh of your visitors as servants or guests of the grand family has produced measurably better improvements in their Welsh than any specialised language courses!"

Oh, and the ideas that Sally collected from the audiences worked very well too. For daily visitors to the Plas there were staged live events such as 'The Rebecca Riots', 'Political Campaigns', 'Revival Meetings', and 'Local Unrest' as well as all the festivals you could imagine. Thus visitors didn't just tour, they were challenged by divisive issues and passionate beliefs, passionately expounded, and all visitors went away changed in some way. Even the least sensitive visitors were heard to let forth a little growl which might one day grow into the roar of *The Dragon Wakes*.

One of the ideas that the audiences gave was framed in a question: "Why, in every city in the world, is there an Irish pub, and not a Welsh pub?"

So, the offer is there if you want to take it up. Myfanwy has written a manual: *How to Make a Pub Welsh* for anyone, anywhere in the world to do. The manual contains sources of merchandise, of tapes, CDs, videos to teach Welsh dances, names of singers, groups, choirs who will tour, descriptions of festivals to celebrate, posters and prints. Also, if you call your pub *The Dragon Wakes*, Myfanwy will send you the software to receive details of 40,000 jobs Britain-wide which are suitable for people with rural skills certificates: for example, relief milking, construction, landscape gardening.

Yes, there can be your own *The Dragon Wakes* near you!

Oh, and the protests against the county's housing plan gathered strength. The demands for local housing needs surveys grew stronger and a public enquiry was called. What happened next? Only the next book will tell…

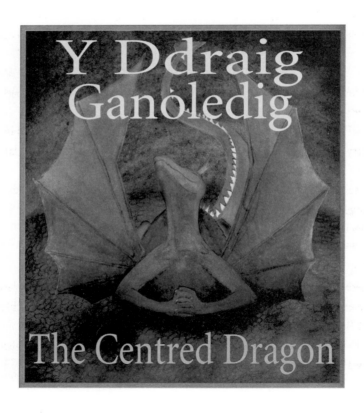

Acknowledgements

Scene 19 has a story version of (1996) Beck and Cowan's eight stage analysis of the spiral development of human existence which I learned from Nick Owen in Italy.

Scene 20 has a traditional Welsh story.

Scene 25 Nick Owen, whose family is from North Wales, has written an excellent international book *The Magic of Metaphor* (ISBN 189983670-5) published in Wales with 77 stories for use by teachers, trainers and therapists. The Dragon Wakes has borrowed elements from Nick's version of that folk tale.

The Trust can be seen at work in a traditional village with pressure from incomers – Stonesfield Community Trust, Home Close, High Street, Stonesfield, Witney, OX8 8PU, U.K. (Stonesfield is a village whose native industry, limestone slates, was ruined by railways bringing in Welsh slate.)

Also see *Short Circuit* by Richard Douthwaite, Green Books, Foxholes, Dartington, Devon UK. Also see The Baratanis Foundation, Keepers Cottage, Pit Landie, Lancarty, Perthshire PH1 3HZ UK

The Farm Project is an idea of the author conceived with a process engineer in Bavaria in 2001. On 7 October 2002 the *Western Mail* reported a similar project, brain-child of archeologists Kevin and Frances Blockley, called **Terra Nova**. See Cumbrian Archeological Projects. Both *The Dragon Wakes* and **Terra Nova** are partly inspired by **The Eden Project** in Cornwall. *Eden* by Tim Smit (ISBN 0-593-04883-0).

The use of stories as therapy is pursued by Milton Erikson: *Phoenix* (ISBN 0-916990-10-9). And by various members of Seal – The Society for Effective Affective Learning www.seal.org.uk

St Fagans is the Museum of Welsh Life near Cardiff, Wales, with wonderful buildings and items from all periods. It also has 'The House for the Future'.

Telecottages (Scene 2) are a room or two in a village with high-tech resources open to training and use by villagers so they don't have to live in cities. There are many in Britain, Sweden, and particularly in Sri Lanka. Email to <teleworker@tca.org.uk>, or call the helpline 0800 616 008, or (00 44) 2467 696 986, or fax (00 44) 1453 836 174.